KISSED BY A DEVIL

Lily DANES · *Eve* KINCAID

A LOST COAST HARBOR NOVEL

Dark & Stormy Books

For the poets

CHAPTER ONE

Nothing good ever happened at parties.

That hadn't always been the case. When she was younger, Anna Belmont had a blast at parties. In high school, she was invited to all of them, and more than once she found herself happily tucked in a corner with the star quarterback. Nothing changed in college, where she spent a fair amount of time behind closed doors with the championship swimmer, or the guitarist in a local band, or a future state senator.

Not that she was a tramp. Her momma taught her better than that, or at least taught her that's what people would call her if she was too enthusiastic with too many men. For her momma's sake, Anna at least pretended to be a good girl. The truth was, she didn't want much more than a few kisses. It was all just a bit of fun.

But Anna enjoyed kissing, and her partners never seemed to mind, so there was no reason to stop pulling handsome men behind closed doors.

Until she pulled the groom of the wedding she was catering behind one of those doors and was promptly fired by the fuming bride—though that really wasn't fair. It wasn't her fault the man forgot to mention his starring role in the nuptials.

Sadly, the bride didn't see it that way. She thought seeing her fiancé's lips pressed against the help's was worth a quarter million dollars of pain and suffering.

Anna's bank account disagreed.

She probably shouldn't have skipped her insurance payment that month, but the red t-strap heels had seemed like a smart decision at the time.

The way Anna saw it, she had a couple choices. She could stick around for a court case that would be a textbook example of drawing blood from a stone, or she could start over.

A month later, Annabel Johnson appeared in Lost Coast Harbor.

The wedding had been her first bad party.

Not long after she arrived in the small town on the Northern California coast, Anna attended her second bad party on Jared Hastings' arm. The good-looking man she'd been dating for a week had turned out to have the depth of a paddling pool. Worse, she caught the attention of Jared's father—who just happened to be the richest man in town. It was the kind of wealth that led a man to investigate his son's date in case she was a gold digger.

Peter Hastings got his money's worth from that P.I.

That was the second party she really should have avoided.

Now, almost three years later, she was at another party, and once again Jared Hastings stood at her side.

"You look wonderful tonight," he murmured in a low voice. The man probably thought he sounded alluring. His eyes never strayed above her neckline. "I'm glad my father invited you as a guest, rather than a caterer."

Annabel held back a somewhat unladylike snort. Peter Hastings would never dream of hiring a local to prepare food for his famed Winter Blues party. Until she was listed in the Zagat guide, the man wouldn't even eat at her bakery.

He did, however, stop by once a month with a large bag filled with cash.

"I think I might leave soon," she murmured. "I don't feel well." It wasn't a lie. Jared's presence made her feel rather nauseous. She'd only attended the party because Peter insisted all the local business owners make an appearance—and Annabel did whatever Peter Hastings told her.

Jared inched closer, trying to improve his view. Annabel cast an exasperated look at her breasts. They always found a way to get her in trouble. She'd considered covering them up for the night, but what fun would that be?

Plus, she'd hoped to see the look on a certain bookstore owner's face the first time he saw her all dolled up.

Then the damn man showed up with a date.

Not that she had any room to complain, of course. She and Declan were friends. Friends who visited every day and made each other laugh, but still just friends—even if she'd spent the last few years imagining Declan Donnelly without his clothes.

In another life, she would have found a way to pull him behind a closed door and have her way with him. She might even have enjoyed more than just kisses.

But that life belonged to another woman with another name. Annabel Johnson didn't get to have boyfriends. She didn't even really get to have friends, not while fifty thousand dollars flowed through her bakery every month. Some secrets made a friendship stronger. Others led to a felony charge. She couldn't risk it.

Annabel kept a smile pasted on her face as Jared dipped his head toward her. It seemed the man was trying to climb inside her bodice.

"Maybe I can convince you to stay. Dance with me." Jared held out his hand, certain she would accept.

Annabel was debating whether it was poor form to fake food poisoning in the middle of a party when her white knight arrived.

"I'm afraid she already promised this dance to me."

For the first time all night, Annabel didn't need to fake her smile. Her entire body relaxed when Declan Donnelly appeared behind her.

Then it tensed up all over again when she turned to face him.

Damn, but the man could wear a suit.

Annabel could count on one hand the times she'd seen him wearing something other than his everyday outfit, which she loved. She'd never thought of herself as attracted to the good boys, but there was something about Declan in those Oxford shirts that stretched tight across his shoulders, and the khakis that showed off his flat stomach and pert butt.

But in that suit...well, someone needed to call *GQ* and tell them they were missing one of their models.

With great effort, she kept her face relaxed and hoped he attributed her sudden flush to the warmth of the room.

She needn't have worried. Declan was too busy glowering at Jared—who was glaring right back.

"Don't tell me my father invited a Donnelly," Jared sneered.

Declan ignored the other man and gestured to the dance floor. "Shall we?"

"Of course. I've got my dancing shoes on."

His gaze dropped to her feet and the red spike heels she'd chosen that night. Declan grabbed two glasses of champagne from a passing waiter and handed one to her. His was gone before she even took a sip.

Before she could comment, he grabbed her hand and tugged her toward the dance floor. Annabel pushed her glass at Jared, who now wore a sulky expression.

Declan pulled her close, his movements as slow and languid as the music. It took every bit of restraint she possessed not to melt against his body. His tall, strong body that was only an inch away from hers.

More than a few of her fantasies the last three years had started just like this.

When the song ended, he didn't let her go.

Annabel tucked her chin and peered up at him. She tried not to flirt with the man. She really did. That way lay nothing but trouble.

But if he didn't want to be flirted with, he shouldn't look so damn gorgeous.

"Is Maddie your date?"

"Mmmm," he said.

Annabel's lips relaxed into a soft pout. Declan was an articulate man. Far better read than she was. There was no excuse for him to avoid complete sentences.

His gaze was riveted to her lips.

"Declan?" She leaned forward and sniffed delicately, catching no hint of the scotch Jared was drinking. There was the champagne, of course, but he wasn't acting soused.

Though his exterior remained as calm as ever, she sensed energy pulsing just below the surface of his skin. He looked normal, but he seemed a little…off.

Her excitement rose, and she made no effort to squash it. So long as she didn't go looking for trouble, she was allowed a tiny bit of pleasure, right?

Declan danced them toward the edge of the ballroom. As soon as they were clear of the other couples, he tugged on her wrist, pulling her down an unfamiliar hallway. The lights were dimmed, meant to discourage guests from wandering, but that didn't slow him. If anything, he picked up speed, moving fast enough that she had to jog to keep up. Then he stopped, and she found herself pushed against a wall in one of the many nooks that decorated the Hastings mansion.

Declan's arms trapped her. A thrill shot through her body at his proximity. At his heat.

"What are you doing?" she whispered.

Part of her felt uncertain. This wasn't the same man she'd known for years, and the sudden change unsettled her.

The other part hoped he never came to his senses.

"Why are you here with Hastings?" he demanded.

Annabel's eyes widened. He couldn't possibly be jealous.

"Jared was talking to me. That's all."

Still, he didn't move. "I don't like seeing you with him." The words came out on a low growl that shot straight to her core.

"Why not?" She hadn't meant to speak in a soft purr, but

the flirtatious words escaped before she stopped to think.

"Because you should be here with me."

When her mouth dropped open in shock, his gaze followed the motion.

Then he leaned forward and kissed her.

Annabel gasped at the unexpected touch. Declan's mouth seemed to know hers already. He coaxed her lips open and teased his tongue against hers.

She rose up on her toes, eager to take everything he offered. For three years, she'd imagined exactly this moment.

Her imagination was woefully inadequate. All those years of parties, of sneaking away for kisses with cute boys—*this* was what she'd been trying to find.

For several blissful seconds, she gave in to Declan's touch. To the hint of salt on his lips and the sweet taste of champagne on his tongue. To the skilled mouth moving across hers with such certainty. She imagined those lips caressing her with the same confidence lower down, and need pooled between her legs.

But a few seconds was all she was allowed. A few seconds to tide her over for two more years.

Annabel wrenched her mouth free.

Declan cupped his hand behind her neck. "I want you." It sounded like the simple words cost him dearly.

Annabel swallowed and forced herself to hold his gaze, to look into those blue eyes darker than any sapphire. She resisted the desire to smooth his dark blond locks or run her hands across his wide shoulders.

Instead, she thought of the thousands of dollars of dirty money hidden in the empty flour tin on the highest shelf in the bakery's back room.

"You're such a dear friend." She gave his hand a gentle squeeze. "Let's not ruin it." The words felt like acid on her tongue, but she spoke them through steady lips, and even managed a sweet smile when she was done.

Declan pushed himself upright. She watched as he transformed himself, the intense expression disappearing under a mask of respectability. The energy coursing through him stilled. "Of course," he said. "I think I had too much champagne. Forgive me."

Once again, he was the man she'd known for years—but for the first time, she wondered just how well she knew her friend. It didn't matter. Whoever he was, she didn't get to have him. Not for another two years, when her deal with Hastings expired.

Only a fool would expect such a man to wait.

It shouldn't hurt as much as it did. By now, she should be used to being lonely.

Annabel sagged against the wall. She was right. Nothing good ever happened at parties, not anymore.

CHAPTER TWO

One month later, Annabel stared at the empty flour tin with a dopey smile on her face.

She didn't need to wait. Not anymore. Not ever again.

For the first time in three years, the tin held no money. No stacks of bills she would deposit in her own account, then use to pay the fake vendors who diverted the funds to Hastings' offshore accounts. It contained no dirty money waiting to be cleaned through her hard work.

She never minded the work. Baking was a joy, and she loved seeing the pastry case filled with cream puffs and eclairs and cupcakes created by her own hands. Two years ago, she'd expanded into small meals, selling soup and sandwiches to an appreciative lunch crowd who wanted an alternative to the local diner. Because of the bakery, she was a member of the Lost Coast Harbor community.

Without that, she couldn't imagine how she'd have kept going. Her nights were cold and lonely, but at least the days were filled with warmth and kindness—and cookies.

It never mattered to Hastings whether she was lonely. He only cared that she came to work every day and gave no one any reason to guess the owner of The Sweet Spot had a spicy past.

Hastings provided the building. The equipment. Everything she required to launch a now-thriving business—and all she needed to do in return was launder cash.

At the time, she hadn't known where the money came from. She never asked. Ignorance might not be bliss, but it beat the alternative.

But a few weeks ago, Peter Hastings was arrested in the biggest scandal the town had ever seen. Every day, it seemed another dark piece of the corrupt puzzle was revealed. Drugs. Guns. Bribery.

And every day, Annabel's smile grew a little more brittle, and her heart jumped a little faster when an unfamiliar face walked through the bakery door. The feds were sniffing around, and she was sitting on fifty thousand dollars she could never explain. Fifty thousand dollars no one seemed to want. The fake vendors' accounts had closed, seemingly overnight, as Hastings raced to cover his tracks, and no one had appeared to reclaim the cash.

Which was why, the day before, she gave the entire amount to Erin Grady to start her mental health clinic. After years of being part of something evil, she figured it was her chance to do something good. The minute the money left her hands, a weight lifted. She was free—more or less.

She still couldn't go home. Hastings made Anna Belmont and her pesky legal obligations disappear as part of their deal. But now that Hastings was under house arrest, awaiting trial for crimes he most certainly committed, she could go somewhere else. Anywhere else.

The minute the thought crossed her mind, an image followed, of a tall man with dark blue eyes and lips that promised all kinds of sin.

A man who'd returned to a polite smile and small talk the day after the party. Declan still visited every day, but he never indicated the kiss was anything other than a mishap. Like his lips accidentally fell on hers, and he was so very sorry about the misunderstanding.

Annabel glanced at the clock and felt a familiar pulse of excitement. He should be stopping in soon for his afternoon cup of coffee and a treat. She'd already set aside the last slice of cheesecake. It was the kind of thing good friends did for each other.

She brushed her hands on her apron and checked her hair. Annabel kept it in an updo at work, because no one wanted to find a curly blonde strand in their soup, but she allowed a few tendrils to frame her face in a way she knew was becoming. She undid the top button on her blouse.

Because for the first time in three years, she was free to seduce Declan Donnelly.

Forget what she said at the party. As much as she valued their friendship, she was more than willing to risk it if it meant a few more of those kisses. She'd never had a problem making friends, but it took her the entirety of her thirty years to find a man who kissed the way Declan did. She knew what her priorities were.

A burst of street noise reached her as the front door opened, and Annabel hurried to the counter. It was late enough in the day that the lunch crowd had come and gone. Otis Spatz, the head of the local Rotary Club, lingered over his coffee and crullers, but otherwise the place was deserted.

Her bright smile drooped when she saw her visitor.

"Hello, Annabel." Jared Hastings leaned across the counter. His hair was rakish, his smirk firmly in place. She was certain he'd spent many hours in front of the mirror practicing both.

Then, with one sentence, Jared turned her disdain into horror.

"I believe you have something for me."

THE BOOKSTORE WAS IN THE MIDDLE OF AN AFTERNOON lull. Declan updated Lost in a Book's website and ordered a handful of magazines, then headed to the rear of the store to shelve that morning's delivery.

It was mostly mysteries, because Annabel had cleaned him out over the last month. So far as he could tell, she went through one a night.

Declan slid two Agatha Christie novels next to Raymond Chandler. Unbidden, an image of Annabel curled up in bed with a book popped into his head. Somehow, he knew she wouldn't be the t-shirt sort. She'd wear some damn negligee that clung to every curve. He wasn't sure if he was more turned on by that visual or by the thought of that gorgeous woman reading for hours at a time. Either way, he needed to fight back the wave of desire that always rose when he thought of her.

It was time to get over this. For more than three years, he'd lusted after the woman—and when he finally took leave of his senses and acted on it, she shot him down.

It was a good thing, really. It reminded him there were

valid reasons he stayed away. At the party, the mix of music, champagne, and low lighting made him think, for just a moment, that the rules didn't apply. That kind of thinking might work for the rest of his family, but it wasn't a good fit for Declan.

He made it as far as Dashiell Hammett when the bell above the door rang.

Declan brushed off his hands and stood, ready to greet the customer.

No one entered. There were no voices, no sound of footsteps. The mystery section was tucked in a corner, away from the windows and out of sight of the rest of the store.

Declan's senses strained toward the front door. After a heartbeat, it clicked softly shut, cutting off the cool February air that rushed inside. That was the only sound. Whoever had entered was working hard to be stealthy.

Declan grabbed the thickest volume he could find, a hardcover compendium of the Sherlock Holmes stories. He gripped it between both hands and eased his way along the bookcase, then peered around the end cap to see who was trying to creep into the store in the middle of the day.

"Sucker!" shouted a too-familiar voice behind him.

Declan barely had time to get the book up before he crashed to the ground. His brother stood over him, grinning.

"Are you *ever* going to tire of that?" Declan grumbled, sitting up easily. He'd have bruises, as he always did after an encounter with Niall, but nothing was injured.

Niall was unrepentant. "Someday you won't fall for it. That's when I'll stop."

"You teach mixed martial arts. You know every move

that's ever existed." He stood until he was almost eye to eye with his redheaded brother. At six foot four, his brother was the tallest member of the Donnelly clan. He had an inch on Declan and two on their oldest brother, Gavin. Naturally, Niall lorded this over them at every opportunity.

"Yep. And if you attended class more than once a week, you might keep up. A few well-executed leg sweeps would serve you much better than that poetry you read." Niall looked in confusion at the volume on the floor. "Dude, I don't think Arthur Conan Doyle is ready to take on a black belt."

"You've read a book?" asked Declan. He only needed to fake his surprise a little. Niall enjoyed playing the fool, and even Declan never knew how much of it was an act. "So what brings you by?"

Before Niall could answer, a large orange cat leapt from the highest bookshelf to land at Niall's feet. The animal twined around his legs, the movement almost ecstatic.

For reasons no one would ever understand, the haughty creature adored his older brother.

Niall scooped him up. The cat draped a white chin across his shoulder, purring so loudly Declan heard the rumble from two feet away.

Declan gave his cat an exasperated head shake. "Pablo, you're a slut."

"Did you hear him?" Niall cooed, dropping into an arm-chair Declan put out for customers. His brother flipped the cat onto his back, the better to rub his belly. Pablo went boneless under his touch. "Did you hear what he called my little Pablo Neruda?"

Declan rolled his eyes. "You don't even know who Pablo Neruda is."

Niall glanced up, all wide-eyed innocence. "Doesn't he play for the Giants?"

Declan snorted. "Philistine. What brings you by?"

"I missed Pablo." He scratched the cat's ears and waited a beat too long. "Also, Dad has a question."

"Uh-huh." Declan leaned against the counter and waited.

"You know about the deal?"

Declan did his best to stay out of his father's business, so he had no idea what Niall was talking about. "Does he want the Stanwick Ranch property?" Declan guessed. "That's back on the market these days, isn't it?"

Niall waved that away. "He was thinking about it, but someone else put in an offer last week. He doesn't feel like fighting for it."

Declan gave his brother a skeptical glance. He'd believe his dad enjoyed wearing tutus and dancing ballet solos before he believed the old man didn't feel like fighting for something.

"Or he doesn't feel like matching the other party's ridiculous bid," Niall amended. "Now Dad's got a much juicier target in his sights."

It took Declan a second to figure it out. The Donnellys already controlled the town's timber and construction companies, though that had never been enough for his father. All his life, Declan had listened to Richard Donnelly complain about the damn Hastings, who owned more of the town than his father wanted them to. The Hastings and Donnellys were Lost Coast Harbor's two founding families, but they played very different roles in town.

The first Hastings to arrive chose to focus on shipping, to Declan's many-times-great-grandfather's amusement. At first glance, Lost Coast Harbor looked like the worst place imaginable to set up a shipping operation. There was a reason this part of the state was known as the Lost Coast. The rugged coastline was formed of steep cliffs no one could build on, and the sea was filled with jagged rocks that menaced any boats that came near. No highways ran through town, and the only way in was a two-lane road that wound through the redwoods.

But Hastings understood something Declan's ancestor didn't. Lost Coast Harbor had a small cove, as did several of the towns up and down the coast—harbors that couldn't be serviced by larger ships. The Hastings fleet filled a niche no one else had seen the need for, and the company's success was a shot in the arm for the growing town. Without the money and jobs provided by Hastings Shipping, Lost Coast Harbor would have faded away several decades ago.

It was bad enough that, over the last century, the Hastings had steadily overcome the Donnellys as the town's most prominent family. They were also a necessary evil, as Donnelly Lumber relied on their company to ship lumber up and down the coast.

And thanks to Peter's current legal troubles, their fleet was struggling to stay afloat. "Are the Hastings selling?" Declan asked, surprised.

Niall tilted his hand from side to side. "Sort of. No more than fifteen percent. Not enough for control, but enough that we can finally ship our product south without being gouged by those bastards."

"Why do the Hastings hate us so much again?"

Niall shrugged. "Habit. Same reason we hate them."

Declan didn't bother arguing. The roots of the feud between their families were lost in the mists of time, and it always seemed like too much energy to dislike all of them. They really weren't so bad.

Well, Jared Hastings was a worthless, entitled ass. And Peter Hastings was currently under house arrest in a San Francisco suburb, because the court thought he was too much of a flight risk in Lost Coast. Having his own shipping fleet was deemed a problem. But the rest of the family were all right, so far as he knew.

"Dad's finally getting that vertical distribution he always wanted," Declan said.

Niall didn't look certain. "Maybe. The deal's far from done, but they need an influx of cash. The feds weren't able to confiscate everything, since the company was also used for legitimate business, but most of its assets are frozen pending the trial. Even so, the family is reluctant to sell. They've had it as long as we've had the timber business, however long that is."

"One hundred forty-three years," Declan said absently. He might resent being a Donnelly, but it was impossible not to know his family's storied past. Anyone who grew up in the area was taught it in fifth grade history.

"Whatever. Anyway, the CEO is out of town this month, trying to work some magic with investors, maybe shut down a few of the depots to save money. Dad's hoping to swoop in while the man's distracted, get a better deal than he otherwise might."

"What does any of this have to do with me?"

"Don't shoot the messenger." Niall lifted Pablo in front of his face, like the cat was speaking the words. "Dad heard you were running for the council seat that opened up, so he sped up the vote. It's in three weeks. As soon as you're on, he was hoping you'd…"

"No."

"You don't even know what I was going to say."

"That he hoped I'd delay some permits? Shut down the dock? Generally make it harder for the Hastings to do business?"

"I guess you did know what I was going to say."

Declan leaned against his counter, arms crossed. "Why would he ever think I'd do that?"

"I think he's still hoping this is just a phase." Niall swept his arm around the room, taking in everything. The well-ordered store. Declan's neat appearance. The apartment upstairs, where none of his family were ever invited. "Maybe he thinks it's time you got back to your roots."

Declan groaned, as he often did when he thought of his family.

The Donnellys were famous in Lost Coast Harbor—or infamous, depending on who you asked. They had been ever since his great-great-great-grandfather breezed into town and snatched up every bit of land the Hastings hadn't already grabbed. Stolen Gold Rush money went pretty far, it turned out, especially when those he'd stolen it from had no idea where to find him. Lost Coast might be in California, but it was a fair distance from the gold-rich foothills outside Sacramento. No one thought to look for a troublesome Irishman in a tiny settlement as far west as one could get without falling into the ocean.

The family's reputation hadn't improved much over the years, though his ancestors established a thriving timber company and built the town's largest construction firm. More recently, Declan's oldest brother opened Lost Coast Harbor's first microbrewery after years of making beer in his dorm room at Chico State. The family had more than enough legal money coming in. No one had to commit any crimes.

His family thought that sounded pretty dull.

The town knew them as the Donnelly Devils. An entire family prone to viewing laws as little more than suggestions. Niall used to race past the police station at midnight, then see how long it took him to outrun the cops. He appeared before the local judge three times, a man who chuckled at Niall's foolish shenanigans, then set a hefty fine the family always paid—along with a significant contribution to the judge's retirement fund. Refusing to be outdone by his younger brother, Gavin stole the cop cars outright, then abandoned them in ditches, cow pastures, and the high school gymnasium. Somehow, those charges also managed to disappear.

His sisters weren't much better.

By now, everyone knew Declan was the outsider. In a family of reprobates, he was the good Donnelly. He owned a bookstore, after all. It was hard to get more respectable than that. So far as the town knew, he'd never broken a single law.

His lips thinned. Even in Lost Coast Harbor, where the townspeople treated gossip like an Olympic event, there were a few secrets. His family made sure of it.

Declan shook it off. He refused to let himself forget, but

this wasn't the time.

Fortunately, he knew one woman who could distract him.

He glanced at the clock, grabbed his coat, and taped the "Be back in 20 minutes" sign to the front door. He swung it open, letting in a blast of cold air, and gestured for Niall to precede him.

Niall bounced from one foot to another while Declan locked up. To an outsider, it looked like he was trying to stay warm, but Declan knew his brother was practicing, staying light on his feet. Niall never stopped practicing.

"What should I tell Dad?" Niall asked.

Declan glanced across the road at the welcoming light of the bakery. A pastry, some coffee, then a quiet night at home with a spy novel by one of his favorite authors. That's all he wanted. Given the choice, no sane person would decide to get involved with whatever scheme his father had concocted.

He stepped into the road and called back over his shoulder, "Tell Dad to fuck off."

He was still smiling when he opened the bakery door.

CHAPTER THREE

Perhaps Jared meant something else. *Anything* else. He couldn't possibly be talking about the money.

When in doubt, play dumb. "We're all out of your favorite soup, Jared, but I could whip up a sandwich for you. You like roast beef, right?"

Jared stepped closer, and she cursed her earlier desire to impress Declan by undoing the top button of her blouse.

"That would have to be one hell of a sandwich," Jared mused. "Would it come in a solid gold wrapper?"

Her smile never wavered. "What do you mean?" Annabel asked, eyes widening. It shouldn't be hard to convince Jared she was a bit simple. He seemed like the kind of man predisposed to believing women were foolish.

To her chagrin, his hard eyes told her he wasn't falling for her act.

Jared glanced at the head of the Rotary Club, who watched them both with interest. Any tension between two people in Lost Coast Harbor had the potential to become the next topic of gossip, and Otis Spatz was plainly hoping to get an exclusive that afternoon.

"You all done there, Otis?" she chirped. Before he could answer, Annabel cleared his empty dishes, then flipped the closed sign. It was only a few minutes earlier than usual. The disappointed man left.

Annabel turned to face Jared. She put her hands on her hips and waited.

Instead of answering her, he stepped around the counter and disappeared into her kitchen. Annabel hurried after him, protesting.

He walked straight to the far corner of the bakery, where she kept her supply of dry goods, and reached for the flour tin tucked behind the two full ones she actually used. He gave it a good tug, expecting it to be heavier than it was, and the empty tin toppled to the ground. The lid popped off as it landed.

Jared looked between the flour canister and Annabel, his brows knit together. "Where's the money?" He looked between her face and the tin. "My father said you kept it in here."

"Ah." Annabel winced inwardly. "About that…"

Jared faced her, his full mouth falling into a pout. With his thick brown hair and classic features, he should have been a handsome man, but he always ruined the effect by acting like…well, like Jared. "Where is my father's money?"

Annabel managed a bright smile, even as she felt invisible shackles wrap around her wrists. "Well, I grew worried when I had no way to get rid of it. Keeping such a large amount here was a big risk for me."

"A risk you assumed when my father made your legal issues disappear."

Mentally, Annabel cursed Peter Hastings. It seemed his promise of silence was contingent on his freedom.

For a brief moment, Annabel eyed her heavy iron skillet. She pictured her fingers wrapped around the handle. She wasn't a violent woman by any means, but she allowed herself to imagine swinging the pan until it crashed over Jared hard enough for him to crumple to the ground, where he would see little birdies circling his head.

The image helped keep her smile firmly in place.

Jared Hastings shoved his hands through his hair and dug his fingers into his scalp. She suspected he was trying to think.

"No one informed me what I was supposed to do," she argued. "It's been several weeks since your father was arrested, and this is the first time anyone has shown an interest in the cash. It seemed reasonable to believe your father was the only one involved. Peter always dropped off the monthly package. I never communicated with anyone else."

Jared took a step toward her, and she held her ground with difficulty.

"It seemed *reasonable* to think my father single-handedly ran a gun and drug ring?"

When he put it like that, it did sound rather foolish. Perhaps she should have taken more time to consider her decision, but she'd been so eager to be rid of the money. The incriminating bills had begun to hound her every thought.

And if she was honest, she hadn't needed much encouragement to get rid of the cash. The only thing that had been holding her back from the rest of her life was fifty thousand dollars in need of a new home. Anyone else would have done the same.

But if Jared Hastings, of all people, believed she'd been stupid, it was possible she should have examined her decision more closely.

Still, nothing to do now but brazen it out. "Well, yes. Your father was the only person I ever saw, and it seemed odd that he'd do his own dirty work if there were others to do it for him. I'm afraid the money is gone now." She managed a self-deprecating shrug.

Jared's face turned an unfortunate shade of red. He loosened his tie, like he was struggling to breathe. "It's...what? Get it back!"

Annabel stepped backwards. She'd been so focused on Jared's weaknesses that she'd forgotten he was over six feet tall and worked out regularly in the town gym.

Then again, she was only a foot away from her favorite chef's knife. She tried to appear casual as she placed the butcher block table between them.

"I can't. It's already gone."

Jared braced his hands on the table. "Where?"

"It's being used to build the new mental health clinic. I gave the money anonymously, so it wouldn't be a problem for you to claim credit. Your family could write it off as a charitable donation," she offered helpfully.

Jared slammed his fist onto the butcher block. Annabel swallowed, then surreptitiously slid open the knife drawer.

"Do you have any idea what you've done?" he demanded. "What my father will do?" He glared at her, breathing heavily, but he didn't step closer.

"I'm sure there's a solution. A payment plan, perhaps?"

She tried to sound reasonable, like she was negotiating with the bank, but Jared's eyes were wild. He wasn't angry, she realized. He was scared—and the emotion was contagious.

She slid the knife drawer shut, no longer afraid of Jared. Whatever he feared, she instinctively knew that was the real threat.

"A payment plan?" He barked out laughter. "My dad's been arrested, half my family's assets are frozen, my father wants to 'borrow' my trust fund, and you think a six-year fixed-interest loan is the solution?"

Jared tapped his fist against the butcher block, three heavy touches while he considered his options.

"It wasn't enough that you gave the money away. That cash is going to the company building the clinic. You handed over my family's money to Donnelly Construction."

"Only in a roundabout way," she insisted. Too late, Annabel recalled that the Hastings and Donnelly families weren't fond of each other. It wasn't at the level of the Hatfields and McCoys, but both wished the other didn't have quite as much power in Lost Coast Harbor as they did.

"If you were trying to screw me, you couldn't have done a much better job."

Her mind raced, trying to come up with a plan. She could sell her car, or maybe take some deposits for June weddings, or...

She gave up. There was no way she could pull together that kind of money.

Annabel deflected. "I don't understand how this affects you."

Jared exhaled hard. "Of course you don't. Let me make

it so simple even you'll understand. My family needs to sell part of Hastings Shipping. We need the money. More specifically, *I* need my trust fund, so this deal has to go through. But my father doesn't want to sell to the fucking Donnellys. He'll be pissed enough to hear his fifty thousand is already in their pockets."

Annabel took a full breath as a real, viable idea occurred to her. "What if I help you complete the sale? Would that take care of my debt?"

Jared's scornful laugh mutated into a thoughtful expression before stopping somewhere around devious. "You know, I bet you could do that."

She nodded eagerly. "Of course I can. I mean…how?"

Jared's happy smile unsettled her. "Declan. He follows you around like a lovesick schoolboy. Just get whatever he knows about his family's business. You can start working off the fifty thousand. Let's say ten grand for every useful bit of information, and the whole debt cleared if any of that information helps complete the sale."

She felt the tightening shackles loosen, just a tiny bit. "And that's it? Once the papers are signed, I'm free?"

"Help this deal go through, and I'll make sure my father forgives the debt—but you'll need to work fast. You have a week. Maybe two."

A week or two till freedom? Annabel could stand anything for a couple of weeks, if it meant she was truly done with the Hastings at the end of it.

Her blooming excitement dimmed as she realized what she'd agreed to do. Abuse her friendship with Declan. Possibly ruin it, if he ever learned that she was spying on his family.

"Declan and I never talk about business. Not his family's, at least." She kept her face calm, her arms loose at her sides, while she sent up one prayer after another that Jared would come up with an alternate plan.

Jared snorted. "I saw how he acted at my father's party. He'll talk about anything if he thinks you might take off your clothes afterwards. He doesn't even like his family very much. All you need to do is lie back and think of Texas."

With great difficulty, Annabel didn't grab her iron skillet and swing it at his face.

She had dozens of questions about the kind of information Jared wanted, but the front door opened before she could ask any of them. She'd forgotten to lock the damn thing. Annabel hurried to the counter with Jared right behind her.

Declan Donnelly's smile dropped, and he stared at her and Jared with disgust.

CHAPTER FOUR

Jared fucking Hastings.

It wasn't possible. Annabel had more sense than that.

Then again, she did briefly date the man when she first arrived in town. And they chatted at the party only a month ago. At the time, he thought he was rescuing her, but now he had to consider the nauseating possibility that she welcomed the man's attention.

Because she looked guilty as hell as she hurried from the back room with the top button of her blouse undone and her curls coming loose. Jared's hair stood straight up, and his tie was loosened.

Declan resisted the urge to tighten that tie around the man's neck until his eyes bulged.

Logically, he knew he had no claim on Annabel. Not only had she turned him down a month ago, but she'd done so while he was on a date with another woman. He didn't have a leg to stand on.

But at least Maddie Palmer was a good person, if not the right one for him. Jared Hastings, on the other hand, was a slug. A lazy bastard happy to spend his life living off his father's money.

He couldn't believe Annabel would overlook all that for a handsome face, but he couldn't deny his eyes.

"Declan!" Her voice was artificially bright. He'd come to know—hell, to cherish—the warm smile she bestowed on him each afternoon. The honest welcome in her voice. This was something else.

"The door was unlocked," he said. "So I thought the sign was a mistake. It's a little early for you."

Over the last year, Declan had learned to time his visits so he arrived five minutes before the bakery closed. That way, he could stay a little longer while she tidied up.

Every day, he looked forward to the thrill he felt when she locked the door behind him. For a few minutes, it was just the two of them.

Declan knew he tortured himself. Annabel made it clear there was nothing between them—and even if she felt differently, he knew in his heart that Annabel was the wrong woman for him. He loved the life he'd built for himself. It was steady. Calming. Filled with small pleasures, like books and wine and good food. Annabel was anything but a small pleasure. He had no idea what would happen if he threw her into the middle of his nice, ordered life, but he suspected she would explode it like a human pipe bomb.

Really, the night of the Winter Blues Ball had been a near miss.

Even so, he couldn't stay away. Seeing Annabel every day—those blonde curls floating around her face, an apron tied tight around her narrow waist, the curves that kept him up nights with his hand wrapped tight around his cock—it was the sweetest torture he could imagine.

If they never touched again, she would still be his friend. The friend who gave him blue balls, sure, but that wasn't her fault. He liked her. He wanted to spend time with her. That was no small thing.

But he hadn't expected it to hurt so much, seeing her with another man.

"I…" She paused, clearly flustered.

"She was showing me the broken sink," Jared said. "This is one of my family's properties."

The man was a terrible liar. Declan doubted Jared had done more than two minutes of manual labor in his entire life.

"The feds haven't frozen the Hastings Properties assets? That's fortunate." Declan met the man's irate eyes with a bland expression.

Jared didn't take the bait. "I hear you're running for the empty council seat. You don't think that's a conflict of interest, with all those Donnelly permits it has to approve?"

"I'll recuse myself if I can't be impartial." Declan never looked away from the other man. "I'm sure your family would do the same…if you had someone on the council."

He let the unspoken implication hang in the air. The council seat was empty because the person who used to hold it disappeared in the middle of the night, just two days after Peter Hastings' arrest. The same council member who always voted in favor of Hastings' businesses and took a surprising number of vacations on Caribbean islands.

The blow landed. Jared ground his teeth, but too soon his expression turned sly. When he spoke, the words were directed to Annabel. "You're clear on what needs to happen?"

She caught Declan's eye for just a second. "Of course," she said, her words more confident than her expression.

"Good. I'd hate for there to be any question about how you'll pay this month's rent."

Declan tensed. There was a weight behind Jared's words he didn't understand, and Annabel's nervous nod did nothing to soothe him.

Jared left. Annabel hurried to lock the door behind him, like she couldn't get rid of him soon enough.

"Annabel? What was all that about?" Declan was beginning to think he should be concerned rather than jealous. Whatever their conversation had been about, it hadn't been a seduction.

If that bastard was bothering her instead of sleeping with her...well, either way, he wanted to punch Hastings in his smug, handsome face.

But when Annabel turned to face him, her expression was once again relaxed. Even playful. "Just re-negotiating the lease. Perhaps you've heard that there were some recent changes to the Hastings business model."

"Couldn't have happened to a nicer family," he muttered, but she overheard. Her laugh was easy and genuine.

Pleasure swelled in him at the sound.

"Sit down," she gestured, then moved behind the counter. He loved watching her work. To see Annabel cross the street was like watching a fifties pinup come to life. Her curves swayed with every step, the movement downright hypnotic. But here, in the bakery, she was a model of efficiency. No move was wasted as she packaged up the now day-old goods for the bargain hunters who would arrive early the next morning.

"I saw Niall crossing the square earlier," she said. "It must be nice, having both your brothers just a block or two away."

"See, I would have gone with traumatizing instead of nice, but yours sounds better."

Annabel wiped down the counter top. "You don't like living close to them?" She sounded a little wistful.

"Sometimes," he said. "When was the last time you saw your family?"

Annabel turned her back to him and began cleaning the coffee maker. "I never pegged Niall for much of a reader."

He let her avoid the question. "Not unless it's Bruce Lee's biography. No, it was something about a deal my dad wants to make."

If he wasn't watching her so closely, he might not have seen the way her body stilled for a second, a small hiccup in her otherwise smooth routine. "The Hastings one?"

She still didn't turn around.

"I guess it's not a secret that he wants a share of the company. You really do get all the gossip here, don't you?"

At last she spun around, and there was no sign of her earlier tension. "You have no idea." She lifted her eyebrows, implying all sorts of salacious knowledge, then returned to her cleaning. "How's the council campaign going?" she asked.

Declan stretched his legs out in front of him. "Well, I told Mrs. Wandsworth I was running, so I assume the whole town knows by now."

Again she laughed, and he smiled with her. The bakery always felt like an extension of his home. It helped that it was warm and always smelled of fresh bread, but it was also comfortable. The chairs were all wide and padded, instead of being those spindly-legged things so many cafes used. Rather than hanging the seascapes that decorated much of the town, she'd decorated with photos of her favorite flowers, fat zinnias and bright gerbera daisies. It felt happy, like the building itself would smile if it could.

Her expression turned a little devilish. "Did you tell Mrs. Wandsworth you planned to host more smutty book club meetings if you won?"

He groaned. Declan doubted he would ever recover from the book club meeting in which a dozen women, including three octogenarians, discussed the literary merits of a BDSM bestseller.

"No, but I told her about the writer's retreat I wanted to start. She rather liked the idea of Lost Coast Harbor as the inspiration for some great work of art, though she made me promise not to let in any of those—and this is a direct quote—'man-bun-wearing hippie types' into her town."

"We will all rue the day her granddaughter introduced her to Tumblr," Annabel said.

And so it went for the next ten minutes, their easy conversation only occasionally interrupted by a rampant burst of lust. This really was the best part of his day.

At last, she carried two cups of coffee across the cafe, then returned with a slice of cheesecake for him.

Declan closed his eyes in bliss as he took a bite. "I didn't think it was possible, but this is better than last week's."

"I adjusted the recipe."

"Let me guess. You added more butter."

"It always seems to do the trick."

He met her eyes and time froze, just for a second, as they held each other's gaze and smiled.

Then she blinked, and the moment was gone.

The silence lasted a heartbeat too long. Declan searched for a safe topic of conversation. "A new stack of mysteries arrived today. I ordered a bunch of Dorothy Sayers for you."

"Is Harriet in these?"

"Of course. You loved *Gaudy Night* so much I ordered all the books that include her."

Her eyes softened, and for a moment he saw a flash of sadness. It passed quickly, and he thought he must have imagined it.

"Thank you. I like Lord Peter Wimsey well enough, but he works so much better when she's at his side."

He feigned offense. "Are you saying a man isn't a strong enough detective on his own?"

Her expression was pure mischief. "I'm saying a woman often sees things a man misses. You lot can be dangerously clueless, you know."

Before he could offer a token protest on behalf of his gender, Annabel gave him a coy smile and a sidelong glance, and he completely lost his train of thought. It didn't help that all his blood was exiting his brain for parts further south.

He was misinterpreting that look. His libido was so desperate for a little action that it was trying to convince his mind of something that wasn't there.

Then she crossed her arms, placed her forearms on the table, and leaned forward. The movement squeezed her magnificent rack between her upper arms, and his libido officially

K.O.ed his brain.

Get it together. Look up. At her eyes. So gorgeous and green and…playful? Okay, not her eyes. Her lips. Full and soft and…moving on. Her hands. Small and a little rough, from days of kneading dough. Hands that would look amazing spread above her head and tied to his bedpost.

In the end, he stared at the laminate table while he fought for control.

Declan mentally scanned his entire body. Polished brown shoes. Khakis. Button-down shirt, ironed the night before. Blue sweater fresh from the dry cleaner. His hair was parted on the right and combed neatly into place.

Eventually, his thoughts settled. His brain might not be fully returned, but at least it was back in charge.

He swallowed the last bite. "I should get back to the bookstore." He made no effort to move.

"Of course." For a moment, she looked indecisive. Like him, she remained at the table. "Did the French cookbook I requested come in?"

When he nodded, her mouth pursed into a perfect O of pleasure.

Declan shifted in his seat. "I can't imagine what you need it for, though. Don't you make up ninety percent of your recipes? You're an incredible cook."

Annabel flushed with pleasure, like the compliment meant something, though he knew she'd heard it too many times to count. She leaned forward a little more, as if to tell him a secret. With great effort, he kept his eyes on her face.

"I'm ashamed to say that my soufflé game has been slipping." She pouted, the movement drawing his attention to her mouth. "I can't get anything to rise."

She leaned back and took a sip of coffee. Her green eyes over the rim of the cup were dangerously innocent.

"I can't believe that."

She swiped a finger across his plate, picking up a missed crumb. She popped it in her mouth.

"Perhaps I could practice on you one night?" Annabel asked. "I need a guinea pig to test my latest techniques."

Declan almost choked on his coffee. Because unless he'd lost his mind, she wasn't talking about soufflés.

He reminded himself that she'd turned him down, insisted they were much better as friends.

So why was she once again leaning across the table, providing an amazing view of her cleavage? Whatever part of his brain still functioned gave up the struggle. All he could think about was his hands on her blouse, ripping it open.

He had to get out of there. Now. Another minute of this conversation and he'd be walking back to the bookstore with his damn cock pointing the way for everyone in town to see.

So when Annabel offered him a teasing smile filled with all sorts of promises, he did what any self-respecting man would do when he was about to make a fool of himself in front of a beautiful woman.

He ran away.

THE NEXT MORNING, DECLAN'S ALARM WENT OFF AT six-thirty, as it always did. He rolled out of bed and pulled on a pair of black sweatpants, then dropped onto the hardwood floor next to his bed. Three hundred crunches and half that many push-ups later, he was almost ready to face the day.

Holding onto a chair with one hand, he lifted the foot of his left leg and grabbed the arch, drawing it backwards. With a slow, steady movement, he pulled the foot closer, stretching out the quadriceps. The muscle didn't want to release—it never did—but eventually it softened enough for him to get through another day without pain.

Afterwards, he made his usual breakfast. A cup of coffee, two soft-boiled eggs, and a piece of wheat toast. He'd always had a weakness for good food, but never first thing in the morning. That was when he set the tone for the rest of the day. When, no matter what happened the previous twenty-four hours, he could hit the reset button. It was always satisfying to feel his body and his appetites fall back under his control.

He sat at his small table to eat, and he checked the morning's news on his tablet. Pablo ate his breakfast at the same time, then eyed Declan as he waited for the leftovers. As soon as the breakfast plate was set on the floor, the cat's pink tongue immediately went to work on the remaining egg.

Pablo always had dry food in his bowl, but he was quite skilled at pretending he was only one egg yolk away from starvation.

Declan followed breakfast with a quick shower. When his thoughts twisted toward Annabel, he slammed the faucet to the right and let the cold stream wash his lust away.

Well, he *tried*. He thought he might need to visit the Arctic Circle to find water cold enough to accomplish that monumental task.

He hadn't been able to get their conversation from the day before out of his mind.

After he dried off, he dressed in a pair of khakis and an Oxford shirt, then walked downstairs with Pablo at his heels. The orange beast decided that was enough exercise and promptly curled up in an armchair for his first nap of the day.

It was Sunday, so most Lost Coast Harbor shops didn't open until twelve. Declan doubted even a third of the town made it to church every week, but they still liked to pretend they were too holy to shop before noon. He didn't mind. It was the best time to catch up on inventory and check the shelves to make sure people hadn't moved a copy of *Lolita* to the self-help section or placed a Stephen King novel in the children's section.

Lost in a Book consisted of two rooms. Some shoppers never made it past the first one, with its new releases table and wall of bestsellers and book club picks. He'd put the children's section there, as well, because he'd discovered early on that it was best to keep the four-year-olds in his line of vision.

The rest of the first room was taken up with general fiction and the most fashionable non-fiction. In other words, the books people happily admitted to reading.

The second room was his favorite room. Row upon row of books of all genres, happily living side by side. Mysteries and science fiction and romance, thrillers and westerns. At least half his customers found themselves in this room every week. Sometimes, they didn't even bother stopping in the front room, preferring to head directly to their favorite section and load up on their literary drug of choice.

Declan pulled out a western by Larry McMurtry and set it aside. He'd already read it twice, but it was calling to him that day.

He would never dream of embezzling cash from his register. Books from the shelves, however…well, those were fair game.

As he walked between the rows, a familiar calm settled over him. While his parents listened to the Sunday sermon in the church across the street, he took a moment to worship in his own temple. Most of the time, Declan thought he believed in God, but books were his true religion. This endless world created by pages upon pages of history and ideas, of stories and poetry. It had always been this way. From the moment he learned how to string letters together to form words, he flew through one book after another. Growing up, his library card had been his most valuable possession.

And when the other boys threatened to beat him up for being, quite literally, a card-carrying nerd, Niall dragged him to his first karate class and made sure he could defend himself. After that, the other boys left him alone.

Declan opened his front door. The rain from the day before had been replaced by a thick layer of fog. He could barely make out the park in the middle of the town square.

Bending down to pick up the stack of local newspapers, he froze at the sight of a pink box wrapped in a large white ribbon.

His gaze immediately sought out the bakery. It was already open for those who wanted a coffee cake with their Sunday breakfast, but he couldn't see anything but the warm light spilling through its windows.

He carried the box inside and opened it slowly, unsure what to expect.

Inside rested two perfect eclairs, her specialty. Annabel

didn't make them often, probably because people would riot in the streets if the bakery sold out before they got their share.

The pastry was flaky, the whipped cream center was light as air, and the chocolate topping was just dark enough to balance out the sweetness of the filling. She knew they were his favorite.

Then he found the note.

One is for you. You can feed the other one to me tonight.

Declan gripped the counter, willing his body to settle while every drop of blood rushed straight to his cock.

Declan stared through the window, cursing the fog. He needed to see her expression. Was she only feeling playful? Teasing him a bit after his abrupt exit the day before?

Because if he didn't know better, he'd say Annabel Johnson was trying to seduce him.

CHAPTER FIVE

Time itself was trying to thwart her. That was the only possible explanation for how long it took the hands of the clock to move to five o'clock.

Annabel spent most of the day in the back room, trying to calm herself with familiar, repetitive motions. She kneaded bread, chopped vegetables, and made several trays of heart-shaped cookies, even though Valentine's Day wasn't for another week. She let Justine and Callie handle the front of the cafe. Every thirty seconds, she glanced at the wall clock and wondered if Declan was doing the same. If he was counting down the minutes till she made good on her promise.

A promise she'd been more than happy to make.

The day before, she'd caught a glorious glimpse of freedom. She could have it again. Jared needed her help completing a deal that Declan's father also wanted. She would help by seducing a man she already desired. Everyone's interests were aligned.

And if it bothered her a little bit that she wasn't being entirely honest with Declan...well, that was a small price to pay. Really, she was *helping* his family. He might even be grateful.

Her assistants got off work a half hour before the bakery closed. Annabel had changed their hours over a year ago, once she noticed the girls had started staying late enough to catch a glimpse of Declan. She couldn't blame them, but she had no intention of sharing their time together.

It was half past four when she finally took off her apron. She spent a few minutes primping. A little powder, another coat of red lipstick. She ran her fingers through her chin-length curls. Annabel performed a quick shimmy, making sure all her curves were still working. Annabel wasn't used to being told no, and she refused to accept that Declan would be the first to do so.

At a quarter to five, Annabel pulled on her knee-length trench coat and cinched it tight, then forced herself to wait. The bookshop closed at five o'clock on Sundays. She shouldn't seem too eager.

Five minutes before the hour, she locked her front door.

Their two shops were catty-corner from each other. She crossed Church Street first, to the large park at the center of the town square. She waited for a car to pass, then hurried across Market Street.

To the locked, closed bookstore.

She peered through the glass, searching for any sign of life. A smug orange face stared back at her.

"Where is he, Pablo?" she asked.

Her impractical heels clacked on the sidewalk as she circled the building, looking for Declan's car. His Volvo wasn't in its usual spot.

He hadn't waited for her.

Disappointment gnawed at her, but she returned to the bakery with the same swivel in her hips and smile on her face.

Unlike Declan, she didn't live above her business, but she still kept a change of clothes on hand. In Lost Coast Harbor, the weather could turn on a dime. Growing up in humid East Texas, she'd dreamed of moving to the mild, pleasant climate of Northern California. It was why, when she needed to run, she'd followed her heart to the out-of-the-way coastal town—only to discover she could have done a little more research. She saw more fog and rain in her first year in town than she had in her entire life to that point.

Annabel exchanged the red heels for a slightly more practical pair of Mary Janes, and she replaced the striped dress with its tight waist and flared skirt for a pair of slim black jeans and a cowl-neck sweater.

She walked the three blocks to her house but didn't go inside. Instead, she climbed into the compact car she seldom used. The poor thing was almost two decades old and barely ran, but it got her to the Hastings mansion.

On the night of the party, the house had been lit top to bottom. Fairy lights were strung between the trees and music poured through every open door and window. It had been exactly what Peter Hastings intended it to be: a joyful extension of the holiday season, a bright spark in the middle of gloomy January.

Now, only a few lights burned. Still, someone was home, so she tapped several times on the heavy oak door.

It swung open, and Jared greeted her with a harsh smile and a rush of whisky fumes.

"Please tell me the deal is completed." He only slurred his words a little.

Annabel arched her eyebrows. "In a single day?"

Jared cursed and walked away from the open door. She assumed he wanted her to follow.

"I'm afraid Declan doesn't want me the way you think he does," she called to his retreating back. "I tried twice, but he didn't respond to either overture."

She was forced to run to keep up as Jared strode toward the rear of the Hastings mansion.

"It doesn't matter," he replied. "It's already too late."

A tremor passed through her, and she reached for his arm. "What do you mean?"

"I mean it's not my problem anymore."

Jared made a sharp turn into a darkened room, and she followed him into a small sitting room decorated in a heavy, masculine style, with brown leather chairs and a bar cart laden with expensive crystal decanters. She could practically smell the money.

Jared went straight to the cart and poured himself two fingers of whiskey.

"Is there another way I can pay off the debt?"

"I said, it's not my problem." Jared added a single ice cube and nodded to the corner. "It's his," he muttered, then dropped into a love seat.

Annabel spun around. Though her heart raced, she forced a smile for the unfamiliar man sitting in the dark corner. "I'm sorry. I didn't see you there."

The man didn't so much stand as unfold from the chair. His arms and legs were long, almost disproportionately so.

He was no more than five-ten, but he gave the impression of being a much taller man, one made of nothing but his extremities.

His face was neither handsome nor ugly. He had pale eyes, pale skin, and light blond hair, like someone had lowered the saturation setting on his appearance. In contrast to his unsettling coloring, the man had the kind of nondescript features that vanished from one's memory soon after they met. He wore black pants, a black sweater with sleeves long enough to dip past his wrists, and a black turtleneck. Other than a fashion sense many goths would declare too dark, there appeared to be absolutely nothing special about him. Still, she fought a shudder.

"I don't believe we've met," she murmured.

The stranger didn't answer. His eyes scraped her from head to foot. He didn't see her so much as consume her, like he was translating an idea of a woman into the reality that stood before him. It was a greedy look, devoid of lust.

Then she was dismissed. The man addressed Jared, though his pained tone suggested he did so against his will. "While I appreciate your attempt at initiative, it was ill-conceived."

"Come on, Fowler," Jared protested. "You've seen the books. We've gotta sell. My father's just in denial."

Fowler raised his eyebrows. They were several shades lighter than his hair. "Your father is many things, but he's not a fool. These are lean times, and he needs your help to get through them. Once he is acquitted, everything will be restored."

Jared took a long swallow. "I'm not signing over my trust fund to pay for some overpriced lawyer." He sneered at the other man.

Fowler studied his fingernails. "That is between you and your father. I am here to ensure that Miss Johnson pays off her debt. If I understand correctly, yesterday you asked her to seduce a man to acquire information about a business deal she knows nothing about. A deal your father has rejected."

"So?" Jared took a long swallow, avoiding Fowler's eyes.

Likely because the eyes of a zombie horde would contain more life than Fowler's did, though Annabel kept that thought to herself.

"Leaving aside the fact that you used this woman's debt to work against your father, it's a ridiculous plan. Not all children are perpetual disappointments to their family," the man said. "Even if the local bookseller knew anything about this deal, there is no reason he would surrender confidential information. Declan may be his family's version of the black sheep, but there's no indication he is disloyal. In fact, at this very moment he attends Sunday dinner."

Annabel's heart gave a happy little jump. Of *course* that's where he was. He wasn't avoiding her at all. He just knew, like all the Donnellys did, that weekly dinners were only optional if one lay in a hospital bed, and even then they should expect a lengthy guilt trip.

The happy flutter lasted only as long as it took Fowler to remember her existence. His gaze returned to her, and she felt pinned in place.

"This means you have a week, Miss Johnson, to acquire an invitation to the next dinner. Peter said you had certain charms." Fowler gestured at her, indicating her body the way an electronics salesman would point to the latest HD televisions.

"I thought my plan was ridiculous," Jared grumbled. "And if you didn't hear, she failed."

"Corporate espionage disguised as pillow talk was ridiculous." Fowler retrieved a pen from his inside jacket pocket. It looked expensive. "Next Sunday, place this in Richard Donnelly's office. There's a small switch on the base. It's voice activated, so don't turn it on until the pen is in position."

She didn't miss the way he wiped his prints before setting it on the desk.

A bug. Annabel swallowed. She'd agreed to ask a few questions and pass on a bit of information. Not betray her friend's trust—or worse, become Lost Coast Harbor's version of Mata Hari.

"I can't do this." Her voice was small.

Fowler continued like she hadn't spoken. "Once you complete this task, half your debt to Mr. Hastings will be erased."

Half her debt. She let herself be tempted. It wasn't much, just leaving a pen behind. But if the pen was worth twenty-five thousand dollars to Hastings, it was the Donnellys who would pay the cost.

She lifted her shoulders in a self-deprecating shrug. "Truly, I can't do this. My charms don't work on Declan."

"Try harder." For the first time, Fowler really focused on her, his pale eyes burrowing into her and demanding she look back. That she hear his words. "If a name can be erased, it can be rewritten. Anna Belmont can be resurrected, perhaps without the burden of her past."

Her breath caught. She wanted to tell him to go to hell. The words were on her lips, and they died there. He wasn't just offering freedom from Hastings. It was freedom from her mistakes. The freedom to return home.

Her own name, free of pretense.

There was little she wouldn't do to put things back the way they were.

She nodded, and Fowler's thin lips twitched into something like a smile.

Without another word, the man left the study. Neither she nor Jared spoke until they heard the front door close.

"Who was that?" she asked, her voice barely a whisper.

"That," Jared replied, "is my father's overpriced lawyer."

CHAPTER SIX

Declan stared at the single eclair nestled in the pink bakery box, still sitting on the bookstore counter.

Annabel had made this eclair and asked him to save it for her.

Of course, that was before he left for Sunday dinner a full hour earlier than necessary. And lingered afterwards to help Bridget wash dishes.

Declan was many things, but he never thought of himself as a coward. He definitely didn't think of himself as the sort to run away from women. He'd never felt the need to do so before.

But other women didn't affect him the way Annabel did. It was that mix of sweet and wicked, the angel's face on a sinner's body.

Declan wasn't attracted to many women. Not really. He'd dated a lot in college, during that brief period of his life when he was surrounded by other readers. He'd stay up late with those women, discussing the relative merits of Wordsworth and Blake as if it were foreplay, then they'd have the only kind of sex one could have on a small twin bed in a dorm room—furtive groping under the covers. Stifled moans. Lots of missionary.

It was fun, and he hadn't missed any of those women when they inevitably stopped seeing each other.

Because it wasn't what he wanted.

One night, after sharing a bottle of merlot, he'd tied his date to the sturdy dorm bed frame. He discovered the power of not just controlling another, but controlling himself. After years of forcing his worst impulses to stay under wraps, he experienced the pleasure to be found in restraint. It had been revelatory.

The next day, the woman told everyone on their floor about the kinky English major down the hall. He learned to be discreet damn fast.

But discretion and small towns didn't mix, so when he moved back to town, he simply didn't date. He hadn't missed it much, at least until Annabel appeared in Lost Coast Harbor.

The day the bakery opened, he'd stepped through the front door, and she looked right at him and smiled. In that moment Declan felt like he was flying. He was a kite that had been untethered, and he spent the next three years alternately chasing and avoiding that feeling.

Declan preferred to be tethered. Grounded. It was why he'd finally asked out the focused and determined Maddie Palmer—then spent every minute they were together thinking about Annabel.

The woman who wanted him to feed her this eclair.

He ran his finger along the side of the pastry, scooping up the rich filling. Before he could eat it, the door opened. Pablo glanced up as the bell rang, confirmed that neither predator nor prey was entering, then went back to sleep.

Annabel stepped inside. She closed the door and leaned against it, watching him.

It was raining outside, and her blonde curls were covered in a fine mist. He tried not to stare at her lips, but he couldn't help a sharp exhale as they softened.

And her eyes…there was something in them he'd only seen once before, in a dark hallway in the Hastings mansion. A look that passed so quickly he told himself he imagined it.

Want. Maybe even a hint of desperation.

"You didn't lock your door."

Declan didn't reply. He wasn't ready to admit he was waiting for her.

Her eyes skipped to the cream filling still balanced on his index finger. "I had other plans for that eclair."

She took slow steps toward him, as if toward an easily spooked animal.

That did it. This might be a terrible idea, but he wouldn't act like a coward again. He met her halfway and raised his finger to her lips. "Show me." He raised one brow in a silent challenge.

Declan waited for the easy, playful laugh that would signal this was only a joke.

Instead, she held his gaze as she wrapped that perfect mouth around his finger and sucked it clean. Want gathered low in his stomach, and he inhaled sharply when she ran her tongue around the tip.

Images flashed through his mind. Annabel across his counter with her ankles in the air. On her knees while he thrust into her mouth. Tied to his bed with silk ropes, completely at his mercy.

Declan wrenched his finger free of her sinful lips and stepped away, putting the counter between them.

"What happened to not ruining our friendship?" His voice was steady.

She leaned on the counter and peered up at him. Her upper arms squeezed her full breasts together, just as she'd done at the bakery. The movement was so practiced he would have felt offended if his brain wasn't melting at the sight.

"I think I made a mistake," she said. "Don't you think so?"

The words felt as rehearsed as her position. She was saying everything he wanted to hear, and it felt wrong.

"What changed in the last month?"

She tilted her head, the better to give him a coy glance. "It's a woman's prerogative to change her mind."

Declan studied her so long that the silence grew between them and became another member of their conversation. At last she lowered her eyes and bit her lip, uncertain.

That small movement pushed Declan's self-restraint to its limits. He wanted to take that doubt away from her. He wanted to control how she experienced the world, if only for a brief time.

She couldn't know it, but her hesitant gesture tested his willpower more than her generously displayed cleavage ever could. Not that he didn't like the view.

But her doubt seemed out of place. It felt like Annabel was an actress playing a part—and she was the only one who knew the lines. This wasn't the friend he'd known for the past few years.

Which meant, for that moment, he didn't need to act like her friend, either. Declan placed one finger beneath her narrow chin and lifted it. Her lashes flew up as his lips met hers, then fluttered closed again.

It was slow and steady, his mouth relearning hers. She parted her lips and offered her tongue, but he drew back. Only when she made a small sound of protest in the back of her throat did he return, giving her the tip of his tongue. He licked softly at Annabel's lush lips, just enough to wet them.

When she stretched toward him, trying to deepen the kiss, Declan gripped her jaw, holding her in place, and continued his slow torture. He took her bottom lip between his and sucked gently, then he released her mouth and ran a finger along her jawline, down the column of her neck, and over the pulse that jumped beneath his touch.

"Is this what you wanted?" he asked, voice low. "Am I supposed to take you upstairs now?" Declan paused just long enough for her glazed expression to turn to confusion. "I don't know what game you're playing, Annabel, but don't make the mistake of thinking I'm a pawn." He stood up straight and walked to the back of the bookstore.

"But…" she managed, and he might be a bastard, but he felt a rush of pleasure when she stumbled over words. He refused to be the only one who didn't understand what the hell was going on.

"If you're serious, come back tomorrow night," he told her. "And we'll see if you deserve more than a kiss."

THAT WAS ABSOLUTELY NOT HOW THINGS WERE SUPPOSED to go.

She practically threw herself at him. Instead of a handshake, she sucked his finger. She gave him the bedroom eyes that always worked, and followed it up with a bird's eye view of two of the most perfect breasts in the county. Any reasonable man would melt into a puddle.

So why was she the one walking home on legs that could barely support her?

That hadn't been a kiss. It was a promise. A declaration that no matter what she offered him, no matter how she tempted, he was in control.

But he told her to come back tomorrow. A thrill zipped through her. She'd turn the tables. She'd convince him to…

To invite her to family dinner, where she would betray him. Her chest tightened at the thought.

It took her a long time to fall asleep, and still she was up before the sun. Bakers didn't get to be night owls, but this was usually the day she slept in a bit. Most businesses in Lost Coast Harbor's town square were closed on Monday, so this was her only chance to enjoy a leisurely morning of French-pressed coffee and whatever treat she saved from the day before.

So there was no reason for Annabel to be in the kitchen thirty minutes later, wrist deep in dough.

One after the other, she moved from bread to pastry to pie dough, sticking them all in the freezer when she was done. Next, she soaked the beans she would use for a winter minestrone soup.

She could only do so much. The Sweet Spot prided itself on serving fresh products, so the pastries needed to wait until the following day.

Seven o'clock, and she was already out of work for the day—but she still pulsed with energy. Her mind kept replaying images from the night before. Declan's lips, so soft and sure. The finger under her chin. The skeptical look in his eyes.

When she wasn't recalling the kiss, she was remembering Fowler and his promise. She could be Anna Belmont again. She could go home, at least long enough to visit her family.

Somehow, she needed to convince Declan to take her seriously. To think of her as more than a friend, more than a plaything. Someone he could invite to Sunday dinners.

A lifetime of never caring if a man wanted her to meet his momma, and now that was the only thing that mattered.

It was still drizzling as Annabel pulled her beat-up hatchback into the road, heading for the meat vendors on the edge of town. They delivered three times a week, but she decided to save them a trip. Thirty minutes later, she had a cooler full of roast beef, ham, and turkey. Afterwards, she visited a local farm to pick up fresh eggs.

All of that was a prelude to her final stop. A way to convince the local nursery owner that she hadn't driven through the rain just to question her about Declan Donnelly.

"You're up early," Maddie Palmer greeted her with a smile, and for a moment Annabel felt like a spiteful toad for using the woman to spy on Declan.

Maddie gestured between the two of them. "You're making me feel like I could try a little harder." Maddie wore blue jeans and a relaxed sweater, a far cry from the professional outfits she used to live in when she was the office manager at Hastings Shipping.

Annabel, on the other hand, wore a slim pair of black pants, a cream sweater that should never have been in proximity to dirt, and a pair of red Mary Jane flats. They were her casual shoes on the days when heels were so inappropriate even she couldn't justify wearing them.

She'd slipped a bit of product into her hair, enough to keep her curls under control, then added powder, mascara, and red lipstick. She never left the house without putting on at least that much makeup.

Standing in front of Maddie's natural beauty, her pale skin and enormous sea-colored eyes, for the first time Annabel felt overdone. Packaged. Was this what Declan liked?

"My mother always said girls should never leave the house without a manicure, lipstick, and a smile." She held out her hands, rough from a morning spent kneading dough. "I decided she'd have to settle for two out of three."

Maddie snorted. "You're still ahead of me. So, what brings you by today?"

"I've heard good things about your Swiss chard."

A low, gritty voice answered. "They're lying. No one says good things about chard."

Annabel turned to greet the man walking through the front door, but he wasn't looking at her. Gabe smiled at Maddie, his eyes so playful and full of love that she almost hated Maddie all over again.

"You're supposed to be studying," Maddie scolded. "It's why you took Mondays off."

"Bree stopped by. She said something about the Internet connection at the cabin being on the fritz, and how was she supposed to take over the world under those conditions. She's currently using your line to test how resistant a new product is to North Korean hackers. Or possibly to hack North Korea. I thought it best not to ask too many questions. But she was distracting me, so I came here." Gabe kissed Maddie on the cheek, then settled onto a stool behind the counter. Annabel got the feeling that, if Maddie's friend hadn't stopped by, Gabe still would have found an excuse to visit.

It took Maddie a second too long to turn back to Annabel. Even though she'd arrived before Gabe, Annabel felt like she was interrupting.

The chasm in her soul, the one she'd learned to live with over the past three years, yawned open. It had been so long, she could scarcely remember what it meant to not be lonely.

Maddie handed her a bag filled with greens. "We should have the early radishes in about a month. Assuming the sun ever comes out again."

"It might be a long wait." Annabel took a breath and blurted out the question. "If you don't mind me asking, why did you and Declan break up?"

She kept her voice low, not wanting Gabe to hear, but she was pretty sure he muttered something about "that fucking catalog model."

Annabel thought she was prepared to hear whatever Maddie might tell her, but she hadn't expected the woman to burst out laughing. "This town," she managed between giggles. "It's like living in the midst of a never-ending game of Telephone, where somehow the message is always garbled by the end. Declan and I went on exactly two dates. One was dinner, no dessert. The other one was the Winter Blues party, and we didn't leave together."

Gabe smiled at Maddie, just a little. If Annabel wasn't mistaken, the woman blushed.

Maddie rang up the purchase, and her expression turned a bit sly. "If I remember correctly, the last time I saw him at that party, he was heading in your direction."

"Oh." Annabel handed her a twenty. "That was it?"

"That was it. I don't know what he wanted, but it wasn't me."

Annabel hated to push, but she needed more. She needed something she could use to garner an invitation to Sunday dinner. "Then why did he ask you out?"

Maddie shrugged. "I think because he's a nice guy, and he wanted to date a nice girl. Other than that, you're on your own. Like I said, it was two dates."

She managed a single nod, then hurried to her car, replaying Maddie's words.

Annabel wasn't a nice girl. Nice women didn't launder money for gun runners. They didn't plan seductions to work off debts. They probably didn't spend three years wondering what their good friends looked like naked, either.

But if Declan wanted a nice girl, she would play that part to a tee.

CHAPTER SEVEN

Declan fell on the ground with a hard grunt. He looked up at his smug brother. "You have got to stop doing that."

Niall grinned. The bastard wasn't even winded. "Come to class Wednesday and I'll give you a break for a week. I've got a *muay thai* specialist visiting this month. You could learn something. Or anything. Learning anything would be an improvement at this point."

Declan rolled to his feet. For him, martial arts had been a way to defend himself when the other kids wanted to pick on the book nerd. Later, he came to appreciate how much discipline was required, but he would never share his brother's passion for MMA. Niall wore every split lip and bruised rib like a badge of pride.

Niall crouched down to pet Pablo as the cat wound around his legs. "Dad wants you to come by tomorrow."

Since their father wasn't there, Declan settled for giving his brother a disgusted look. "He could call. It would be easier than sending you every time."

"Would you pick up?" Niall countered.

They both knew the answer. "I was there for dinner last

night. Why didn't he talk to me then?"

Niall shrugged. "I didn't ask."

"Did you give him my message?"

"To fuck off? Yeah. He laughed. Come on, Dec. Dad's the one who taught us to swear. You really thought that would stop him?"

Declan groaned. "I was hoping to convince him I haven't spent years playing the nice Donnelly all so I can get elected to the town council and immediately act like a corrupt bastard."

Niall's eyes sharpened. "So you admit you're just playing?"

Declan leveled an even stare at his brother. "This again?"

Niall shrugged. "Well, we've never resolved it."

"It's resolved. You just don't like the answer."

Niall deliberately nudged a stack of books. "Because it's stupid. One mistake when you were seventeen shouldn't change who you are."

Declan straightened the pile of presidential biographies. "You know as well as anyone this is who I am. I always have been."

"There's a crashed car that says otherwise." Niall opened a book and cocked his head, as if confused by the words. It was a little too casual. "Come on, Dec. Everyone has more than one side to them. You aren't as boring as people think you are."

Declan plucked the book from his brother's hands. "I really am. Tell Dad I'll stop by tomorrow."

Niall rolled his eyes. "Fine. Now, please, I'm begging you, show me you have some idea how to defend yourself."

Niall rose into a crouch. At least this time, he gave Declan some warning.

"Damn it, Niall. You have got to find a better place to do this." Declan ducked around the new releases table to avoid his brother's grasping hands.

"If it makes you feel better, you can come into my studio and read Shakespeare." Niall grinned, enjoying himself too much.

There were a couple feet of empty space between the table and the counter. Declan headed for them, trying to minimize the damage.

His brother was the better fighter. Of that he had no doubt. He was also overconfident after two surprise takedowns in a week.

Niall raced at him. Declan feigned uncertainty until Niall was only a foot away. At the last second, he twisted to the side, sending his brother rushing past him.

"You bast—" Niall laughed as Declan yanked his brother's right arm behind his back. He got a foot behind Niall's knee and forced him to the ground.

Laughing, Declan smacked the back of Niall's head. "Who's the sucker now?"

"Oh my."

Both Donnelly brothers looked up at the quiet sound. Annabel stood in the open doorway, her green eyes enormous.

"Well *hello.*" Niall stood in a single fluid movement.

Declan's smile disappeared in an instant. With great effort, he didn't growl at his brother.

"Annabel is here for a book."

"Really? After hours?" Niall leaned toward him and whispered loud enough for the people on the next block to hear. "Is it the *Kama Sutra*?"

Declan punched his brother in the arm. The bastard laughed.

"I'm going, I'm going." Before he left, he gave Declan a cunning look. "Mom's starting to get worked up about you-know-what. Maybe if you bring Annabel to Sunday dinner, she'll relax for a bit."

Somehow, Annabel's eyes widened even more. "Dinner?"

"Ignore him," Declan said. Niall was being ridiculous. None of his siblings brought dates to Sunday dinner. It was a horrible thing to do to someone they liked. "Every two years, my mom gets worked up about the lack of grandchildren in her life. We've learned to ride it out."

For once, Niall didn't appear to be joking. "She's really on the warpath this time. If you don't want to be set up on blind dates with your cousins' best friends, at least pretend like you're dating someone. It'll make all our lives easier, trust me. If you're going to insist on being the boring Donnelly, at least go the whole way. Marriage, kids, minivan, etc. You two would have beautiful babies." He winked at Annabel on his way out.

ANNABEL STRUGGLED TO FIND WORDS. HER MOUTH HAD gone dry as soon as she stepped through the door to find the two brothers fighting. She knew Declan was strong, but Niall had the kind of muscles that would make the Hulk think twice. It shouldn't have been a contest.

But Declan hadn't needed brawn. His movements were flawless. Not a single wasted motion.

And when he stood over the other man and laughed, his face so open and free, she wondered why she'd never seen this side of her friend before.

His smile had set off something in her chest. The way he moved…well, that had an effect further down.

She stepped toward him. "Family dinner?" It couldn't possibly be that easy.

Declan glared out the window, as if he was hoping to burn a hole in Niall's retreating back. "The general rule of thumb with Niall is to ignore him."

"He's just tormenting you, like brothers do."

That caught his attention. "You sound like you know."

She cursed her thoughtlessness. Over the last few years, she'd learned to say nothing about her past. Not her family, or her hometown, or even how she learned to cook. When people asked, she always turned the questions back on them. In her experience, most people preferred talking about their lives to hearing about someone else's.

But this time, she found herself answering. "Not me, but my cousin Lola has a little brother that drives her crazy. He'll be sixteen this year." Annabel lifted a hand to her mouth, as if to prevent more words from escaping. She caught herself, dropping both hands to her side. She forced her fingers to relax and allowed her lips to curve. "But I'm not here to talk about that."

Declan arched an eyebrow, his earlier levity vanishing. "Why are you here?"

She fought the urge to fidget under his scrutiny. "You said to come back. Was this a mistake?"

"I'm still trying to figure that out."

Annabel tried reading his expression. Though his features were steady, his eyes burned.

At last, he broke the stare and walked away. Declan was halfway up the stairs before he glanced back at her. "Are you coming?"

Annabel inhaled and followed him without argument. Somehow, she could never get the upper hand with Declan. It didn't bother her as much as it should have.

Her eyes widened as she stepped into his apartment. Somehow, she'd known he wouldn't have the typical bachelor pad of leather and glass, or a messy kitchen filled with take-out boxes, but she'd imagined something simple. Predictable, even.

Instead, she stepped into an unexpected mix of natural and industrial. Tan sisal rugs lay beneath a coffee table made of wood and metal. The couch was covered with far more throw pillows than she'd expect from a single man, each with its own distinct texture. He'd decorated with large paintings of abstract landscapes. The far wall was exposed brick, while the near one was covered in floor-to-ceiling bookshelves. At some point, most of the walls had been knocked down to create an open plan that resembled an urban loft more than a small-town apartment. It was too large to be called a studio, but there were no doors or screens between the bedroom, living room, and kitchen.

The living room was pristine. Annabel doubted she could find a speck of dust if she went looking for one. Large plants stood in the corners. The overall vibe was a thoughtful, well-considered space. It wouldn't look out of place in a design magazine.

Her gaze was drawn to the king-sized bed against the brick wall. A dark wood nightstand and heavy metal sconce lined each side. She averted her gaze before her mind began to imagine what they might do on that bed. She strolled to the bookshelves and studied the titles.

"You don't have enough books downstairs?" she teased.

Declan stood in the middle of the room. "Those are for other people. These are mine."

Annabel ran her hand along the spines, knowing she touched something Declan loved. "You have a lot of poetry," she said.

"Does that surprise you?"

It made parts of her grow dangerously warm, but she chose not to mention that. "A little. I've never seen you read it before."

At last she turned to him, though she kept the distance between them.

"Why are you here?" Declan repeated his question from earlier.

The truth popped out, unplanned. "I couldn't seem to stay away." He didn't need to know her words were true on more than on level.

He made no movement, but she felt the tension in the room increase. Annabel stepped toward him, unable to resist the pull between them, so strong it was almost tangible.

Halfway across the room, she stopped, uncertain. "Who are you?" she blurted out.

He blinked, the tiny movement his only sign of surprise. "I don't understand."

"Are you my friend Declan, the sweet guy I've known for

years, or the one that pulled me down a corridor and kissed me like a starving man? Or are you this cold stranger in front of me?"

Declan's lips quirked. "I feel many things right now, but trust me. Cold isn't one of them."

Like he summoned it, heat wound through her body, and she took another involuntary step forward.

With the men in her past, Annabel always felt like she was in control. It wasn't difficult. There was little she couldn't accomplish with coy glances and a push-up bra. Two days ago, she'd imagined it would be easy to seduce the man she'd reluctantly rejected a month ago.

Annabel got the feeling Declan was still deciding whether or not he would be seduced.

She would help him figure it out. Too much rode on his decision.

Annabel raised her fingers to her top button and popped it open. His gaze dropped to her hands as she popped a second one loose, revealing the white lace bra underneath.

"Who are you now?" she asked.

Declan exhaled through his nose. His body was drawn tight as a bow, every muscle carefully contained. "One more," he told her.

"Answer me first."

"I'm the guy who's going to rip that blouse off if you don't do it first."

Need pooled between her legs.

She undid another button, then the last one, tugging the top loose from her waistband. One inch at a time, she slid it from her shoulders. Declan didn't just look at her. He *feasted* on the sight of her.

It was going to happen. Her breathing grew shallow as the realization hit her. After years of wanting him, tonight she would be in his bed. The thought almost made her giddy with relief.

It was followed by a sharp twinge. She'd imagined this moment for so long. If Fowler hadn't appeared in town, she'd still be standing before Declan. Still be counting the moments until he was inside her.

Except, if this had been her choice, it wouldn't feel tainted. She wouldn't lose Declan's friendship when he learned the truth.

She froze. Could she really do this?

"Take off your skirt." Declan's eyes were so dark they were almost royal blue, and not once did he lift his gaze from her. The longing she saw on his face made the decision for her. She thought she'd do anything to see that expression again.

She began to remove her heels, but he shook his head.

"Just the skirt."

Annabel had kissed her share of men, but none of this felt familiar.

Declan had accused her of playing a game, but she began to suspect she wasn't the only one—and she'd never played by his rules before. If her soaking panties were any indication, she very much wanted to learn them.

She slithered the skirt over her hips, then stepped lightly out of the circle of fabric. Annabel stood before him, wearing only red heels and white underwear. Declan's breath caught, and a sense of power swelled in her chest.

At last, he stepped forward, though he still stopped more

than a foot away. Declan reached out and drew a line with his index finger from her lips to her collarbone. He slid his finger between the valley of her breasts and lower, then hooked it inside the lace underwear and tugged. "Come here." His voice was deep and a little rough.

Annabel took the final step to close the distance. He was much taller than she was, and in her heels she still needed to tilt her face up to him. Her breasts brushed the soft fabric of his sweater. She shivered at the touch, her nipples hardening.

This time, she expected his kiss, but she was still unprepared for the rush she felt when his mouth slid over hers. He wasn't playing with her the way he had the night before, though his kiss was every bit as assured. He knew exactly how to coax her mouth open, how to tease her tongue with his until she pressed herself flat against him, needing to erase the lingering space between their bodies.

But still he held back. While his slow touches drove her wild, she felt his restraint in the way his fingers grazed over her shoulder. The way he cupped her jaw, resisting her attempts to intensify the kiss.

She broke free, unable to stand the excruciating torture, then slid her hands down his sweater, lifting it enough to place her hands on the warm skin underneath. Annabel traced his hard abs, fingers skimming along each brick of muscle. He expelled air and wrapped his arms around her. It was the first time she felt his embrace, and she longed to melt against him.

"How do you manage this on a pastry-a-day diet?" she murmured.

He laughed, the sound warm and unexpected. The Declan

she thought she knew best returned, and she leaned into him, welcoming the sound.

"Blame Niall. That's a good rule in general, but he's had me in martial arts since I was five."

"Isn't he only a year older?"

Declan nodded. "And a taskmaster by age six. But I don't want to discuss my family now, Annabel." He pressed against her, walking her backwards toward his bed.

His family.

She stumbled. She couldn't do it. Not like this.

But she couldn't *not* do it, either. Fowler had made the cost abundantly clear.

She didn't get to choose whether or not she slept with Declan.

Her arousal vanished. For the first time in Annabel's life, she felt like a whore. It didn't matter whether it was money or information. She was being commanded by another to use her body. Fowler might as well be her pimp.

Her knees hit the edge of the bed and she fell backwards. Declan lay beside her, still fully dressed.

She turned her head to the side. "I can't."

For one second, he was still, then he pushed himself forcefully away. He sat on the edge of the bed, watching her. "That's okay. Can you tell me why?"

"It's not because I don't want you. I do. But not like this." It was the truth, as much as she could tell.

"Like what?'

His eyes were so intent, it seemed impossible that he wouldn't see through every falsehood.

But somehow, the words that came out sounded so sincere. She was almost ashamed of herself for being such a good liar. "It's too rushed. We've been friends so long, but we've never been on a date. I'm afraid this isn't who I was raised to be." An idea came to her, a terrible, awful idea, and she sent up a silent prayer for forgiveness for what she was about to do. "I haven't even met your family."

Declan continued to stare at her. "My family?" he repeated. He sounded vaguely amused. Annabel felt exposed, lying before him in her skimpy underwear. She sat up, and his gaze dropped to her bra as her breasts swayed. He swallowed. "You want to meet my family first?"

At that moment, Annabel was thankful her dating life had been non-existent for so long. It almost made her seem like a respectable woman, the sort who might insist on being in a committed relationship before they slept together. "Don't worry about it," she said, understanding and considerate. "We haven't dated, so of course it's too early for that. My momma was a bit old-fashioned, and I guess I caught more of it than I meant to. But we can wait. Whenever you're ready. If you want this to be anything more, that is."

That time, she didn't need to fake the hitch in her voice. Until then, it hadn't even occurred to her that Declan might only be in this for a night.

Annabel scooted off the bed and moved toward the pile of crumpled clothes. Straight-legged, she bent over to pick them up, presenting Declan with a fine view of her ass. He might not succumb as easily as the others had, but he was still a man. If the universe hadn't wanted her to flaunt her assets, it shouldn't have been so generous when it was handing them out.

It sounded like he spoke through gritted teeth. "I don't think that's a good idea."

Annabel stood so fast the blood drained from her head. Once again, Declan had resisted her.

She was yanking her skirt over her hips when she heard his quiet footsteps move toward her. He stopped so close she could feel the heat of his body.

"I'll walk you home," he said.

CHAPTER EIGHT

Declan decided to wait three days to visit his father. He had enough free time, but the old man needed to realize that his entire family didn't jump the minute he snapped his fingers. Declan sent a quick email his dad would probably never see, then spent the week doing inventory with Pablo's help.

Every afternoon, he watched the minute hand of the clock swing past a quarter to four, and four days in a row, he didn't cross the street to visit. It didn't feel right, missing their daily chats, but he couldn't face her. He couldn't tell her why he was willing to sleep with her but not invite her to meet his family when he couldn't entirely explain it to himself.

Declan was used to understanding his own mind. He preferred it. And for the life of him, he couldn't understand how he felt about Annabel. He wanted her. He liked her. She appeared to be interested in him. Logically, he knew those three things meant they should at least try dating.

But something held him back. No matter how much he wanted her, he couldn't overlook the one-eighty she'd pulled in the last four weeks. Something felt off. And the way she'd responded to him Monday night, with soft eyes waiting for his next command—it was almost too good to be true.

Although it pained him, he needed to avoid Annabel until he figured out what he wanted.

Instead, he finally gave in and visited his father. Better to see the old man now than face his wrath on Sunday, with much of the family there to weigh in and pick sides.

His parents lived in the same house all his ancestors once called home. While the Hastings chose to build a mansion in the trees, separated from the town they helped build, the Donnellys were right in the thick of it. They lived in a sprawling Victorian just south of the harbor on the corner of Gold and Tidwell. It was the first house built in that part of town and still the largest.

If Declan ever needed evidence that he came from a long line of utter bastards, all he had to do was look at the streets where his family lived. His ancestor chose the names based on the metal that helped pay for the house and the man whose treasure he stole.

These days, the south end of town was considered the fanciest part. The streets were wide, the gardens were manicured, and the driveways mainly held German cars.

It was only a couple blocks long—Lost Coast Harbor wasn't a town that could support too many houses that cost more than half a million—but it was where he'd grown up. Where he'd played in the streets with his brothers, and read in the treehouse whenever he could sneak away, and eaten a ridiculous amount of Irish food prepared by a mother who'd never set foot outside the United States.

The place was home, but it was also the bane of his existence.

His mother swung the door open. Dark-haired and blue-eyed, she was the obvious source of Gavin and Bridget's coloring—except unlike them, she barely passed five feet. "Declan!" She rose on tiptoe to kiss his cheek. "Niall says you have a new girlfriend."

Declan made a mental note to beat the shit out of Niall at their next sparring match. "It's not like that," he told his mother's retreating back. She was already heading to the kitchen, where he expected to find a snack that could feed an entire basketball team.

"Bring her to family dinner," she called over her shoulder, ignoring everything he said. "I want grandchildren."

He followed her, because if he didn't, she'd chase him around the house until he listened.

And his family wondered why he didn't pick up the phone.

"We're not dating yet. And women don't get pregnant from Irish stew, Mom."

"Yet, is it?"

He cringed. Where had that come from?

His mother glanced back at him, looking far too pleased. "It's a start. Niall says she's the owner of The Sweet Spot. I like her."

"You barely know her. You like her coffee cake, that's all."

"Any woman who cooks is a good woman. She's pretty, too. And I'll get to know Annabel when you bring her to Sunday dinner. I haven't met one of your girlfriends in a long time. You're overdue."

"She's not my girlfriend, Mom."

His mother crossed her arms and stared at him. Though

Declan had his father's coloring, he'd inherited that particular expression and knew exactly what it meant. It was the one that said she would wait as long as it took for the answer she wanted.

And while he could return the expression, he knew his mother would win. She'd had a lot more practice.

Declan bit back a groan. "I'll think about it."

Molly stared at him for several more seconds, but at last she nodded. "That's a start."

"Why aren't you bothering Gavin and Niall about this? They're older than me."

His mother harrumphed. Of course she'd already hit up the others. No wonder Niall had been so quick to throw him under the bus.

"Niall is still sowing his wild oats, and Gavin…well, I can't even get him to talk about the subject. At least I have one respectable son." She patted his cheek lightly and handed him an immense corned beef sandwich.

Declan carried the sandwich into his father's office and handed it to the old man. "Mom forgot I'm a vegetarian again."

"More for the rest of us." His father took a huge bite and gestured for Declan to take a seat.

Declan needed to move several files off a chair before he could sit down.

As usual, Richard Donnelly sat in the midst of chaos. It wasn't so much an office as a collection of documents organized according to the principles of surrealism. The desk held at least a dozen picture frames filled with images of his wife and children. There was a blotter, a few paperweights, lots of scattered fountain pens, and a ten-year-old computer his father turned on as little as possible.

Richard reluctantly pushed the sandwich aside and leaned forward. Declan might as well be looking into a mirror, thirty years in the future. His father had the same dark blond hair and dark blue eyes, the same straight nose and clean cheekbones. There weren't many days growing up when someone hadn't told him he was the spitting image of his father.

That wasn't entirely true, though. He had his father's face, and he got most of his height, but Niall was the one who'd inherited the man's brawny build along with his gruff voice.

"Took your sweet time." His father had a tendency to grouse, but it never really sounded like he meant it. Even when he yelled, his family knew he was just letting off steam. It was when he was quiet that they needed to worry.

"I own a business, Dad. I can't drop everything without a good reason, and you didn't give me one."

"I thought your brother was clever enough to come up with a good lie."

Declan didn't bother hiding his snort of amusement. "We're talking about the same Niall?"

His father tilted his head in acknowledgment of the point. "Now that you're here, tell me what you know about Hastings Shipping."

It took great effort not to walk out. "I already told Niall I'm not getting involved."

Richard continued like he hadn't spoken. "You dated Maddie Palmer when she was the company's office manager, right?"

Declan threw his hands up. Two minutes in his father's

company, and already he felt like a frustrated teenager. "Two dates! We didn't even really kiss."

"Two dates and you didn't kiss? Do we need to have a talk, son?" The man's blue eyes damn near twinkled at his own joke.

"If you're asking if Maddie told me secrets you can use against the company, the answer is no. C'mon, Dad. Yes, most of the Hastings family are bastards, but the head of the company isn't so bad. Can't you just wait till he's back in town, then make the deal without working some angle?"

Richard's brow creased. "What fun would that be?"

Declan rolled his eyes. "Anything else?"

"I've been doing some informal polling about the council seat. It sounds like you're in good shape, but you'll want to hit up the head of the Rotary Club to solidify the victory. Otis likes fly fishing, so pretend you know something about that."

"I'm not going to help you with permits if I win."

His father waved his hand. "Help, don't help. Makes no difference to me. But for some reason you want to win, and this will help."

Declan nodded, a little chagrined. Sometimes he forgot that his father wanted to see him happy, even if they had different ideas how to go about it. "Thanks, Dad."

"Good. One other thing." He nodded at the tottering pile of folders on the right corner of his desk. "Grab the top one."

Declan flipped it open, afraid it would contain incriminating information he'd need to blot from his memory. Instead, it held a photo of a man who looked to be his early forties. He was on the skinny side, with long limbs and pale eyes. Declan tilted it slightly to study the image.

"Does he look familiar?" his dad asked.

After a second, Declan gave his head a slow shake. Looking at the photo gave him an unexpected sense of deja vu, but he couldn't recall ever seeing the man before.

"That's Victor Fowler. He's been in town the last few days, staying at The Capital."

Declan flipped through the file, and his father's interest became clear. "Hastings' attorney?"

"Sort of. He works for the same firm as the trial lawyers, though there's no record of him appearing in court or signing his name to any motions. I want to know why he's here."

"To help with the damn contract you're so desperate to sign?"

"He's not a lawyer, Dec. Not really. He may have passed the bar, but that was a long time ago. He's the pit bull, the one sent out to manage things when the proper attorneys don't want to get their hands dirty. They've got one of those at the firm we use, and she's damn handy. Whatever he's doing here, it's shady at best. I know a law-abiding, future councilman like you wouldn't want that kind of element in our town."

"At least try to be subtle when you're manipulating me, Dad. What do you want?"

"You live in town, and he's staying in the town center. All I need you to do is listen to the gossip from your customers. We all know our fellow citizens can't ignore the presence of a stranger for long."

There was no point arguing, and the task didn't sound too arduous. Declan didn't have a prime location for the town gossip—that was the diner or the local barber shop and hair salon—but he heard his fair share. It wouldn't be a bother to pass it on. "I'll let you know if I hear anything."

His father blinked, seeming surprised that Declan agreed so easily. "Great. Oh, while you're in an accommodating mood, do me a favor and bring that baker to Sunday dinner, okay? It'll get your mom off my back."

And that, Declan remembered, was why he did his best to avoid his family the other six days of the week.

Chapter Nine

Annabel checked her reflection six times. Three of those times, she removed the thin belt that cinched in her waist and brought her other curves into stark relief, and the other three times she put it back on.

Temptress for Declan, or good girl for his family?

She still had no idea why he'd changed his mind, but on Friday evening he'd phoned with an invitation to Sunday dinner. Maybe her mother had been right all along about that whole cow and free milk thing.

In the end, Annabel left the belt on. Her dress was a pale cream color, and that was close enough to innocent.

At precisely six o'clock, there was a knock on her door. She checked her makeup once more, then strolled through the house like she had absolutely no reason to hurry.

When she opened the door, she realized she should have taken a bit longer. Maybe done some yoga and meditation to settle her mind and body—because she had no idea how she was going to calmly get through the night next to a man who looked like this.

Other than the night of the party, when he'd looked devastating in his suit, she'd never seen Declan wearing anything other than a neat pair of khakis and a button-down shirt, often paired with a crew-neck sweater. He looked great in those, sexy as hell in a preppy kind of way. In black jeans that fit a little too well and a v-neck sweater the same color as his eyes, he made her skin tingle, like it was just waiting for his touch.

It had been almost a week since she visited the bookstore, and seeing him felt like she was finally taking a deep inhale after days of shallow breaths. It was disconcerting to realize how much she'd missed him.

Annabel had grown used to being alone. She didn't like it—in fact, she hated it—but for years it had been a necessity. She couldn't risk involving someone else in her questionable activities.

Now Declan stood on her porch, looking devilishly handsome, and all her heart wanted was to invite him inside and simply spend the evening with him. They could chat, or cook a meal, or curl up on the sofa and watch a movie. Right after they tore each other's clothes off, of course.

That sounded like a small piece of heaven, and for a moment she resented his family for intruding on her fantasy.

If Declan felt the same, he kept it well hidden. Instead, he studied her from top to toe. His perusal ended on her ankle-strap heels, one of her favorite pairs. "How many red shoes do you own?" he asked, a little bemused.

"If you want, I'll give you a fashion show later." She leaned forward and deliberately pitched her voice lower. "Maybe I'll just wear the heels."

His eyes darkened, but instead of replying, he held her

coat for her, then gestured toward the Volvo. She picked up a bakery box and headed for the car.

Declan stepped ahead of her, opening the passenger door a moment before she reached it. He didn't do it the way some men did, as if they were acting the role of a gentleman and expected praise for their efforts. For him, it was easy and natural.

When he walked around the front of the car, she tried to only ogle him a little.

In silence, he buckled his seatbelt, started the car, and adjusted the heater so it was aimed at her bare legs.

"I want," he said.

She blinked at him, needing a moment to understand that he was responding to her offer of a fashion show. "Well. Let's see how this evening goes."

A hint of amusement crept into his eyes. "Good point. After meeting my family, there's a fair chance you'll run home and blockade your door against all Donnellys."

Then he smiled, open and comfortable and everything they seemed to have lost this week, and she returned it, a little giddy.

They made idle conversation on the short drive to his parents' house. She told him the latest antics of the town's crochet group, who'd started gathering at her bakery, and he shared the horror story of the last book club meeting, when fifteen women and three men dared to take on *Odysseus*.

"I think they were trying to make up for their previous choice," he said.

"Oh dear," she murmured. "That's James Joyce, right? Quite a jump from BDSM."

"I don't know. Many college students would consider Joyce torture."

Her mouth twisted. "I've never even attempted to read him. I fear I'm not particularly well-read."

His brow drew together. "You read all the time."

"Mysteries, mainly," she said. "And cookbooks. Not serious books. Not like you read."

Declan shook his head. "You're not in high school. Books aren't supposed to be homework. Read what you love. I happen to enjoy those so-called 'serious books,' so people think I read proper books. I also love westerns and thrillers, especially spy novels."

"And poetry," she reminded him.

"And poetry," he agreed. "I'd be a pretty lousy bookseller if I thought people should only read the kind of books I like. Though really, more people should read Pablo Neruda."

"I'll ask him to show me some of his work."

Declan snorted. "That cat would write nothing but sonnets about tuna. If it makes you feel better, almost no one's read *Odysseus*. If they tell you they have, they're probably lying."

"Have you read it?"

He slid his eyes toward her, and his lips quirked in a small smile. "Of course."

She straightened her skirt and tried to recover from the look he'd just given her. "Any news on the council race?" Annabel understood almost nothing about town politics. Until recently, she'd never had a reason to care. "You must be a shoo-in." He certainly had the "women with eyes and hormones" vote locked down.

"There's more than a week before the vote, but it looks good. My father says I need to kiss up to the head of the Rotary Club. Otis Spatz apparently holds a lot of sway over the seventy-year-old-man demographic, and they all vote. He's known for his strong opinions, too."

Annabel studied his profile. Straight nose, strong chin, a defined jaw. She couldn't find a single flaw. "And what do you have strong opinions about?"

He glanced her way. "How much we're going to regret this dinner," he said with exaggerated solemnity.

Declan turned the car onto Tidwell and drew to the curb, then put it in park and turned off the engine. Both movements were a bit slower than necessary. "Looks like Bridget's already here. That's her car."

"The red Thunderbird?" It was a newer model convertible. She'd left the top down.

"My sister isn't known for her practicality," he said. "Last chance to call this off. You don't need to prove anything to me. I already respect you." His smile turned more than a little wicked. "I'll still respect you in the morning, too."

She swatted his shoulder and jumped out of the car before she launched herself at him, family dinner and Fowler's orders be damned.

When Declan met her on the sidewalk, he was still grinning. Every moment with him, every additional facet she discovered, she liked him just a little more.

It was easy to return his smile, so long as she didn't think about the pen in her handbag.

Her heart twisted.

She would do almost anything to clear her debt and

reclaim her name. She just hadn't expected anything to be quite so difficult.

THE FRONT DOOR SWUNG OPEN, AND LIGHT AND NOISE poured out. Annabel wanted to run inside and join in the fun.

A family lived here. A loud, boisterous family who bickered and teased and loved each other. If she closed her eyes, she could almost pretend it was her own.

Perhaps, when this was over, she could arrange another trip to see her family. Maybe they'd spend a week in San Diego, or even find a nice vacation spot on the Mexican coast. After three years in rainy, chilly Lost Coast Harbor, Annabel wouldn't turn down a week in the sun.

She gripped her slim clutch handbag, feeling the outline of Fowler's pen. All she needed to do was drop it off, and she'd be one step closer to freedom.

And maybe leaving the pen wasn't such a terrible thing to do. Not *really*. Obviously, Fowler was up to no good, but if Richard Donnelly was on the up and up, then no one would hear any incriminating information.

Nope. Even she couldn't convince herself of that.

Declan squeezed her arm as they stepped into the foyer. "Just remember," he whispered. "Use small words, avoid any sudden movements, and don't, for the love of God, listen to a single word my mother says about our future."

Our future. The words shouldn't make her feel so warm.

Together, they moved toward the voices.

"Dec!" A tall dark-haired woman came barreling around the corner, a half-full pint glass in her hand. "We were taking bets on whether or not you'd chicken out." Declan's sister sized up Annabel. "Or whether you would. Gavin said you seemed too sweet for this family."

Declan made a strangled noise.

"I don't know about that, but at least I brought something sweet." Annabel held out the bakery box.

Bridget Donnelly lifted the lid to peer inside. "Apple cake? You better run now. Mom will be fitting you for a wedding dress as soon as she sees this."

Declan's hand tightened on her arm. "Bridge, if you throw me under the bus, I swear…"

His sister swatted him. "That was all Niall. Don't be too mad. Mom won't stop talking about grandchildren. Last week, Gavin told her he had his sperm tested and they're slow swimmers. Total lie, of course, but it shifted her attention to Niall. He's too proud to pretend his boys aren't up to snuff, so Niall reminded Mom that he was traveling to a lot of tournaments these days and would be a lousy father."

Declan gave a long-suffering sigh.

"I have three sisters, too," he reminded Bridget.

"But Elizabeth and Neve are smart enough to stay away until one of us pops out the next generation. I told Mom that I'll cancel a date every time she mentions the words 'biological clock.' She hasn't said a thing in months, though I know it's driving her mad. It's all on you now."

Annabel bit back a smile at Declan's expression. "Help me take one of them down, Bridge," he said. "Which older brother is pissing you off the most this week? We know it's not me."

"He likes to pretend he's my favorite," Bridget mock-whispered to Annabel. "Well, Gavin brought the last party keg from this year's winter ale, so I like him right now—but Niall stole a sixteen-year-old bottle of scotch the other night. Said a Donnelly had no business drinking Lagavulin. Let's get him."

As they approached the kitchen, Declan dropped Annabel's arm, and her skin felt exposed and cold. It was because of his mother, she insisted. When any sign of affection was viewed as the first step toward grandchildren, of course he was going to be cautious.

She still missed his touch.

The kitchen was huge—even larger than the bakery's—but before she could study the bakeware and appliances, she was swallowed up by the rest of the family.

A tiny woman with dark hair reached her first, and gave her a quick head-to-toe study. "Good hips. I knew my son would choose well."

Declan closed his eyes and took a long inhale. "Annabel, this is my mom, Molly."

Unsure how one greeted a woman who'd already assessed her fertility potential, Annabel pressed the bakery box into the other woman's hands. "I brought dessert."

Molly opened the box and gave a small, satisfied smile at the sight of the traditional Irish cake. "I knew it," the woman repeated, then busied herself with the many pots on the stove.

Niall grabbed Annabel in a hug. "Thank you," he told her with great feeling. Annabel eyed the empty pint glass in his hand and wondered how long ago he arrived.

Gavin waved to her. Donnelly's Pub was only a block away

from the bakery, and they frequently saw each other in town, though they'd never had a reason to move beyond small talk. Declan's oldest brother had the same coloring as Bridget— dark-haired with lighter blue eyes than Declan—and when he grinned, she saw he had the same easy charm as his sister. "Annabel, you may be the bravest woman in all existence."

She laughed. "That may be overstating the case. It's just dinner. I'm hardly your first visitor."

All four Donnelly siblings were taller than she was, and they seemed to have a long, silent conversation over her head.

"How long *has* it been since your last guest?" she asked, suspicion growing.

"Niall brought a girlfriend home from college once," Bridget offered.

Annabel's eyes narrowed. More than a decade had passed since the red-headed Donnelly was a student.

"And Bridget's prom date in high school, because otherwise Dad wouldn't let her go," Niall added. "And Gavin's wife, of course."

For the first time since she arrived, the group grew silent. They stared at Niall.

"I mean, there is no wife. She is a figment of my imagination." Niall's voice dropped into a monotone as he stared off into the middle distance like he was hypnotized.

Gavin plucked the empty glass from his hand. "You're cut off."

At her side, she could actually feel Declan growing tense. Uneasy.

Before, she'd been curious why he changed his mind about inviting her. Now she was bursting to know. Imaginary wives aside, guests obviously weren't a regular thing. Only serious partners were asked to Sunday dinners.

Was that what Declan wanted with her?

She swallowed. The idea of Declan in her life for more than a half hour every afternoon wasn't just tempting. It felt like a gift. A good, handsome man who constantly made her smile—and made her body sing with his touch.

If they were dating, it meant she mattered to someone. It meant she had value beyond her ability to move money and stay quiet about it.

And it made what she was about to do that much worse.

"Excuse me," she murmured to the others. "Where is the…"

She had to do this. Now, before she changed her mind.

"I'll show you," Bridget said, shaking her head at her brothers. It was a small, exasperated movement, and Annabel suspected she'd made it many times over the years.

Declan's sister led her down a long corridor, and though she kept up with Bridget's easy chatter, Annabel couldn't recall a single thing she said. She was too busy scanning each room she passed, looking for the most likely spot to plant a bug.

"Dinner's in five, Dad," Bridget called.

Annabel's breath caught as the man himself emerged from a room just ahead of them. He shut the door behind him but didn't lock it.

"Hello, Annabel." He studied her once, with a little more reserve than the rest of the family had shown, then he offered the same grin that made her weak in the knees when his son did it.

If Declan looked like this in thirty years, his wife would be one lucky lady.

Something inside her clenched at the thought.

"Interesting choice," Richard murmured, as if to himself, then wandered down the hall, headed for the dinner table.

When Annabel emerged from the bathroom a minute later, the hallway was empty. She wasn't going to get a better chance.

She hurried to the closed door and tapped lightly. When no one answered, she eased the door open. The office was empty.

Annabel took one deep breath, then stepped inside.

CHAPTER TEN

I f she was a sensible woman, Annabel would have escaped out the bathroom window by now.

Why the hell had he invited her? All he knew was it had been some deadly combination of his family's unrelenting demands and the fact that, if he was honest, he rather liked the thought of dating Annabel. Walking through the front door with her on his arm hadn't been nearly so bad as he'd feared. It almost felt...right.

He'd never hear the end of it if she deserted him before taking one bite, so when the others carried dishes to the table—every meal in the Donnelly house was served family style—he went in search of his date.

His date. He shouldn't enjoy those words so much.

Maybe he should stop second guessing everything and just enjoy it. Even if he didn't understand why she was suddenly interested in more than friendship, he wasn't going to turn down the chance to find out.

There was just something about her. She was sweet and sly, wanton and old-fashioned, and the combination was deadly. He couldn't take his eyes off her, and he always wondered what she'd do next.

Just look at that dress she wore tonight. Virginal white that flared out from the waist. It would have been practically demure, except for the belt that emphasized every sweet curve and those heels that made her legs ten feet long and tilted her perfect ass until all he could think about was lifting the white skirt to her waist and driving into her.

The white skirt that was disappearing into his father's office.

Declan crept forward, not wanting to make noise on the hardwood floor. Annabel should have emerged as soon as she realized she was in the wrong room.

What the hell was that woman up to?

She'd left the door open an inch, and he pushed it inward a little more, enough to watch her move around the room. Whatever she was doing, she was so preoccupied she didn't even glance his way.

She looked worried. Her brow was knit together, and her movements were jittery. She glanced between the bookshelf and the desk and gnawed on her lower lip.

She withdrew something from her purse. A pen. She tapped the base, then dropped it on his father's desk.

Shaking her head, she snatched the pen up and hurried to the bookshelf. She stood on her tiptoes and dropped it behind a row of binders.

Annabel took two steps toward him. Before Declan could back away from the door, she rushed back to retrieve the item.

Her eyes darted to the wall clock, and he studied her face. Annabel's expression was hounded. Panicked. He felt an answering fear claw its way into his chest.

He barely caught himself before he pushed the door open and tried to smooth the line between her brow.

He had to know what she was doing.

When she used her skirt to wipe the pen clean, then held it carefully between the folds of the fabric as she placed it on the bottom shelf, he had his answer.

Declan backed away and hurried into the powder room next door. He gripped the bathroom counter so hard he thought he might break the marble. The fear in his chest transformed into a dark, pure rage.

It wasn't just his date who'd crept into his father's office. It was his friend. No matter what she'd said or done this last week, he'd never thought she was truly devious.

He listened to the sound of her heels moving away. When the gentle clacking sound disappeared altogether, he headed straight for the bottom shelf in his father's office.

Please let it be empty. She could have changed her mind at the last minute. Maybe she hadn't really betrayed him.

But it was there. The small pen that wasn't really a pen, because most pens didn't have a small button on the base. When unscrewed, they didn't reveal a tiny network of electronics.

Declan put it back together, then turned it off and pocketed the pen.

The rage settled into a low simmer, but now it was joined by a second, unexpected emotion. Intrigue. If she was going to throw away their friendship, he was damn sure going to learn why.

He took a second to mentally review himself. Hair

combed. Clothes neat. Bland expression in place.

Declan returned to Sunday dinner with his family.

EVERYTHING CHANGED WHEN SHE CLOSED THE CAR DOOR, trapping them in his sedan. Her nervous chatter was met with curt nods and monosyllabic responses, if that.

The air between them grew heavy. Oppressive.

She'd never wanted to talk to Declan as much as she did at that moment. She wanted to hear his version of his family's stories, learn about the two sisters who hadn't been present, ask why she was the first woman he'd ever brought to family dinner.

But Declan kept his attention on the road and made no attempt to break the charged silence.

It was a marked change from dinner. Barely a minute passed without one of the siblings teasing another, and the parents had long ago stopped trying to mediate their children's battles. Collectively, the family was high-spirited and clever, and Annabel needed to pay attention to keep up with them. Molly only made one or two comments about grandchildren, though she cast several thoughtful glances Annabel's way.

As much as he complained about his family, it was clear Declan belonged with them. Whereas Niall didn't seem to take anything seriously, and Gavin turned everything into a story, and Bridget appeared to always be on the edge of bursting from her seat, Declan was the calm voice of reason. He leaned back, only interjecting comments at the proper moment. No word was wasted, but more often than not his dry wit and perfect delivery had the table in hysterics.

She'd laughed and made conversation and tried to ignore the tightness building in her chest with every passing minute.

Because she liked this family, and she quite liked their son, and she didn't know how she could look any of them in the eye without despising herself a little for what she'd done.

That damn pen. She should have just dropped it on the desk in plain view. Richard seemed a bit absent-minded, and his desk was so cluttered she suspected a small car could disappear under the mess, but perhaps even he would notice it wasn't his pen.

If Richard Donnelly figured it out on his own, it wouldn't be her fault. She'd done what she was asked.

But no. She chose to hide it. To see her deal with Fowler through, so she was one step closer to freedom. She'd put her own needs first.

They stopped moving, but Declan didn't turn off the engine. His hands gripped the steering wheel, and his jaw remained locked.

She peered out the window. They were in the town square. Declan was parked outside the bookstore.

Outside his apartment.

"Should I drive you home?" he asked, not looking at her. "Or would you like to come up?"

Her breath escaped in a rush, and her fear vanished. It had just been the usual tension of a first date, the uncertainty of not knowing how the night would end. Declan was nervous. She would have been, too, if she hadn't had so much guilt to distract her.

"I'd like to come up," she said, her voice low.

Declan gave a single nod and stepped from the car. Annabel smoothed her skirt, taking a moment to settle her nerves. A blast of cold air hit her as the passenger door was yanked open. She placed her hand in his and let him pull her from the car.

It wasn't a gentle touch. Electricity shot through her body.

The walk upstairs took too long. Declan's steps were measured. Careful. Whatever uncertainty he'd felt in the car, it vanished as soon as she took his hand.

By the time they reached his apartment, she was breathless with anticipation. Last time, she'd insisted they stop before it went too far. Tonight, she had no such intentions.

It was going to happen. Just the thought made her nipples tighten.

Declan gazed at her chest with bold eyes, and she swallowed her nerves.

"Do you have anything to drink?" she asked.

Declan raised an eyebrow. "You need booze to be with me?"

"Of course not," she protested, but he was already in the kitchen, uncorking a bottle of red wine. "But it might help with the nerves."

"Why are you nervous?" He returned with a full glass, but he didn't so much walk toward her as glide. Every step was measured. Planned.

"It's been a while," she admitted, taking a grateful sip. That was the truth, at least.

He circled her, and she let herself stand still and accept his scrutiny.

"Is that the only reason?" He spoke behind her, close enough that his breath warmed her neck.

She took another sip and chose honesty. She had so little to offer him, she might as well give what she could. "You make me nervous, too."

He tugged on the zipper that ran along her spine, pulling it down a single inch. "Why?" His voice was liquid.

She hesitated, and he yanked the zipper backwards, tightening the neckline against her skin.

"Why?" he repeated.

Because you unsettle me. Because you are a good, honest man who deserves more than me. Because you're a controlling bastard, and I never want to say no. Because you are a completely different man than you were when this evening began.

Instead, she dipped her chin to better display the zipper. "Because I want you," she said.

Long seconds passed when he didn't respond. He didn't seem to breathe, let alone move.

Then he tugged her zipper down another inch, and then another. When he'd lowered it enough to reveal the strap of her bra, he paused.

"It matches your dress."

It almost sounded like an accusation.

"Well, yes. A darker color would show through the fabric."

Declan plucked the strap, letting it snap back against her skin. She started, the glass in her hand shaking.

"Don't spill the wine," Declan warned. "No matter what I do. No matter how I make you feel."

Annabel tried turning to see his face, but his hands gripped her hips, holding her in place. He kept an inch of space between their bodies. She inhaled his scent, warm with the hint of linen.

She felt his lips against her left ear as he learned forward to whisper. "You should be in black. Or red. Because however you may pretend, we both know you're not innocent."

Annabel stilled. "What do you mean?"

Declan pushed her dress to the side. He grazed his lips down her neck and across her shoulder. She shivered.

"Watch the glass," he reminded her.

Annabel took a long sip. Less wine meant less chance to spill. She thought she felt him smile against her shoulder. It was the first time his mood had lightened since dinner, and she leaned into his touch.

Maybe he was only teasing her. She'd hardly behaved like an innocent the last time she'd been in this room.

Declan's lips returned to her neck. He sank his teeth into the delicate skin, the movement slow and steady, and she gasped as the pleasure began to tip over into pain—and the pain contained a pleasure all its own.

A moment before it became too much, he released her, then blew gently across the skin. She knew he'd left bite marks.

Her breath escaped on a soft sigh. She arched her back and tilted her hips toward him, wanting to feel if he was hard for her.

Instead, he held her in place, keeping that single, torturous inch between them. He outlined the shell of her ear with his tongue. He whispered to her, the words so low it took her a second to understand—and once she did, the blood he'd heated seemed to freeze.

"I know what you did," Declan said.

CHAPTER ELEVEN

One moment, she was soft, almost melting into him. The next, she was so stiff he thought she would shatter if he touched her wrong.

Annabel turned her head to the side, offering her profile. "I don't know what you mean."

He had to give her credit. She recovered fast, and when she stepped out of his arms and spun to face him, her expression was adorably confused.

"I know what you did," Declan repeated.

She blinked several times, as if she had trouble seeing him clearly. "That sounds like an accusation. What, exactly, do you think I did?" Her lips pushed out a little in a gentle moue. He wanted to suck on that bottom lip, feel it grow swollen under his tongue.

Goddamn it. This wasn't the plan. He hadn't had much of a plan, really, when he invited her up to his apartment. There'd been some vague idea that they'd talk. Maybe she would confess. Then he saw her, standing in the same spot she had a week before, and he flashed to how she'd looked in her underwear, nothing but curves and pale skin and those damn heels.

She said she was nervous because she wanted him. Maybe it was another lie, perfectly told, but the words seemed to strip his capacity for reason. Because damn it, he still wanted her, too, no matter what she did.

If neither of them told the whole truth, did that make them even?

He wondered if she felt the space between them the way he did. Felt the emptiness where their bodies should be touching, or the cold air where there should be only heat.

Declan forced himself to meet her wide green eyes. She was giving an Oscar-worthy performance, but he saw something move in their depths, the barest hint of the panic he'd witnessed earlier.

He wanted to be angry. Anger was a tidy emotion, easily explained. Though he still felt the sting of her betrayal, there was nothing tidy about his feelings. He wanted to yell at her and demand an explanation. He wanted to make the fear that dwelled within her disappear.

And God help him, he still wanted to see her undressed, in nothing but a pair of red heels.

The uncertainty was too much. Of all the questions he wanted her to answer, he somehow blurted out the same one she'd asked him. "Who are you?"

The question hung heavy in the room.

Annabel's lashes dropped. "Does it really matter?"

Declan's chest grew tight at her non-answer. "Yes."

She kept her eyes lowered as she stepped away from him. "This was a bad idea."

He didn't remember moving, but when he looked down,

his fingers were wrapped around her upper arm. "But maybe, just for tonight, it doesn't need to matter."

At last, she lifted her eyes to him. "And tomorrow?"

Tomorrow, he would discover who she really was, but at that moment, all he wanted was proof her behavior hadn't been only about gaining access to his family's house.

Declan already suspected her flirtatious looks and tempting poses were rehearsed. He could accept that. He couldn't accept that every kiss was calculated. Every soft moan planned.

Tonight, he needed to prove that she could only control so much. "Tomorrow doesn't exist. Not yet."

Her eyes widened, but she nodded her understanding.

"There are two rules." He ran one hand along her upper arm and watched as goosebumps formed under his touch. "Are you ready to hear them?"

Annabel gave a silent, almost eager nod.

"You don't mention this to anyone else."

Hurt flashed in her eyes. "You're ashamed?"

Declan stroked her cheek. "No." He should be. He was about to hop into bed with a woman trying to harm his family, all because his ego refused to believe her desire had been feigned. But somehow, shame was noticeably absent. It would return the following day, and he'd pay the cost then. "I'm not ashamed," he said. "I'm private, and I want to remain that way."

"I won't kiss and tell."

"Good. Rule number two. Whatever you give me tonight, it will be honest. If you can't show me who you are the rest of the time, you *will* show me who you are when you're with me—and it will be the truth."

Her nod was slower this time, but she agreed.

They stood a foot apart, not moving. Neither seemed ready to take the next step.

Annabel recovered first. She gave him the barest hint of a smile. "Do we seal it with a kiss?"

Who could resist an offer like that? He took her small chin in his hand and brushed his lips across hers.

She placed her hands on his shoulders and eagerly rose on tiptoe, trying to follow his lips as he pulled away.

"There," he told her. "As binding as any contract." Declan nodded toward the other side of the room. "Put the wine-glass on the nightstand, then get on the bed on your hands and knees."

She only hesitated a second before obeying.

As soon as she was in position, Declan grabbed the hem of her dress and threw it over her waist, revealing her pale, flawless ass.

He exhaled through his teeth. Soon, he would skim his hand along that sharp flare from her waist to her hips. He would dig his fingers into her soft skin while he slid inside her one careful inch at a time, drawing out the torture as long as he could.

But for now, he only wanted to look at the round curves that narrowed to her sweet thighs. To stare at that thin scrap of white fabric between her legs, already wet enough to mold to her gorgeous pussy.

Annabel twisted to look over her shoulder, and he gave her a light warning smack on her ass. His breath caught as he waited to see her reaction.

She gasped, but she didn't move away.

"Keep your eyes on the wall. Don't look at me until I tell you." His voice was steady, giving away none of his uneasiness. Half of him expected her to jump up and run from the room.

The other half wasn't surprised when her lips softened and her eyelids grew heavy. She returned her gaze to the wall.

"Spread your legs wider."

This time, she didn't hesitate. If anything, she was eager to show more of herself to him.

"I'm not going to undress you. I'm not going to kiss you again, not on your mouth."

Annabel whimpered, and he gave her another smack, this one heavier than the first.

"Do you have something to say?"

Her curls bobbed as she shook her head, and he ran his hand over the red mark, soothing it. She exhaled at his touch.

"Are you comfortable?"

She nodded.

"You can speak, Annabel. I didn't say you couldn't." In fact, without her face to guide him, he found he very much wanted to hear her voice. Her body spoke volumes with its small shudders, the way her breathing changed every time he touched her, but it wasn't enough.

"I'm comfortable." A little sass crept into her voice. "Your sheets must have a high thread count."

Declan was glad she couldn't see him bite back his smile as he slapped her ass again.

God, those gasps. This time, there was no doubt that she loved it. His cock strained against his zipper, and he reached into his waistband to adjust himself. Pre-come had already gathered at the tip, and he wet his finger.

Declan knelt on the bed and pressed against her, letting the outline of his cock slide between her perfect cheeks. He leaned forward until he could touch her lips with his finger, and he painted them with his arousal.

Her tongue darted out, and he could barely breathe while he waited. Every step he took, he feared it was one too far, that any minute she would ask him why they couldn't just have missionary sex for a while.

Oh hell. The thought of his hips between her legs as he pounded into her, her nails digging into his back, their lips meeting in desperate kisses, threatened to send him over the edge. He took several long breaths, battling the desire to pull out his dick and slam it into her hot body.

Desire? Who the hell was he kidding? It was practically a *need*, a desperate craving to be balls deep inside her flesh.

"Do you like the way I taste?" His voice was ragged, and he stood up to retrieve the wine glass resting on his bedside table. Declan took a long sip and waited.

Though she remained facing forward, her gaze slid toward him. "More."

She earned another slap from his free hand.

Her body rocked forward.

"I asked if you were comfortable because you will remain in this position until I'm ready for you to move. You will not adjust your hands or widen your knees further unless I tell you. I have placed you exactly where I want you, and that is where you will remain."

He waited for her to protest. She said nothing.

Declan dipped another finger into the wine and ran it across her lips. "Wrap your mouth around it. I want to feel your tongue on my skin and imagine it on my cock."

She whimpered as she took the tip of his finger in her mouth. Her tongue circled it. The sight of her red lips wrapped around him sent his control spiraling again.

He wrenched his hand away and moved out of her line of sight.

Declan stood behind her with the glass of wine, and once again he dipped a finger into the liquid. He drew it across the width of her body, from one hipbone to the other, then followed it with his tongue.

Annabel shuddered, but otherwise she didn't move.

He placed the glass on the floor and sat on the edge of the bed. Declan grazed his hand across her panties, across the hot flesh underneath. He slid the flimsy fabric down her thighs and lifted each knee just enough to pull them off completely.

He stared at the sight of Annabel exposed, the pink flesh slick with her arousal. He hadn't thought it was possible, but his dick grew even harder.

Declan spread her lips with one hand, then ran his fingers across each revealed fold, learning the hidden parts of her body.

Declan slid a single finger inside, then added a second. Annabel's muscles tightened around him.

"Grind against me," he told her.

She moaned and pushed backwards onto his hands, then whimpered in protest when he withdrew.

One last time, he covered his fingers in the wine, then drew them down her right inner thigh, then her left. He braced himself on his elbow and licked upwards on either side, stopping just before he reached her lips. She tried wiggling her hips closer, and he almost let her. He couldn't wait any longer to taste her.

Declan dropped to the bed and positioned himself between her legs, looking up at her glistening cunt.

"Now you can move," he told her, grabbing her hips and pulling her down. Her thighs widened until she was just an inch from his mouth. Declan inhaled, taking her scent into his body. He turned his head to bite one of her inner thighs. Annabel squirmed, but his hands were locked on her hips, holding her in place.

Declan bit her thigh again, then gave her a long lick from her opening to her swollen clit. He pulled back enough to nibble her other thigh, then returned to her center, blowing warm air across her core.

She was gasping, shaking with the effort to get closer to him. A surge of triumph hit him.

He fitted his lips against her pussy, claiming her. God, even here she tasted like sugar. Sweet and musky. He hauled her closer, burying his mouth in her flesh.

He tried to be slow. He tried to cover her with long, steady licks, but as her taste dripped onto his tongue, he felt almost frenzied. He couldn't get close enough. He slid his tongue deep inside her, letting her heat encircle him.

His cock was in pain, trapped against unforgiving fabric. Declan moved one hand from Annabel's left hip, and she immediately dropped down on that side, rubbing herself against his mouth. She knew exactly where she wanted his tongue, and he let her guide him to the right place.

With a sigh of relief, Declan unzipped his pants, letting his dick spring free. He'd planned to be inside her already, but right then all he wanted was to feel her come on his lips and taste the rush of her release.

He fisted his cock and began stroking in long, rough movements.

He tilted his head to reach her clit. His tongue flicked over it, picking up speed with each of her gasps. He took his mouth away only as long as it took him to speak. "Drop onto your elbows."

Annabel obeyed, her forearms flat on the mattress. With her arms entirely supporting her weight, he was free to use his other hand. He slid his fingers inside her, thrusting with long, steady strokes. His lips latched onto her clit, pulling the hard nub into his mouth. She ground against him, her small gasps turning to cries, and those cries grew louder with each thrust.

He imagined that tight heat wrapped around his cock, and he stroked faster, wrapping his palm around the tip to bring pre-come down the shaft. Again and again, matching each stroke to the fingers thrusting into Annabel's hot pussy.

For a single second she froze, every muscle of her body tense. Even her cries quieted.

Then she screamed, and her body seemed to fall apart around him. Her hips pressed hard against his mouth, her legs shaking uncontrollably. Declan groaned against her flesh, feeling her orgasm pass into him, and that loosened his last thread of control.

He came hard, hot streams falling across his chest. Declan's head rolled back, and his guttural groans mixed with the last of Annabel's cries.

They didn't move for several long seconds, both needing time to find their breath. To remember how their bodies normally worked.

And Declan needed a few moments to remember who he was.

At last, she fell sideways onto the bed, and he levered himself into a sitting position.

Unwelcome reality intruded.

Did he cuddle her now? For a second, he allowed himself to picture it. He would take off his shirt and wrap her in his arms, his skin warm against hers while he murmured sweet nothings until they were both ready to go again. He would take off his pants this time, and she'd ask questions about his scar, ones he didn't want to answer.

Or did he remember who she was when she wasn't with him?

Tomorrow, he'd vowed to figure out who that was.

Tonight, he needed to get the fuck away from the woman who seemed to have climbed inside every pore of his being. He'd wanted to prove that her attraction to him was real. All he'd succeeded in proving was that, where Annabel Johnson was concerned, he couldn't be trusted to make the right decision.

He jumped up and headed for the shower.

"Declan?" Her voice was sleepy and satisfied, but a hint of uncertainty crept in.

He knew he was already ruining it, but he couldn't stop himself. Didn't want to. Whatever this was, it needed to be ruined.

"You can see yourself home. If it's too far to walk in those shoes, take my car. The keys are on the counter."

He closed the bathroom door behind him. For good measure, he locked it.

CHAPTER TWELVE

Damn straight she was taking his car. Three-inch heels and he thought she would walk home?

While her legs still shook after what he did to her?

The man was a *bastard*. Forget her previous debate about whether he was the sweet guy she'd known for years or the commanding, irresistible man who took what he wanted. He was just a jerk.

A jerk with a *really* talented mouth, but still a jerk.

She didn't care that she only lived five blocks from the bookstore, or that she'd walked home from the town square hundreds of times in all kinds of heels. *He* didn't know that.

Annabel had heard about the "wham bam thank you ma'am" version of sex, but she'd never been through it herself. It was safe to say she didn't like it. And the fact that it was Declan, of all people, who introduced her to that unpleasant experience only made it worse.

Declan. Sweet, kind, funny Declan. The clean-cut, slightly nerdy future councilman had just thrown her out on her ass.

She fumed as she turned the key in the ignition. Did he

think she did that with just anyone? A bit of fun, like watching a movie? But if they'd watched a movie, he probably would have let her stay long enough to watch the credits.

He *kicked her out.*

She pulled out into Market Street and followed the one-way street around the park, then headed north to her little bungalow.

Annabel had offered him a part of herself no one had ever seen. She wasn't entirely sure *she* had seen it before. She hadn't orgasmed. She'd fallen apart. In one hour, he'd shown her that all those boys she used to play with were just that. Boys. Every man she'd ever kissed, ever dated, now felt like a rehearsal for the real thing.

There was no excuse for his behavior. No excuse other than…

She stomped on the brakes when the memory returned. The car screeched to a stop in the empty road.

Declan knew what she'd done.

It wasn't possible. No one knew except Jared, Peter, and Fowler. She had no doubt Fowler would expose her if it was convenient, but she'd given him no reason to do so. Peter couldn't accuse her without incriminating himself. Even Jared wouldn't be that stupid.

Her breath grew quick and shallow. She yanked hard on the wheel, pulling over a block from her house and slamming the car into park. She leaned her head against the steering wheel and fought to calm herself.

If Declan knew she laundered money, the man could ruin her.

Annabel waited until her breathing was steady, then

schooled her features into a mild expression and returned to the road. When she hit the turnoff for her street, she kept going. Fifteen minutes later, she pulled into the Hastings driveway.

It was almost midnight, but that didn't stop her from striding up to the door and ringing the doorbell. When no one answered straightaway, she kept pushing it, each ring longer than the one before.

The door swung open to reveal a scowling Jared. "What the hell is wrong with you? You're waking the entire house."

Annabel glared at him. "You're the only one who lives here, now that your father's in prison."

"And the servants, and my mother."

"Oh." She paused, sad to see her righteous indignation thwarted so easily. In her defense, she wasn't used to visiting people with live-in servants, and by all accounts, Patricia Hastings took to her room after her husband's arrest and had yet to reappear.

Jared gestured for her to enter. "Come in. If someone wants to know why you were here tonight, let's at least provide a believable story."

She felt physically ill at just the thought of a late-night tryst with Jared. Almost better to have rumors flying about a suspicious midnight visit than about a possible affair.

With another death glare at Jared, she crossed the threshold.

When she entered the sitting room, she made sure to check all the corners. She didn't doubt that Fowler could emerge from the shadows like a vampire, but she wouldn't make it quite so easy for him this time.

Jared collapsed onto a brown leather armchair. He looked tired, but surprisingly he also looked sober. "What's so important?"

"I left the pen in Richard Donnelly's office."

He managed a smirk, though it wasn't up to his usual standards. "I knew you'd get to Donnelly. How'd you do it?" Jared leered at her. "Like I even need to ask."

Someday, if there was a just and fair God, Annabel would have the opportunity to kick Jared Hastings in the balls.

"Just tell Fowler I'm done."

"Done?" He shook his head, laughing. "Aren't you the optimist? You heard Fowler. This is a good start, that's all. The debt still exists."

"Then figure out another way to clear it. Something legal."

"Are you drunk?" Jared nodded at the loaded drink cart. "Then pour me one, too, so I can catch up."

"Declan knows. I don't know how. I promise, I was careful. I did everything the way your father told me. But he knows about the money laundering."

He leaned forward, mouth slightly agape. "Okay, now I really do need that drink. Vodka rocks."

He waited for her to pour. Gritting her teeth, she threw several ice cubes in a glass and added two fingers of vodka. Then, because he looked a little too pleased that she was serving him, she did the same for herself.

She didn't touch her drink, but Jared gulped his down. "Does he have proof?" he asked.

"I don't know." She should have asked. Should have demanded more information. She'd been so happy to be distracted by him. Even more than that, she'd been happy

Declan was willing to be distracted. For a short while, she'd forgotten her crimes, and she thought he had, too.

Jared ran a hand through his hair. It was longer than usual, like he'd missed his usual hair appointment. "You better find out." He stood and poured himself a second drink. "I won't tell my father or Fowler."

"But they need to know why I can't keep spying for them," she protested.

"Annabel, evidence is disappearing left and right. Witnesses are changing their minds or moving out of town. What do you think will happen if they learn your secret isn't so secret?" He grimaced. "Donnelly's a smug prick, but he doesn't deserve to have Fowler after him."

"Oh." She dropped onto the love seat. "Thank you," she whispered. Two words she never expected to say to Jared Hastings.

He shrugged it off. "Find out what Declan really knows before you panic. For now, Fowler wanted me to give you this once the pen was in place." Jared opened one of the wooden cabinets. He withdrew a small case and handed it to her. When she pushed the clasp, the lid sprang open.

Annabel's only exposure to spy equipment was through Bond films, but even she could identify recording equipment. It was a simple device, with a speaker, a slot for an SD card, and a few buttons to toggle the machine between record and play modes.

Jared dropped back into the armchair. "The bug you left behind only transmits about five miles. Something about radio frequencies. I wasn't listening that closely, to be honest. So not far enough to reach out here, but it'll make it to your house. Or the bakery."

"What about Hastings Properties? You have an office in town."

"I'm not the one with a debt to clear," Jared reminded her. "So unless you recently found twenty-five thousand dollars in your couch cushions, you'll walk out of here with this case. Someone will come by every evening to retrieve the recording."

Her debt. Her risk.

This was the cost of her freedom. Her name.

Her only other choice was throwing Declan to the wolves, and that would never be an option.

She closed the case with shaking hands. "This is it, right? After I do this for you, I'm done."

"That's not my decision to make." Jared almost looked at her with pity. "This isn't what I wanted, either. I'm still in favor of the deal. None of us are getting what we want out of this."

She wanted to say something cutting, or dump a carafe of water over his head. *Anything* that might make her feel better about this moment. But as satisfying as it would be to blame Jared, this wasn't his fault. He was just the messenger.

Perhaps Jared was only capable of being a decent human being once or twice a week, because he leaned forward and said, "You should probably keep giving it to Declan, just in case. It seems to be working for you."

That *was* his fault, so she had no compunction about chucking her full drink into his face.

For the first time since she arrived, she almost felt like smiling.

~

Declan was pretty sure he was going to break something. Possibly his tablet. He was already gripping the edges so tightly he was surprised the screen didn't shatter.

Annabel was at the Hastings mansion.

He'd feel guilty about becoming the sort of guy who followed a woman, except this particular woman kept going to the wrong places.

Years ago, he'd installed a GPS system in the Volvo after Niall borrowed it a few too many times without asking. When his brother commandeered the car for a week-long trip to Vegas, Declan decided it was time to do something. Niall still took it all the time, but at least now Declan knew where to find it.

He'd never used it to track someone else. Until now.

As the small green dot began moving again, he finally relaxed his hold on the device. She was leaving.

Declan dropped onto the edge of his bed as his breathing returned to normal. She'd only been there ten minutes. She wasn't spending the night.

He didn't doubt that Jared could be a ten-minute wonder, but Annabel needed a bit more finesse than that. He almost smiled at the memory.

Declan tossed the tablet onto his bed and began pacing. Some wire had come loose in his brain. Was he seriously more worried about whether she was fucking Jared Hastings than whether she was fucking over his family?

It wasn't hard to connect the dots. A bug in his father's office. A midnight trip to visit the family currently negotiating a high-stakes deal.

Annabel was working for the enemy.

A few minutes ago, he'd been feeling like an utter bastard. Now, he was pretty certain she deserved far worse treatment than he'd given her. Annabel might not know it, but she'd just declared war.

Declan picked up the phone and dialed. When it went to voicemail, he called again. This time, his brother picked up, his voice thick with sleep.

"Niall, get to the bookstore first thing tomorrow."

DECLAN AND PABLO WALKED DOWNSTAIRS AT EIGHT-THIR-ty. Niall was already waiting outside, even though it was raining.

"You that eager to buy a book?" Declan asked, unlocking the door and inviting his brother in.

Niall hung his coat on the rack, then shook off the drops that still clung to his short hair.

"Pablo needed a belly rub," Niall said, bending down to scoop up the orange cat.

Declan moved behind the counter and began clearing the previous day's work. He'd never ended a day so unorganized, but the night before, he'd been unable to think about anything but Annabel from the moment he flipped the sign in the window to closed.

Just over twelve hours, and it felt like everything had changed.

At least it was Monday. He had a day off to get organized.

Niall dropped into his favorite armchair. Pablo immediately began kneading his heavy sweater, purring so loudly they'd hear him in the next street. "I'm also here because I can't remember a single time my little brother summoned me to appear. I'm dying to know what's going on." He scratched the cat's head and eyed Declan. "Did you knock her up already?"

"No!" Declan didn't mean to shout.

Niall shrugged. "Wow. That certain? Sorry to hear that, man. If it helps, she's probably too good for you, anyway. No man should get a woman who looks like that *and* cooks. It's not fair."

"She's not perfect. Trust me."

"Oh, really?" Niall raised his eyebrows. "Out with it. What's going on?"

Declan took a deep breath and pulled the pen from his pocket. "She put this in dad's study last night." He tossed it to his brother. "It's a bug."

Niall caught it one-handed and studied it from every angle. Silently, he pointed to the button on the base.

"I turned it off," said Declan. "It's not recording."

"So sweet little Annabel is spying on us?" Niall seemed torn between annoyance and admiration. "What's she looking for?"

Declan waited, saying nothing.

Niall figured it out. "Oh. The deal you want no part of?"

Declan leaned his forearms on the counter. "I might be changing my mind about that."

Niall's lips twisted in thought. "Is this about helping buy out part of Hastings Shipping or getting back at Annabel?"

He'd expected his brother to be more enthusiastic. "Can't it be both?"

"I suppose." Niall shrugged. "I don't know. She didn't do anything Dad wouldn't do. Or Gavin, or me, or Bridget."

"None of you ever lied to me about it."

Whatever Niall was going to say next, he changed his mind at the last second. "You sure about this, Dec? I mean, I don't agree with any of the choices you've made the last decade or two, but they mattered to you."

He wasn't a stupid kid anymore. This time, he had a plan. "I'm sure."

At last, Niall's face broke into its usual grin. "Please, please tell me this involves you breaking the law."

"Of course not. I'm about to be a councilman." As soon as he spoke to Otis Spatz. With everything going on, it kept slipping his mind.

"You better not have summoned me here to *uphold* the law."

"Not at all." Declan tried not to smile. He was answering the first shot out of necessity. He wasn't supposed to enjoy it. "We're going to help the Hastings break it."

His brother leaned forward. "What did you have in mind?"

Declan nodded at the pen in Niall's hand. "How many times have you been told you sound just like our father?"

Niall's eyes lit up in understanding. "This," he declared, "was worth getting out of bed early."

Chapter Thirteen

Annabelle stared at the recording device. The light hadn't turned on yet.

Fowler said that, once turned on, the bug was voice activated. Maybe Richard Donnelly didn't start work until mid-morning.

Though it was Monday, she needed to get to The Sweet Spot. Tomorrow was Valentine's Day, so she should spend the day preparing several extra batches of heart-shaped cookies.

There was no reason for her to take the receiver to work. No reason at all, except that she *really* wanted to know what was being recorded.

An hour later, she rolled out cookie dough in the bakery kitchen with the receiver positioned on a shelf above her and the volume turned up.

She was so lost in the comforting movement of transferring cut-out pieces of dough to trays and baked cookies to the cooling racks that she jumped when Richard Donnelly's gruff voice came through the speaker.

"About time you got here."

"You saw me last night, Dad." The other voice was exasperated, and much too familiar.

Annabel froze in the middle of the kitchen, still clutching a tray of cookies. Just his voice, so low and cultured compared to his father's, sent a shock through her.

She'd never forget how filthy that refined voice could sound.

"Fair point," Richard agreed. "So now that you're here, let's talk business."

Declan groaned, and Annabel bit back a smile. He might be one of the most contained men she knew, but his father could still make him act like a petulant child. Parents did have a gift for that.

She felt a sudden pang for her mom. Just a little more of this, and they could once again share the same last name.

"Dad, I have the bookstore. That's my business."

"You're a Donnelly. If it has our name on it, it's your business. And if you stop avoiding your responsibilities, we can finally get our name on the shipping company."

Annabel stopped rolling out dough, all her attention fixed on the speaker. This was the reason she'd bugged Richard's office.

It was what Fowler wanted.

Annabel wiped her hands on a towel, scrubbing off the dough as fast as she could. Her small fingers wrapped around the memory chip and wrenched it out of the device.

She stared in horror at the small SD card. Her heart thudded in her ears, the sound a taunt. *Yes-no, yes-no*, it murmured over and over.

She could leave it out. Blame it on a technological malfunction.

And even if Fowler believed her, the debt would continue. The Hastings would still own her, and her past would never be erased.

She shoved the memory card back into the machine.

Closing her eyes, she sent up a quick prayer that neither man said anything damaging.

Richard was speaking. "The price they're asking is ridiculous. How many accidents did they have at the docks this year? They should be paying us to take some of the burden."

"Dad, do you have the money or not?"

"Of course I do," the older man grumbled. "It's just not liquid at the moment. I need you to handle that."

Annabel furrowed her brow, but when Declan spoke, he sounded more resigned than confused. "What do you need me to do?"

"I bought a bunch of gold bars when the price dropped. Felt appropriate, given our family's history. Now I need them turned into cash. They're already in a safe and everything. Drive to the Bay Area and bring back the cash in the same safe, and we'll have the money we need. I even offered a fair price, which should make you happy. I just want this over with."

"Dad, I'm a little busy. Get Niall to do it." His voice almost vibrated with tension.

"In that stupid yellow sports car of his? He'd be pulled over in a second, and I'd rather the cops not play asset forfeiture with seven million dollars. Take the Volvo. This is your family, and we need this. At least try acting like a Donnelly."

Declan gave a heavy sigh. "Fine. Load up the trunk. I can't go until Wednesday morning, though."

"That's okay."

There was a soft thud, almost like a fist against flesh, then the sound of a door closing.

After a second the red light turned off.

She'd heard rumors about the Donnelly family for years. Most of the stories took place long before she arrived. She'd always assumed they were exaggerated, the salient details adjusted as needed to produce an interesting story.

For the first time, she wondered what it really meant to act like a Donnelly.

Well, there was no better time to find out.

"TWICE IN ONE WEEK?" MADDIE SAT IN THE MIDDLE OF A circle of plants. She appeared to be either repotting them or performing some complex ritual. "The radishes are still several weeks away."

"I'm not here for radishes." She took a deep breath and prepared to ask Maddie yet another inappropriate question, but her mind skipped to thoughts of thick slices of baguette slathered in butter and topped with paper-thin pieces of radish. "Wait, will you have the French Breakfast variety?"

"That's the plan." Maddie stood and brushed the dirt from her hands. "So what brings you by?"

"Declan." The word burst out, like she'd been waiting to say it all morning. Mortified, she glanced around the nursery, afraid she'd see a shopper she hadn't spotted earlier.

Maddie smiled at her. "It's okay. We're alone."

"How soon she forgets."

Annabel started and sought out the source of the woman's voice that seemed to be coming from somewhere in the rafters. "Bree?"

Maddie's best friend closed her laptop and shoved it into a backpack, then climbed down from the loft. Bree skipped the ladder, choosing to hang by her fingers before dropping lightly to the ground.

"What were you doing up there?" The loft looked cold and damp, even by Lost Coast Harbor standards.

"Best spot for Maddie's wi-fi," Bree said. "My Internet line won't work for more than two minutes at a time. If the president of Coastal Telecom doesn't get his shit together soon…"

Maddie regarded her friend with love, humor, and a tiny bit of fear. "You can't blackmail the head of a corporation because you chose to live in the middle of the woods in a cabin with spotty Internet access."

Bree shrugged. "Then he shouldn't have posted such interesting photos to that dating site." She dropped her backpack on the counter and jumped up to join it. She perched on the edge, her legs dangling.

Annabel watched her with a touch of envy. While Maddie moved with the grace of a dancer, Bree had an effortless cool. Her bleached blonde hair and eight-hole Doc Martens helped with that image, but it was really her air of confidence that did the job. Bree gave off the impression that she did what she wanted when she wanted, and really didn't give a fuck what anyone else thought.

"Sorry," Maddie said to Annabel. "I didn't forget she was here."

Bree harrumphed in disagreement.

"I just know that Bree keeps secrets. You're fine."

Bree acknowledged the point. "So long as you're not messing with my Internet connection, your business is your own." Her eyebrows lifted. "And did you just say Declan is your business?"

Annabel hesitated. "I don't know either of you well, and I realize this is inappropriate, but…"

Bree waved off her concerns. "Pfft. I gave up appropriate for Lent in 2005 and never bothered to pick it up again. What do you want to know?"

"Declan is…" Annabel began.

"Nice? Sweet?" offered Maddie.

"Hot?" Bree suggested.

Annabel glared at her, and Bree held up her hands in mock surrender.

"He's awful." Annabel finished. "I don't understand him. I was hoping you could tell me a little about him."

Maddie's brow drew together. "Well, he's nice and sweet. And hot," she added, before Bree could jump in. "He's respectful."

The other women looked at Annabel in surprise when she snorted.

Maddie shrugged. "That's it. I can't say I know any of his secrets."

Annabel pursed her lips in thought. "But he has to have some. Everyone has secrets."

Bree looked unconvinced. "Everyone does, but sometimes they're pretty boring. I can't see Declan having anything worse than a hidden porn stash. Probably something kinky. The straight-laced guys are always the worst."

With great effort, Annabel kept her face impassive. Even so, she thought she saw a ghost of a smile on Bree's face.

"Well," she murmured. "Thanks for answering me. I know you didn't have to."

"If it helps," Maddie said, "the general opinion in town is that he doesn't want to be like the rest of his family. You've heard about them?"

"The Donnelly Devils." Everyone knew that much. "But I thought that was in the past. No one's stolen a cop car or been arrested in years."

"Uh-huh," Bree said. "Go to the back room of the pub one night with a bit of money and a strong opinion about this year's Final Four. Bridget will be more than happy to help you out."

Annabel's eyes widened. "If everyone knows, why don't the cops stop her?"

Bree laughed. "The cops and the Donnellys have an understanding no one else seems to understand. From what I hear, Valerie Childs is counting the days till she can hand the police chief badge to someone else. My guess is she's more than happy to look the other way until then."

Did Declan know Bridget was a bookie? If he was willing to overlook his sister's questionable activity, why couldn't he do the same for her?

Bree watched her closely. Annabel got the feeling she didn't miss much. "And then there's the scar, of course," Bree said.

Annabel stilled. "Scar?"

"You know, on his thigh."

Maddie glanced at her friend. "I forgot about that."

With great effort, Annabel didn't kick the slim brunette in the shins for seeing Declan's thighs before she did.

The woman seemed to catch her thought. "I forgot about it because it's been so long. We were still in grade school."

Bree picked up the story. "And Declan was in high school. He's about the same age as my brother, so they had P.E. together. Senior year, Declan just showed up in the locker room with a huge-ass scar on his leg. No explanation. And when people asked about it, he started wearing sweatpants, no matter how hot it was. No one ever learned how he got it."

"He *is* private," Annabel said, but her curiosity was piqued. And by piqued, she meant that she wanted to run to Declan and strip off his pants to see the scar for herself.

Only for the scar. Really.

"Sorry we couldn't help you more," Maddie said.

"But you did help. Thank you." She gave the women a small smile and headed for the exit.

Maddie stopped her. "You know, you can visit even when you don't have questions about Declan."

Annabel nodded, then hurried from the room before they could see the tears forming at just the thought of having real friends again.

CHAPTER FOURTEEN

Step one was complete, even if Niall had made a few last-second changes. Declan should have seen it coming. There was no way Niall would risk his precious baby when a boring old Volvo was available. At least the GPS tracker meant he'd get it back.

The trap was set. His car, theoretically stuffed with enough gold to make or break the deal, was parked on a dark side street that, years back, had experienced a string of robberies. The townspeople complained and motion sensor cameras had been installed so that the police could monitor the area.

Niall had friends in the police department. Several members of the department trained at his studio, and they'd be happy to give Niall a sneak peek at the video.

Now they had to wait and see who took the bait in the next day or two.

To Declan's surprise, step two involved following his father's instructions. It was time to look into Victor Fowler. Somehow, Hastings' attorney was involved in this mess.

A surge of anger hit him. If Fowler was involved, that meant the lawyer was screwing with his family—and using

Annabel to do it.

He wrenched his mind back from that particular edge. Thinking of Annabel never seemed to lead anywhere good.

Declan pulled open the wooden door, one of the few parts of The Capital Hotel replaced in the last fifty years. The hotel had been built at the turn of the last century, when the town reluctantly agreed that they might want guests from time to time, and then was more or less left to age with whatever grace it could manage. Lou, the current owner, had inherited the place from his father, and he acted pretty resentful of the fact.

That day, Lou sat behind the reception desk. Declan grimaced. The man usually worked in the back office or, more often, in the bar.

"Jimmy off today?" He forced himself to sound casual. Jimmy was young, sweet, and frequently confused. It would have been a lot easier to get information out of him. Lou was, on his good days, a cranky bastard. On his bad days, he mainly communicated through grunts.

"Yeah. Something about labor laws. Probably beats paying him overtime, though." Lou didn't sound sure about that. He glanced over Declan's shoulder into the bar, his expression almost longing. It was harder to sneak shots at the desk.

"I understand Mr. Fowler is staying at the hotel," Declan said. "I was hoping to meet with him. How long will he be here?" He kept his voice mild.

This must by why his dad asked Declan to look into the guy. Niall would have just grabbed Lou's collar and demanded the information while smiling and threatening to choke the owner. A little finesse might be the better choice.

Unfortunately, Lou didn't agree. "I don't give out guest info."

Declan nodded, the very picture of understanding. "Of course. I'll run up and ask him. Can you tell me his room number?"

Lou just looked at him.

"Right. Confidential." Declan was surprised to discover Lou cared enough to guard his guests' privacy. Maybe Niall's approach would have been more effective. He nodded at a phone on the desk. "I know you can put a call through, at least." Lou had stubby fingers, but Declan should be able to see the numbers he dialed.

"There's no point. He's out."

It was clear Lou had no interest in taking a message, and Declan couldn't imagine what that message would say. This had been a fishing trip, nothing more. "It's okay. I'll catch him later."

Declan wandered toward the front door. At the last second, he turned left into the bar.

Once, it had been a gathering spot for the town, but that was before Gavin opened the pub, which offered better beer and ambiance. The old-timers still showed up here on occasion, and it had karaoke on weekends, since Gavin flatly refused to allow that anywhere near his bar.

On a Monday afternoon, the place was empty. Declan settled into the corner, next to a window. The spot allowed him to see both the street and the hotel's entrance.

He didn't entirely know what he was waiting for. He doubted this Fowler guy would walk in and announce his plans to the hotel lobby. Still, any information was better than none, and he had no other plans that day.

He ignored the text from Niall, asking if he was coming to the evening *jiu-jitsu* class.

The bar offered a bunch of thoroughly adequate beers. Nothing as good as what Gavin made, but it was drinkable. He ordered a pint, pulled out a small book, and settled in to wait.

It was a slow day. Most tourists only came to Lost Coast Harbor in summer. The rain, fog, and cold kept them away the rest of the year. He suspected the place would be busier the next night, when locals decided to celebrate Valentine's Day in the old hotel, but at that moment the place felt deserted.

Declan read twenty poems and was halfway through his second beer when the outside door swung open. He sat up straight, but it was only a short older man with thick glasses.

Ten minutes later, he'd finished the slim volume and the drink and was ready to call it a day. The sun was setting, and he'd already wasted enough of the day.

The door swung open, but it still wasn't Fowler.

It was Annabel.

She crossed the lobby, and his eyes tracked every movement. She wore slim black pants instead of her usual dresses, and flat black shoes. The different clothes changed her gait. Her hips still swayed with every step, but the movement was less pronounced, the steps a little more spry.

"Lou!" She called brightly, holding up a small pink box. "I have a delivery for Mr. Fowler. Can you tell me his room?"

Declan would have expected the man to be charmed by Annabel. Instead, Lou scowled at her. "Why does everyone keep asking? I don't know anything about the guy."

Declan couldn't see Annabel's face, but the surprise in her voice was obvious. "You don't know what room he's in?"

"Of course I do. But I'm not telling you. You can leave the delivery here. He'll get it when he returns."

"Nice try, Lou." Her voice was a little too bright, an unsettling contrast to Lou's surly tone. "But I'm not leaving this eclair where you might be tempted to eat it. I'll come back later."

Her charm had zero effect on the ill-tempered owner.

Annabel spun around and, for a single second, she allowed her cheerful expression to drop, and Declan saw her as he rarely did. Unguarded.

She looked exhausted, and afraid, and in that moment he realized there were worlds he didn't know about her—and in those worlds, he might find an explanation for why she hurt him.

Then she spotted him, and the mask fell into place. It wasn't a sweet expression, however. It was scorn.

She strolled toward him, the movement of her hips once again falling into that hypnotic sway. Knowing it was exaggerated for his benefit did nothing to lessen its effects.

After several interminable seconds, she reached his table. She took in the empty glass and the book at a glance. "Drinking in the afternoon?"

"It's my day off, too." He nodded at her more casual outfit. His face remained calm, but his cock stirred to life. Declan was grateful for the table between them, especially since her eyes kept straying toward his legs.

Declan needed a second to process this version of Annabel. He thought she was perfect in the tidy outfits she wore in the bakery. He'd thought she was flawless in her pale blue dress at the ball. This woman standing before him…she was breathtaking.

The black jeans stretched over her hips, the fabric soft and a little faded from several washes. She wore an open cardigan—red, of course—but underneath she had on a simple white blouse, tied at the waist. He knew she wore makeup— the red lipstick gave that away—but for the first time he saw a few freckles scattered across her nose, and her eyes were unlined. She'd pushed her curls away from her face with a simple headband, and there was a smudge of flour along her jaw.

It was both the most and least perfect he'd ever seen her, except for one small detail.

She looked at him like he was an especially repellent insect.

She was the one who used his friendship and his desire for her to get an invite to Sunday dinner. Who was working with the Hastings family. Who planted a damn bug in his father's office.

So why the hell did he feel the need to apologize?

"Will you join me?" Declan indicated the other seat.

"If I do, how long will it take you to ask me to leave?"

He refused to answer, though he winced inwardly.

After several seconds, she sat down, though she perched on the edge of the seat, like she might hop up at any moment.

She raised her eyebrows at the book. "More poetry?"

He slid it across the table, and she flipped through it, stopping to read a few lines here and there. "Who's Swinburne?"

"One of those deviant English poets. The country did

turn out its fair share. Still, some of his early work is rather compelling."

Annabel pushed the slim volume back to him, every movement deliberate. Contained. "Do many women make my mistake?"

His brows drew together. "Mistake?"

"The mistake of thinking a guy who reads poetry will be sweet. Romantic. Sensitive."

He couldn't look away from the accusation in her green eyes.

"I…" He stumbled over the words. He hadn't thought he'd gone so far the night before. Perhaps a day apart had convinced her he was an over-controlling deviant, after all. "I thought you liked it."

"I *liked* being tossed out like so much garbage?"

Oh. "I thought you meant…" he began. "We agreed. One night."

"Really? Because I only remember one hour."

Considering everything she'd done—everything he *knew* she'd done—Annabel shouldn't have the upper hand in this conversation.

"You're acting pretty superior, considering what you did." He tried to stay calm. Impassive. The first one to shout always lost.

Somehow, the words came out louder than he intended.

"What did I do, exactly? Undress for you? Let you touch me until you were so turned on you couldn't keep your hands off your own cock?"

Declan swallowed. "Just tell me why, Annabel. I thought we were friends. These last years…was I really just another customer?"

Hurt flickered in her eyes. "I thought we were friends, too."

"Then fucking tell me the truth," he demanded, dangerously close to shouting.

Annabel stood, disgusted. "I wanted to know who you were. I got my answer. You're a jerk."

He glared at her and gestured for the bartender to bring him another beer.

She turned away and froze. Declan peered around Annabel to see what caught her attention.

Instantly, he recognized the man from the picture his father showed him. In the flesh, he looked stranger. The black clothes that covered him from head to toe provided a harsh contrast to his pale looks. Fowler was also leaner than in his photo, and more self-contained.

More menacing, too.

A memory flared in Declan's mind, gone before he could identify it.

Fowler's gaze locked on Annabel. The man was heading toward the front door, rather than away. He must have slipped in while they were talking and was already on his way back out.

His attention shifted to Declan, and something flared in the pale depths. Something that felt a lot like rage.

But the man only nodded at them. "Miss…Johnson," he murmured, before stepping into the cold night.

Annabel left the hotel without another word. Her steps seemed to drag, as if she was being pulled against her will.

She left the bakery box on the table. Declan lifted the lid.

It was empty.

A pint glass landed before him, and a second, smaller glass followed. It was filled with a brown liquid.

The bartender gave him a sympathetic glance. "I saw your expression when Annabel walked out. I got the feeling you could use this."

Declan threw back the whiskey. The man wasn't wrong.

CHAPTER FIFTEEN

It had been foolish to reinterpret Fowler's instructions. She was supposed to wait for him to pick up the recordings.

But when five o'clock rolled around, and no one stopped by the bakery, she grew agitated. Was he coming there, or to her house? The thought of that man in her space made her squirm. His presence would contaminate her home.

So, instead of waiting for him, she'd visited the hotel, hoping to drop off the memory card and be done with the whole thing. He couldn't be mad that she'd shown a bit of initiative, could he?

Of course he could. She got the distinct feeling Fowler would be happy if she never had an original thought.

Still, there was no reason for her to be so nervous. The man had asked her to get close to Donnelly. Fowler had no way of knowing that, during their entire conversation, she hadn't thought of Hastings or a bug or her former name, not once.

She'd been too busy trying not to claw Declan's eyes out. Or jump in his lap. Really, it had been a fifty-fifty chance of either.

As angry as she was about the way he'd treated her, she couldn't fault him. Not really. If she'd discovered one of her good friends laundered money for the town's most notorious criminal, she'd probably be upset, too.

Annabel sighed. This would be much easier if she wasn't afraid, deep down, that Declan was in the right.

Still, he should have at least offered her a glass of water before throwing her out. That was just good manners.

Her doorbell rang. Annabel glanced at the wall clock in surprise. She'd only returned home twenty minutes before.

With her hand on the doorknob, she took a long breath to settle her nerves, then checked the peephole.

Declan glared back at her.

It seemed their earlier argument wasn't over. She swung the door open.

"What's your connection to Fowler?" He didn't ask so much as demand.

Annabel felt her jaw begin to drop and caught it just in time. "I have no idea what you mean."

"Don't lie to me. You've done enough of that."

The words weren't slurred, and he was steady on his feet, but there was a sheen to his eyes she never seen before. It made him look wild. Unrestrained.

It set her nerves on end. "I don't believe you have the right to insist on honesty from me," she said. "Honesty being a by-product of respect, after all, and I don't remember you offering that last night."

"Damn it, Annabel." His hand slapped against the front door, the movement frustrated rather than violent. "Let me in. Let's talk about this."

She shook her head hard enough for her curls to hit her cheeks. "There's nothing to talk about." She peered over his shoulder. He needed to leave before Fowler showed up.

"Expecting someone?"

"Of course not."

He braced his hands on the doorframe and leaned forward, though he never crossed the threshold. "Is there someone else?"

She stared at him with wide eyes. This time, her surprise was unfeigned. "What on earth are you talking about?"

"You're blocking the door, refusing to let me in."

"You—" She poked his chest to emphasize her point "—do not get to ask that question. You don't get to kick me out, then act like a jealous boyfriend."

"I'm not jealous. I just don't want you to date other guys." His eyes were dangerously sincere.

"I hate to argue with your drunk logic, but that's what 'jealous' means."

"Can I come in?" he asked again.

A dark sedan moved down the street.

"No! You're drunk."

"Afraid you'll take advantage of me?" His smile was downright wicked. For the life of her, she could not keep up with Declan's moods—and she didn't have time to question his multiple personalities at that moment. About a hundred feet from her house, a car door slammed.

"You need to go. Now."

His face dropped at her inflexible tone, but he didn't argue. He pushed himself back to standing and took a minute to compose himself.

She shut the door before he finished.

She remained there, her forehead pressed against the wood, and waited for the sound of his footsteps. It took too long, and they were too slow when he finally left.

She held her breath, waiting. Please. Please don't let him cross paths with Fowler.

Declan wouldn't be driving, so she strained her ears, hoping to hear footsteps moving away, but he was too quiet.

Five minutes later, she was still standing in that spot when the doorbell rang again.

This time, it was Jared Hastings standing on her doorstep.

"What are you doing here?" She rose on tiptoe to look over his shoulder. Mrs. Wandsworth lived across the street, and Jared Hastings paying the baker a nighttime visit was the kind of scoop that would make her the star of the diner's next gossip session.

"Invite me in," he muttered.

Seeing no other option, she swung the door open and gestured for him to enter. "Is Fowler coming?"

"He sent me." Though the man pouted, he still looked around her house with interest.

Over the last few years, she'd done a lot to make the place feel like hers, even if it was a rental. She didn't want to see the home she loved through Jared's eyes. Annabel knew the place was a bit overdone. She'd decorated with soft, pale fabrics and accented it with all the glitzy pieces she could find—a chandelier dripping in crystals, gilt-trimmed tables, gold-striped pillows. It was hard not to feel glamorous when she curled up on the couch, but she doubted Jared would appreciate that fact.

"Pretty," he said, and she couldn't tell if it was a compliment or not. "But we should do this somewhere else."

Annabel held her ground. She liked this room. It was closer to the door.

"Fowler told me to stay away from windows. He also told me to take a plain car and not to linger in the doorway. He doesn't want the Hastings family connected to you any more than we have to be."

"Then why didn't he come himself?"

Jared snorted. "Because he wants to be connected to you even less. We can at least come up with a plausible reason for my visit." He gave her body a quick scan, almost out of habit.

"Never going to happen, Jared."

He shrugged. "If you say so. For now, I just need to hear the recording. Where should we sit?"

"If you head toward the back of the house, you'll find a small sunroom. It's not well-heated, but it's private." She picked up the recording device and followed him down the hall.

In theory, the room offered a bit of cheer on cold days, but the single-pane windows provided such poor insulation that she rarely used it. Even now, she felt the tendrils of chilly air sneaking past the weak glass.

Jared already sat on one of the wicker chairs that faced the large windows. He gestured for her to take the seat next to him.

"I thought we only needed to swap out the SD card."

Jared rolled his eyes, though she didn't think the gesture was meant for her. "Of course not. That would be evidence. I've never met a man more paranoid." He moved the switch from record to play. "Though maybe you gave him reason. For someone who spent the last three years doing what you have, you don't seem to have any idea how to be a criminal. It's a wonder you didn't bring my dad down years ago."

"No one ever sent me to a conference on advanced money laundering techniques," she said tartly.

He looked at her in surprise, as if he didn't know she was capable of jokes.

Jared turned on the device. It only took a few minutes. After the morning's conversation, Richard must have worked quietly for several hours. There was a phone call in the late morning that consisted mostly of "uh-huh" and "no," then the door slammed. Richard ran several businesses, so it made sense that he wouldn't remain in his office all day.

When the recording ended, Jared pulled out his phone and typed a lengthy text. He fidgeted while waiting for a reply, and she refused to break the silence.

At last, his phone beeped. Jared read it aloud. "He thanks you for your service and says, much to his shock, you earned your keep this week. I'm just quoting." Jared tucked the phone back into his pocket. "He says he won't need to follow-up until later this week."

A couple of blissful Fowler-free days. It was almost enough for her to forget that he was probably planning something awful with the information she acquired for him.

Jared stood and stretched. "You still seeing Declan?"

Annabel raised her eyebrows. "Those were my instructions."

He didn't look pleased about that. "He's so fucking sanctimonious. How can you stand it?"

She ran through all the adjectives she'd use to describe Declan. Frustrating. Unpredictable. Infuriating. Sexy as all hell. "He's not that bad," she said instead.

Jared shrugged, unconvinced. "Whatever. Fowler said to keep stringing him along, but I think Declan's served his purpose. You can move on." She thought his pained expression was meant to be a come-hither look.

Annabel stood up, more than ready for him to leave. "I'm happy where I am."

His confusion would have been cute, if it was on any face other than Jared's. He took a step toward the hallway before pivoting back to her. "Crap. I almost forgot."

She cringed as he sat back down.

"Fowler wanted me to give this to you." He pulled an envelope from his pocket and unfolded it. "Said something about a carrot and a stick."

She gripped the back of her chair and stared at the item in Jared's hand like it was covered in poison. If the carrot had been the promise of her name returned, something awful was in that envelope.

Annabel refused to be a coward. She wrenched it from Jared's fingers and tore it open. Inside were five typed pages detailing three years of identity fraud. The sixth page was a photocopy from a book of sentencing laws. One paragraph was highlighted. The mandatory minimum for identity fraud was two years. Scrawled on the bottom was a short note. *When the deal's dead.*

Her hands shaking, she raised her eyes. "What does he mean by this?"

Jared plucked the papers from her hand and skimmed

them. "I'm sorry." He seemed to mean it. "I think he's letting you know that you're not off the hook yet."

Blood drained from her cheeks. She couldn't even draw breath. For a moment, it felt like her entire world froze. "He can't do this. There has to be an end." Rage overtook her, and she ripped the pages in half. She tore the paper again and again, until small pieces fluttered to the ground at her feet. It didn't erase the words. They were never going to give her name back. It had all been a lie. All of it. "I won't do this anymore. The cost is too high."

Jared shrugged. "I hate to tell you this, but it will be a lot higher if you don't. That's how my family works. Find a way to do it. You're way too pretty to go to prison."

DECLAN MADE IT HALFWAY DOWN THE BLOCK BEFORE HE turned around.

She had someone in there. He knew it.

It was possible it was the beer that was so certain, but he was still going to listen to it.

Most nights, Declan drank wine. A glass with dinner. If it was an especially good vintage, he might allow himself two glasses. It relaxed him.

Apparently, three beers and a generous shot of whiskey relaxed him a little too much.

What—or who—was she hiding?

He was still two hundred feet from her front steps when a familiar figure moved into the beam of the porch light.

Jared fucking Hastings.

CHAPTER SIXTEEN

Declan paused, considering his options. A smart, reasonable man would leave. He already knew what kind of woman Annabel Johnson was. Granted, he seemed to forget every time he saw her face. And, okay, her body. Or heard her voice. Or watched her brows draw together when she was confused or saw her face smooth into a pleasant smile when she lied.

God, he even adored the way she lied. The damn woman should come with a warning label.

In the end, two things kept him from doing the smart, reasonable thing and walking away.

The first was that Jared fucking Hastings had just stepped through her front door. No way was Annabel going straight from Declan's bed into the arms of that smug prick.

The second thing was that he was still pretty drunk.

Decision made, Declan crept back toward her home. He caught the bluish light of television screens through her neighbors' windows and hoped most of them had settled on their couches for the night. This would be a bad time for Mrs. Wandsworth to be spying through her front window.

First, he moved toward the front room, trying to look confident enough that no one would mistake him for a peeping tom.

Annabel's lights were on, but the sheer drapes were closed. He could make out the vague shapes of her furniture, but it didn't look like there were any people in the room.

Declan hesitated only a second before slipping around the side of the house. He'd never been inside Annabel's home and could only guess at the layout.

Despite being so close to town, it hadn't been built during the late eighteen hundreds like so many others in the area. This street had borne the brunt of an earthquake sometime during the forties. The quake destroyed several of the town's original Victorians. Most of them had been lovingly rebuilt, but one was razed to the ground by a transplanted Los Angeleno. The man had moved to Lost Coast Harbor after a series of notorious Hollywood flops. He'd missed the small bungalows that populated his former neighborhood of Los Feliz, so he decided to recreate one of the red-roofed stucco homes in his new home.

The first window had frosted glass. Probably a bathroom. As expected in February, it was closed, so he kept walking. The next windows were large and also closed. Heavy curtains hung across them, blocking his view. Declan weighed his options, then chose the stupidest one possible.

In his defense, the window was unlocked, so he wasn't doing the breaking part of B&E. It slid open easily.

For a moment, he was angry that Annabel had made herself so vulnerable.

As he climbed through the open window, Declan discovered his judgment wasn't the only thing that was impaired. Though he had no problem climbing through the window, he struggled with the dismount. His feet became tangled in the curtains. Declan fought for balance, but that seemed to have vanished with the third beer. His landing was cushioned by thick wall-to-wall carpet, but the floor still shuddered around him.

He held his breath and waited to see if anyone heard, but no footsteps moved toward him. After a second, he picked up the quiet murmur of voices.

Declan rolled to his feet, finally remembering some of his martial arts training. He was in a bedroom, one with so many mismatched pieces of furniture and so few personal touches it had to be a guest room.

He wondered what Annabel's bedroom looked like.

Focus, you idiot.

Once he was standing, he felt more steady. The adrenaline of the fall seemed to have burned off some of the booze. While he might not be able to wrench his thoughts fully from the image of Annabel in bed, it was possible the beer wasn't *entirely* to blame for that.

He sat on the bed and removed his shoes. With one hand on the wall to steady himself—just in case—he followed the voices down the hallway.

A few seconds later, he stood outside another room. He didn't risk peeking through the doorway, but he could hear them easily enough—and for good measure, there was a bathroom just behind him, one he could duck into quickly if they moved.

That was becoming a strange new habit of his.

Jared Hastings' voice reached him. The man sounded as superior as ever. "You're still seeing Declan?"

"Those were my instructions." Declan closed his eyes, his worst fear confirmed.

"He's so fucking sanctimonious. How can you stand it?"

"He's not that bad." Annabel's voice was pure and clear, and he wanted to fall into the sound. There was something so sweet about it, though it didn't match the woman he was coming to know.

That woman didn't mind getting a little dirty.

He blinked as he processed her words at last. He wasn't *that bad*? What the hell did that mean? That was the kind of vague statement a person made when it was too much bother to really defend someone. Like, he might need to bathe more, but at least he didn't spit on nuns.

On the other hand, perhaps she was saying he wasn't as bad as she'd accused him of being earlier. That was a much better interpretation, Declan decided.

Annabel's voice dropped, and he forced himself to pay attention. He'd missed a full minute of their conversation while attempting to parse four damn words.

"I won't do this anymore. The cost is too high." She sounded afraid. If Jared Hastings made her feel that way, he was going to pummel that asshole's perfect face until it was unrecognizable. No jury would convict him, not if they were forced to listen to Jared for more than thirty seconds.

Damn it. He'd missed Jared's response again. He only picked up the last bit. "Find a way to do it. You're way too pretty to go to prison."

Prison?

Whatever this was, it went far beyond some stupid local business deal.

Declan almost missed the sound of footsteps. He dropped into the bathroom a split second before Jared emerged from the room.

The man walked straight to the front door and left.

Prison?

The word echoed in his head. He was still trying to make sense of it when Annabel decided to use her powder room and came face-to-face with the man who'd broken into her house.

Her scream cut off as soon as she recognized him, though the panic lingered a second too long. She smacked him in the chest, hard enough for him to grunt.

"What are you doing? What did you hear?"

Declan raised his hands in a gesture of surrender. "I'm sorry. I didn't mean to scare you."

"What, exactly, did you mean to do?" She glared at him, and he had the uncomfortable feeling he deserved it.

"I wanted to know…I mean, it was Jared fucking Hastings. Why was he here?"

Her green eyes practically sparked with her anger. "You're jealous, and you're drunk, and you think that gives you the right to break into my house and ask questions?"

He tried to protest. It wasn't that cut and dried. This was a complicated situation, though he couldn't quite express why.

"Get out. Get out get out get out." She pounded on his chest to punctuate each word.

He stepped out of her reach, only stumbling a little. "I'll go. We'll talk tomorrow."

She advanced on him. "You think so? You think we're ever talking again after you invade my space, after you…" She caught herself.

What else had he done? He tried to remember, but his muddled brain didn't offer much help.

They were at her front door. With one hand, he scrabbled for the door knob and pulled it open. He stepped onto the porch in a hurry, then paused for a second, just to look at her.

God, she was so beautiful.

If they hadn't been ruined before, he'd just messed it all up. Except, he reminded himself, she messed it up first, so he didn't know why he felt guilty.

Maybe it was because, for the second time that day, he caught her look of fear and exhaustion. The look of a woman overwhelmed by what she faced.

And he'd been the one to put it there.

For a moment, he felt completely sober. "I'm sorry," he said again, knowing it wasn't enough. He turned away.

"Wait!"

He spun around a little too fast. The world wobbled, but at least he was able to see her face again. Her lovely, lovely face.

Okay, maybe he wasn't quite sober.

"Get back in here."

He hurried into her foyer, realizing as he stepped over the threshold that his shoes were still in her guest bedroom.

"You're going to tell me exactly why you're here."

He nodded dumbly, and she sighed.

"But first, I'm going to make you a cup of coffee while you find your shoes."

Five minutes later, she returned to the living room with a French press carafe on a silver serving tray. Several slices of crusty bread slathered in butter sat next to it.

"Eat," she commanded. "Soak up some of that beer."

"I only had three pints."

One of her eyebrows arched, unimpressed with his argument.

"And a shot," he conceded. "A big shot." It seemed unmanly to be a lightweight, and he didn't want Annabel thinking of him that way.

The bread looked really good. He tore off a piece, then poured the coffee into a mug and added sugar. There was no milk, he noticed. Because, of course, Annabel knew how he took his coffee.

They'd been friends for years. They knew so much about each other. He wondered how it stacked up against the mountain of things they didn't know.

She waited until he dusted off two slices of bread and half a cup of coffee. "Why did you break into my house?"

"I…" He stopped. He couldn't think of a single lie that justified what he'd done. Only the truth had a chance of excusing his actions. "Because I can't make heads or tails of what you're doing. You put a bug in my dad's office, but you're mad at me. You're upset about how things ended last night, but you didn't even want to date me. You were instructed to."

Her lids lowered. "You heard that?"

He didn't bother to reply.

"It's not what you think," she began. "Wait. You know about the bug?"

"Of course." He blinked at her. "I told you I did last

night."

"You didn't, you said…you said you knew what I did."

Declan took a long sip of coffee, trying to hurry sobriety. "What did you think I meant, Annabel?"

She brushed it away. "It doesn't matter."

"Whatever it is, could it send you to prison? Is that what Jared was talking about?"

After a moment that lasted so long it felt suspended in time, she gave the smallest of nods.

He closed his eyes. If he looked at her, he knew he wouldn't be able to think straight, and he needed whatever faculties he could still gather. "What did you do?"

When she didn't answer, he opened his lids a crack. She sat upright on the couch, staring at her hands. "I don't want to talk about it."

That wasn't good enough. The woman before him had gone from friend to date to enemy to criminal, all in the space of a week. If there was information that could help him understand, he needed it. "Was it something violent?"

Her answer was quick and steady. "Nothing like that."

"Did you steal something?"

She shook her head. "I don't want to play twenty questions."

Declan stood, glad to find himself more steady on his feet. It was a small room, and he paced from one side to the other. Twice he did this, then came to an abrupt halt. "Right now, there are three things I don't know. Three things that bother the hell out of me. Why you could go to prison, why you put a bug in my dad's office…and whether any of what passed between us was real. If I go home, I won't be able to sleep because the damn questions will keep me up all night. I need some answers, Annabel."

"I'm not going to tell you what I did, because I don't want to go to prison."

"You think I'd turn you in?"

She shrugged. "Everyone says you're the good Donnelly. The future councilman. I don't want to put you in a position where you have to choose. It's better that you don't know."

He started pacing again. "I'm not *that* good. I've been around my family my whole life. I think I've learned how to keep a secret."

His words seemed to trigger a memory for her. Annabel's eyes dropped to his legs. "How did you get your scar?"

Declan stopped moving. "Who told you about that?"

"Just a bit of town gossip."

"Old, forgotten gossip," he pointed out. "Have you been poking around my past?"

"Of course." Her retort was a little sharp, and he was perversely pleased to see her spirit return. It was a marked improvement over the quiet, withdrawn woman too afraid to answer any questions. "I was tired of waiting for you to tell me."

He sat back down, only a few inches of space between them. "I never lied."

Her chin jutted forward. "That's not the same as the truth."

Declan exhaled. "I suppose you could say the scar is my secret. Want to trade?"

Her mouth rounded as she considered. Even now, moments after recalling the week that changed his life, his body noticed the expression. His body wanted him to hurry up with the whole baring-of-souls thing so they could get back to what they started the night before.

"Which of your questions will I answer?"

Whatever her crime was, it sounded like it was in the past. There was no rush. Obviously, the pen was the most pressing issue. Knowing the full story behind why she left it in his father's office might prevent further sabotage against Donnelly businesses.

None of which explained why he said, "I want to know what was real."

She swallowed, and he made no effort to change his answer.

"You first," Annabel told him.

He held her gaze, looking for proof that this was the right choice. That she wouldn't blame the man he was for the choices he made at seventeen.

"Whatever we say, it doesn't leave this room?"

Annabel looked amused. "You really do like your secrets, don't you?"

He flushed, remembering that he'd made a similar request the night before.

She took pity on him. "Consider this a circle of trust." She glanced between them. "A line of trust?"

His lips quirked. "A couch of trust."

She nodded. "That'll do. Now start talking."

CHAPTER SEVENTEEN

He sank into the couch. Maybe if he acted relaxed, his memories would follow suit and not clench up like they always did when he tried to recollect that night.

"My family tends to do things a little differently than other families."

Annabel smiled at the reminder. "They're not nearly as bad as you make them out to be."

"They're wonderful." He must not be fully sober yet. "I mean, they're good people when they're not running the local law enforcement ragged. They never hurt anyone. It's all just a game to them. But it's not a game I wanted to play. While my siblings were off looking for every kind of trouble they could find, I mainly wanted to hide in the treehouse and read."

"Sounds like a pretty good way for a ten-year-old to pass his time."

He chuckled. "I was seventeen when I stopped. The thing is, my family teased me all the time, but I was still one of them. And I wasn't completely hopeless in their eyes. I still went to parties. I got drunk a couple of times, until I figured out that it wasn't worth my dad's reaction."

"He got angry?"

"I wish. He'd march into my room at six the next morning with a pair of cymbals. Seriously. Then every half hour after that until I got out of bed."

"It dissuaded you from teenage drinking, so I guess it worked."

Declan snorted. "He wasn't trying to dissuade anything. He was having fun. Anyway, that's how it was growing up. We hung out together, then I went off to be the book nerd and they went off to raise hell."

"What changed?" Annabel moved to face him, and her knee brushed his leg as she changed position.

He gave a rueful laugh. "Even book nerds can raise a bit of hell. Junior year, the school offered this study program in the summer. An intensive course split between Oxford and Cambridge. I was desperate to go. It wasn't just a chance to learn in a more challenging environment, or hang out in the Bodleian Library, though those were major selling points."

"You really are a nerd." Both the tone and expression were teasing. For a second, it felt like they were back in her bakery.

"Never doubt it. But the trip would also give me a chance to meet with some Oxford dons. I could try my hand at the A-levels and go through a couple interviews. Until then, I'd never dared imagine that could be my future—four years in the UK, attending one of the best universities in the world, completely separate from my family and their insanity. As soon as I heard about the program, I was obsessed. I asked my parents for the cash, but I forgot about my dad's policy. Donnellys earn their own damn money."

"How much was it?"

"Three thousand dollars. I knew Niall and Gavin could get that money in a week, so I tried thinking like them. I even learned how to hot-wire a car. I stole one, drove it halfway down the block, then panicked. I put it in park and ran away. I learned how to pick locks, but I was too scared I'd get caught. I refused to sell drugs. While, at seventeen, I would have happily considered escort work, there was little demand for my services."

"Mmm-hmm." She lifted an eyebrow, and he almost blushed.

What were they talking about?

"So what options were left?" she asked.

Right. That. "None that I could see. One day, I went for a long walk in the woods, because it felt like the proper setting for my despair. I tripped over a metal box that hadn't been fully buried."

She leaned forward, intrigued. "Please tell me it held pirate treasure."

"Better. Forty thousand dollars."

Her mouth dropped open.

"I was dragged to Sunday school my entire childhood, but that might have been the first time I was certain God existed. And not too far away from the first box was another one, also full of money. This was a ways out of town, next to this old abandoned barn. There weren't any houses nearby, so I had no idea who it belonged to."

"What did you do?"

"I took three thousand dollars, of course. I ran home and gave it to my father. He counted it, studied me for a long while, then said, 'I guess that's Europe sorted.' He never asked me how I got it. That's the second part of his policy."

He ran his hands through his hair, feeling the stands spike up.

"I could have stopped it there. I meant to. But it kept eating at me, the thought of all that money, just sitting there in the trees. Someone had to use it, after all. It might as well be me. I told myself I'd use it to travel to Prague and Rome and have all sorts of cultural experiences, like a noble purpose could justify stealing the money."

"Only you would consider a visit to the Coliseum noble."

She still looked at him with kindness, even understanding. He braced himself for the end of the story. "I started to pilfer the money. Just a little bit at a time. Soon I was back there every day, grabbing another hundred dollars or so. Just five bills out of hundreds. No one would miss them, right? Then one day I had this moment of panic. What if the barn wasn't really abandoned? So that day, I peered inside. It still had a dirt floor, and the wood was rotten, and no sensible person would live there...but people were working in it. They were running a printing press."

"I'm guessing they weren't printing pamphlets."

"Nope. Genuine counterfeit American money. Thousands of twenty-dollar bills. Paper money is actually made from a cotton-linen blend, so there were stacks of fabric waiting to be printed, dried, and cut, then placed in a couple of metal cases. Three men were working in the barn. As soon as I spotted them, I backed away and hurried home."

He didn't pause. Didn't wait for her response. The words flowed from him, as fast as he could speak them before he lost his nerve. "Niall was in my room when I got back. He'd been away on some wrestling trip, so he only just heard that I came up with the money. Unlike Dad, he had no problem asking questions. When I didn't answer them, he got my wallet off me and found another six hundred dollars inside. And that was the first time I thought Niall might secretly be a genius, because he looked at this perfect twenty-dollar bill and asked why the flag on the White House was pointing right instead of left."

Annabel hung on his every word.

"He wanted to know where I got it, and I refused to tell him. So Niall figured out how much time had passed between school letting out and me getting home, and he saw the mud on my boots from tromping through the trees. He made a pretty good estimate of where I'd been that afternoon, though it was still a pretty big area. I swear, I don't even know what came over me. I thought Niall was going to race out there and grab the metal boxes. There's a pretty strong finders-keepers attitude in our family, and I didn't want to fight him for it. So I ran downstairs and out the door. He started shouting when I got into his car. I figured he couldn't follow me if I took the Trans Am."

"Wow. He's always had terrible taste in cars."

He knew she was trying to lessen the tension, and he appreciated the effort. "Always. So I hot-wired the thing—turns out I was a natural—and peeled out. I knew he'd be in Gavin's car within minutes, so I drove as fast as I could. I needed to park far enough from the barn that no one would see the car, then get to the money on foot. But it was already getting dark, and the fog was thick that night. Too thick for the speed I was driving. I roared to the barn at full speed, and it seemed to appear out of nowhere. I slammed on the brakes, and the whole car swung around. I crashed through the rotting wall and slammed into the printing press."

Declan closed his eyes, fighting the wave of memories. The screech of tires and the crunch of metal. The roar of flames and the thick black smoke billowing out of the barn's broken walls. The screams.

Annabel's hand slid into his, and he clutched it like a lifeline. "Turns out the generator ran out of fuel that night, so they had a bunch of oil lamps going while someone refilled it. When I knocked down the wall, I also knocked down several oil lamps, and one of them broke open, right next to the replacement fuel for the generator, which was right next to a fat stack of money. The whole place went up. The three men ran out, their clothes and hair on fire. Two of them got away, but the other one didn't make it more than ten feet before he collapsed. He was in the hospital for months, recovering from third degree burns." His voice thickened, and he needed to stop talking for a bit. Annabel held his hand and didn't push.

"I know he was probably some low-life criminal, but he didn't deserve that kind of pain. I did that to him, and I couldn't even help the guy. I was trapped in Niall's smashed car with a twisted piece of metal buried in my thigh. There was blood everywhere. I watched it spill out of me and wondered if this was how I died."

Annabel moved closer. She pressed against him now, and he thought she was comforting herself as much as him. "I'm very glad you didn't die."

He managed a laugh. "Me too. That was Niall's doing, and Gavin's. They found me easily—all they had to do was follow the flames. Niall lifted me out of the car, breaking every guideline about how to deal with injured people, then Gav drove us to the hospital. Me and the other guy both. From there, it was just a matter of watching my father cover everything up."

He exhaled and wondered if the hollow feeling within was relief. The burden hadn't been removed, but it had been shared. It was both a start and the most he could hope for.

"No one ever knew?" she asked.

Declan shook his head. "Someone knows. A lot of people, probably, all of whom found their wallets a bit heavier that month. The guys who escaped definitely know. But Niall's car was towed to a less incriminating spot for an accident, and the printing press disappeared. The fire was put out before it spread to the forest. From what Niall says, half the barn is still standing. I haven't gone back out to see it. The counterfeiter was never charged, but I imagine a lifetime of burn scars is punishment enough. And that, Annabel, is how I got the scar on my thigh."

Annabel took his other hand in hers. He looked down at their joined hands. "Look at that," he whispered. "We made a trust circle after all."

She took their hands, still joined, and ran them across his left thigh, looking for the ridge of the scar. He guided her to the correct spot, and she traced the long line of raised flesh.

"It's so big," she murmured.

"Of course it is." A teasing note dropped into his voice, and she responded with a playful pinch.

"Is this why you're so determined not to act like a Donnelly?"

Declan ran his thumb across the keloid scar. The wound had been too deep and jagged to heal well. "What I did that night, the damage I caused…I can't forget it. In the hospital, I realized I don't get to be as flexible about the law as the rest of my family. I wasn't meant to be that guy."

Annabel didn't look convinced. "You fell into the role pretty easily."

"And look how it turned out. I like the choices I've made. I really do. I'd much rather own a bookstore than a…a…" He tried to think of a suitable criminal activity.

"A gambling ring, for example?"

"Exactly." His smile already felt easier.

She rose up enough to throw one leg across him, then settled into his lap. "So now you rein yourself in," she said. "Make sure you and the rest of the world know that night was a one-time-only thing."

Declan tried to focus as her heat transferred to his body. "It *was* a fluke. It took all summer for my leg to heal. I never got anywhere close to Oxford and ended up going to Northwestern. I learned my lesson."

"If it was a fluke, why do you try so hard to control yourself?"

"It's not that hard."

"You don't date," she said. "Based on the pastries you eat, you should be twice your size, so I'm guessing you have a rigid workout schedule. You're a vegetarian. Until tonight, I've never seen you drunk. There's something inside you that's just bursting to get out, and you refuse. You build brick walls around yourself."

Declan held up a hand and ticked off his answers on his fingers. "I dated Maddie."

She interrupted. "Why didn't that go anywhere?"

Because she didn't excite him. Because he *only* felt controlled with her. "I think we bored each other." He ticked off the next fingers. "I like being healthy, so I exercise. I'm a vegetarian because my mother forced so many beef sandwiches and bowls of Irish stew on me that I feared I would start to moo. I decided to give the cows a break for a while, and it stuck. Maybe there is something inside me, but that's where it's going to stay. That wild side…for me, it's dangerous."

"Okay." She moved close enough that her breasts brushed his chest. "And controlling other people? Why do you do that?"

The grin he flashed was wicked. "Because it turns me on."

Her breath hitched.

Declan's fingers dug into her hips, holding her in place. "I believe you owe me an answer now. Are you only here because you were ordered to seduce me?"

Annabel leaned back enough that he could see into her eyes. They were green and crystal clear, with no hint of subterfuge or evasion. "Yes, I was instructed to do so, but no one needed to put the idea in my head. I've wanted to sleep with you since the first day you walked into my bakery."

Chapter Eighteen

Declan gaped at her, his surprise almost comical. "Since the first time," he repeated.

"You were wearing a blue-striped shirt. It looked freshly ironed. It was your work outfit, though I didn't know it at the time. A button-down, khakis, and polished brown shoes. Your hair was parted differently back then. A bit more to the right."

"You remember all that?" His hands tightened on her hips, more like he was holding on than trying to hold her in place.

She ran her hands through his hair, then smoothed it back down. "You were so put together. So neat. I thought it would be tremendous fun to mess you up a bit. But you were a customer, and I..." She trailed off. Some secrets, she wasn't ready to share.

Perhaps his story should have made her feel better. He'd made mistakes, too, born of greed and stupidity. Mistakes that caused others to suffer. But he'd been a kid, and she'd been a grown woman. He paid for his crime, if not via the law then through his own guilt. She'd done everything she could to erase the past.

She lifted her shoulders in a delicate shrug. "It doesn't matter how I felt. Until the party, you were never more than polite, so I didn't believe you were interested."

His eyes were soft. "Your hair was tied back, so I couldn't tell how long it was, but a few curls had come down. That was the second thing I thought about, how much I wanted to wind one of those curls around my finger. You wore a dark blue dress. It came to your knees, and the skirt swayed every time you moved. You had a necklace made of beads, large red ones, and it was the first time I saw those damn red heels. Why is it always red heels?"

Annabel stared at him, unmoving.

"I remember, too," he told her.

She'd never wanted to kiss someone so much in her life.

But she wasn't ready to stop talking, either. "My momma raised me to behave a certain way. To be sweet, even demure. Skirts always came past my knees, and shirts were always buttoned. I was a good girl once, so I followed my momma's orders. One Sunday morning, all these people at church were whispering about a new woman in town. They acted like the Whore of Babylon was sitting in the third pew from the back, but when I looked at her, all I saw was a pretty lady. Her blouse was buttoned, and her skirt was long enough— and then she stood, and I saw these red heels. That's all it took. Ten years old, and I decided that as soon as I had my own money, I was going to wear nothing but red heels." She glanced down at her now bare feet. "I broke a lot of promises, but not that one."

He opened his mouth to speak, but she feared he'd ask about those broken promises. Annabel hurried to fill the silence. "You said your second thought was about my curls. What was your first thought when you met me?"

His smile was wistful. "I thought I'd found a woman I wanted to look at every day for the rest of my life."

She tried to respond, but there were no words. Annabel feared he was still drunk.

Declan said nothing else. Offered no explanations or caveats. He let the words hang in the air between them, heavy and full of promise and regret and boundaries she wasn't ready to cross.

Instead of responding, Annabel bent her head and pressed her lips to his.

He returned the kiss, soft lips meeting again and again, building a slow charge between their bodies. Declan swung his legs onto the sofa and leaned against the arm, pulling her across his body in the same motion.

It felt like restraints were being removed, the hundreds of minutes of not touching vanishing with each kiss. With his lips against hers and his large hands gripping her back, she relaxed into the desire flowing through her.

Between their bodies, she felt his cock lengthen, but she didn't press closer to him. Whatever this was, whatever they were, it was fragile, and she didn't want to move too fast.

His hand slid up her spine to cup the back of her neck, and she sighed at the touch.

He pulled back just far enough to speak. "Taste me."

Annabel eased her tongue into his mouth and ran it over his teeth, then along the inside of his cheeks and across his lips. He did the same to her. When at last their tongues danced together, they did so with a growing need. Declan threaded one hand into her curls. His fist tightened as the kiss deepened.

Part of her never wanted to move. If she spent a lifetime on that sofa, with his hard body below her and his lips claiming hers, it would be time well spent.

But another, much louder part needed his cock inside her.

His thoughts seemed to mirror hers. "Do you want more?" he asked. "Do you want me to touch you the way I did last night? Do you want to ride my fingers or my mouth? Or something else?" His hips twitched underneath her, and a small moan escaped.

He kissed her again. He kissed her like he was starving, like he couldn't exist without the taste of her lips, without her tongue twining around his with the same ferocity he felt.

Declan ripped his mouth away, breathing heavily. He pushed against her chest, urging her to sit upright. She still wore her white blouse, loosely tied at her waist. He plucked at the knot until he held one side of her shirt in either hand.

He yanked his hands apart, popping the bottom button. He stroked the delicate skin of her midriff before tearing the next button free.

Annabel rocked toward him, arching her back in blatant invitation. Declan tore the final button free. Her blouse hung open, revealing another cream-colored bra. Her pink nipples were visible through the thin fabric, the rigid tips pressing against the material.

Declan bowed his head to her breasts and covered them with light kisses. "*And all her face was honey to my mouth, and all her body pasture to mine eyes*," he murmured against her skin.

Annabel's breath hitched. She couldn't remember a moment in her adult life when she'd felt so adored.

With steady hands, he eased the blouse from her shoulders. The fabric pinned her upper arms to her sides. "Put your hands behind your back," he ordered, "and grab your wrists. Don't let go."

Almost shaking with eagerness, she obeyed. Declan slid his hands under her ass, then lifted her until her breasts were at eye level.

He pulled one hard tip into his mouth, sucking on it through the fabric. When he rolled it between his teeth and tongue, she writhed against him, so he did it again, a little sharper, then repeated the movement on the other side.

"Declan…" she gasped.

He ran his cheeks over the swell of her breasts. When he pulled back and saw the red scrapes caused by his end-of-day stubble, he did it again, a little rougher. "I like seeing you marked by me." He ran his mouth over the same flesh, biting just a little too hard before soothing it with his tongue. Annabel clutched her wrists and struggled to stay upright.

"You act so sweet," he murmured, "but you like it dirty, don't you?" He eased her down his body until she was only an inch above his cock.

She moaned in protest, squirming against his hands. Wanting to feel him pressed against her.

"Why do you pretend, Annabel? What are you covering up?"

She whimpered. The words were too real. They threatened the delicate truce they'd forged that evening.

Declan felt it, too. He stared at her a second longer, at her face and breasts and her legs straddling him. Then, as if it pained him, he placed her back on the couch and swung his feet to the floor. "I can't do this."

The space between them was so quiet she could hear the refrigerator hum. Hear the ticking of the clock. She was afraid to speak and didn't want him to, either. She feared what he would say.

He was the first to break the silence. "I want this. My entire body is screaming at me right now, calling me every name in the book because I don't have you on your back right now with your ankles around my ears."

She gulped. He wasn't making this easy.

"And when it's over, and my arms are wrapped around you, I'll remember that I still know nothing of your past, and apparently it's a bad one. I'll remember that you're working against my family and won't tell me why. And then I'll hate myself, and maybe hate you a little, and I'd leave. An hour or two from now, you'll be alone and cursing my name."

She could see it too clearly, and the image crushed her.

Declan rose, and she followed. Several feet separated them, their postures almost formal.

"I'm going to leave now, before we give each other any more reason for regret. Maybe tomorrow, you'll trust me a little more, and you can tell me what I need to know."

He opened her front door and stepped through, and she felt the threshold as a line in the sand, a barrier she needed to cross if she had any hope of not spending all her nights alone.

It took all the courage she possessed, but she raised her eyes to Declan. Whatever he saw there made him pause. Wait.

"I didn't want to betray your family. I thought I had no choice." She took a deep inhale and gave him one piece of her answer. "I'm afraid Fowler owns me."

CHAPTER NINETEEN

At exactly six o'clock on Valentine's Day, as soon as the bookstore closed, the door to the bakery opened. A second later, she heard the lock click into place.

All day, she'd been on edge, waiting for this moment. She knew he would come. The night before, she'd closed the door on his questions, unprepared to give him more information. Unsure how much she was willing to share.

More than once, Annabel looked across the street to find Declan at the window, staring back at her. Every time, her breath caught, and once her hand shook enough to spill the cappuccino she was carrying.

When he didn't arrive at four as the bakery was closing, she was almost relieved. She wasn't ready yet. Her stomach still felt twisted, and no matter how many times she rehearsed the story in her mind, she couldn't find a version where she didn't sound like a foolish girl who jumped into one bad decision after another rather than deal with her own mistakes.

As her momma might say, you couldn't put lipstick on a pig.

Then she realized he was waiting until they'd have more

than twenty minutes to chat. When both their schedules were clear for the night and she had hours to spill her secrets.

What had seemed important, even vital the night before felt like a rash decision in the bright light of day. Well, the drizzly, overcast day. The weather matched her mood. With each passing hour, she remembered details his caresses had helped her to forget—things like false promises and real threats.

She quite liked Declan. Like was such a weak word for what she felt, but she wasn't prepared to assign a stronger one. She also wasn't prepared to go to prison for him if he chose to use her confession against her.

Declan didn't join her in the back room. He wanted her to come to him.

She couldn't help her small smile. The man did like being in control—and God help her, she loved it.

She stood and brushed out her skirt, then removed the headband she often wore while working, letting her curls spring free. For once, she didn't bother to touch up her makeup. He'd already seen through her, in so many ways. Red lipstick could only mask so much.

She walked into the cafe. Though her heart raced, she kept her steps slow. Declan's eyes locked on her as soon as she stepped through the swinging door. His blue gaze pulled at her, those sapphire-colored eyes making her breath catch the way they always did. Despite that—or perhaps because of it—she kept the counter between them.

Declan didn't bother with small talk. "What do you mean, he owns you?"

Annabel was tired of lying to him, but the truth still felt

too immense. Too dangerous. The truth was, she was scared.

So she crossed her arms, shrugged, and gave him a pleasant smile. "It means we're on opposite sides in your family's war."

He crossed the room and leaned against the pastry case, so close she had to tilt her head to meet his eyes. The pastry case was empty, though she'd set aside a single red velvet cupcake for Declan—because it was Valentine's Day, and she couldn't resist. This didn't seem the right moment to give it to him.

"Damn it, Annabel. Don't retreat now. What's going on?"

Retreat. He made it sound like a battle lost. "I just told you. According to your family, I'm one of the bad guys." She kept her voice light and sweet. "Would you like a cup of coffee?"

The corner of his eye twitched, and she turned her back to fetch the coffee. The tic was such a small movement, but she knew for Declan, it was the equivalent of most men throwing a tantrum.

She returned with the cup of coffee. He took it automatically.

"Why did Fowler ask you to seduce me?"

Annabel suspected he had several variations on that question, all designed to reveal her true motives.

He waited for her to answer the question. The eye twitched twice more.

"Because Fowler needed me to get inside your house, and I think we all know where my charms lie."

Declan glared. "That's ridiculous."

"Is it? Would it have been better if he sent me after Niall?"

"Of course not," he growled. "But that's not what I mean.

Why did he ask *you* to seduce me?"

"We seem be to be going around in circles. As I said, he owns me. I don't want to tell you why. Let's just say the penalty for refusing him would be high." Except that hadn't been true in the beginning. Back then, he'd only offered the carrot. The stick came later.

"A man tells you to seduce another, and you just do it?"

"If it's my best option." She put her hands on her hips and tried to stare him down.

Declan hissed in a breath. "Have you done this before? How many times has Fowler sent you after some man?"

She glared at him, then picked up the red velvet cupcake and threw it at him. Hard. It landed smack in the middle of his face before crumbling to the floor.

Declan gaped at her for a second, then grabbed several napkins off a nearby table. He scrubbed cream cheese frosting from his face.

"Are you seriously asking if I'm Fowler's whore?" Annabel's voice rose. She stepped around the counter and advanced on Declan. "I tried *not* to use you."

He scowled. "You didn't try very hard, did you?"

A shadow fell across the room, and they turned as one to find Mrs. Wandsworth and her bridge group peering through the window, looking like they wished they had a bag of popcorn.

It was almost magic. One second Declan looked like he was in danger of erupting, and the next he was smiling at the women. He even opened the door to tell one of them their book club picks arrived that morning, and they should come in any time to get their copies.

Annabel tried to hide her astonishment as Declan chatted for a few minutes, acting for all the world like a man who didn't have cake crumbs in his collar.

She felt as if her vision cleared. She imagined blinking away the tumultuous last week until the man she used to know was revealed. The clean-cut and kind-hearted bookstore owner, the respectable man running for city council. For a moment, it was like he reappeared in her bakery.

The intense, demanding Declan had been a surprising discovery, and an irresistible one. But this was the man she'd first met, the one who'd been the closest thing she had to a friend. She still wanted him, as much as she ever had.

When he at last convinced the older women to leave and turned back to Annabel, she was still staring at him in wonder. "Who *are* you?" she whispered.

His dark blue gaze settled on her, and she didn't have a hope of looking away.

"We seem to keep asking that," he said. "You haven't answered yet, either."

She only knew she'd formed a small O with her mouth when his eyes dropped to her lips, and she forced herself to relax. "Let's get away from the windows."

Only after he followed her into the kitchen did she realize she'd given up the small protection the cafe offered. As soon as they were truly alone, it felt like electricity ran across her skin.

Declan leaned against the heavy butcher block table, his hands gripping the edge. She was glad she'd already dropped the plastic cover over it. Without it, she suspected he'd leave fingernail marks in the wood.

"Why does Fowler own you?" he asked again.

"I can't tell you."

"Why not?"

Fresh off her glimpse of the kind man she knew he was at heart—when they weren't driving each other crazy—she dropped the pretense and offered him as much honesty as she could. "I can't trust you."

His lips tightened. "You don't trust me."

She gave a rueful laugh. "That's the problem. I do trust you, though goodness knows why after you didn't tell me that you found the transmitter. Or after you broke into my home, let's not forget that. But that's not what I said. I said I *can't* trust you. It would be very stupid of me to do so."

Declan's hands clenched on the table, as if he fought to hold himself in one place. "I could have turned you in. If not to the cops, to my father. I've been carrying that damn pen around for two days, wondering why I haven't told anyone. I don't know why I didn't, except…I *couldn't*. You say you can't trust me? Well, I can't betray you, even when I know I should."

Annabel opened her mouth, then closed it when everything she wanted to say seemed like too much. Too honest, and too true.

She tried again. "I laundered over a million dollars for Peter Hastings."

She didn't know why she did it. Maybe she was ready to stop carrying the secret. Perhaps she wanted to admit aloud why she'd been forced to have such a small, private life.

Or perhaps she just wanted to know how Declan would look at her when he learned the truth.

His face was impassive, but at least he didn't walk straight to the police station. "Explain."

She wet her lips, unsure where to begin. For a desperate moment, she considered throwing herself at him, using her lips and hands to distract him.

Somehow, she knew it wouldn't work this time.

"I don't always think before I act," she began.

Declan raised an eyebrow. "I'm shocked."

"Do you want to hear this or not?"

He gestured for her to continue.

"Well. This is how it started. I accidentally made out with the groom at a very expensive wedding I was catering. It was my first big job."

Both his eyebrows went up. Annabel wasn't sure how most "how I got into money laundering" stories started, but she suspected her path was atypical.

"She was one of those Texas debutante types. It was her day, her chance to be a princess, and it turns out princesses don't like seeing their prince's hands on the servant's ass. She filed suit for a quarter million dollars. I had no insurance, no hope of paying it, so I ran. I didn't know he was the groom, if that helps. The stupid thing was I didn't even like him. I was bored, and it seemed like a fun way to pass the time."

"That was the stupid thing?"

"You're really not making this easier. Anyway, as soon as I arrived in Lost Coast, Jared asked me out. I didn't know much about him, but I thought it would be a nice way to get out and meet people. His father thought I was a gold digger, so he looked into my background and discovered a court in Texas had filed a default judgment when I didn't show up. I owed the full amount, and a warrant had been issued for my arrest. So he offered me a choice. I could stay in town and launder money through the bakery, and he'd make my old name go away, or he'd tell the Texas authorities where I was." The words spilled out, eager to be heard.

Declan didn't move, though his hands continued to grip the table. "Why didn't you run a second time?"

"Because it was exhausting. I liked it here. I never thought I'd like rain and fog after decades in Texas, but I do. This is a weird little town, but it feels right. Plus, while everyone knows everyone's business, no one wants the government to interfere too much with their lives. They didn't care that the hologram on my ID wasn't quite right, or that my social security number doesn't exist."

"So who are you?" Declan asked, one more time.

"I was born Anna Belmont."

"Anna." The word sounded unfamiliar in his mouth, too short.

"That's not my name anymore." She paused. That had come out of nowhere. She still wanted to be Anna Belmont, the woman with a family and a valid ID and the freedom to live her life, but Annabel was the name Declan called her. She wasn't ready to give it up.

He didn't push it. "That's what they have over you? That you used to launder money? But that means you have power over them, too. You can testify against Hastings."

For a moment, she let herself hope. It passed quickly. "The thing is, Fowler isn't a very nice man."

Declan's expression hardened. "No, but he's still just a man. We can find a way to get you free of him."

We. She couldn't remember a single word ever sounding quite so nice. "And then I'll go straight to prison. If I step out of line, they've got me on identity fraud. If they send the right info to the right prosecutor, I'm looking at two years."

"And you're too pretty for prison," he said, recalling Jared's words. "That was it, wasn't it? Do I have the full story now?"

There was so much more to it. He had the lines, but the true story was in the shading. In the years of loss and loneliness and regret, when the brightest part of her day was when the handsome bookstore owner paid her a visit.

"That's it," she said.

Declan stood perfectly still for a long time. Then, out of nowhere, he smiled. "The Hastings family is powerful. They have a lot of reach, I'll give them that."

Annabel raised her eyebrows, waiting for him to explain his sudden good mood.

He bent at the waist, leaning forward as if to tell her a secret. "The Donnellys are *also* a powerful family, and my father likes nothing more than beating the Hastings. Let us help you."

It was so tempting to put her fate in someone else's hands and let them solve her problems. Let them find a way to keep her out of prison. All she had to do was believe in the family whose trust she'd abused.

"Can I think about it?" she asked.

"If it helps your decision, my dad would probably pay you to testify against Hastings. He'd think you were doing him a favor."

She couldn't help laughing. "Try to remember I'm still a felon. I can't exactly walk into the police station, give my report, and hope they think I'm too cute to lock up."

"That's exactly what would happen. Bring doughnuts as well, and they might not even charge you."

"You know some cops are women, right? Or gay? Or not into blondes?"

"It's for the best, really. I don't have time to fight them all for your attention."

His expression barely changed, and it took her a second to realize he wasn't entirely joking.

"You...still want my attention?"

He smiled, and it was like the sun coming out in a dark room. "Annabel, I've spent the last week half hating you, then hating myself for not staying away from you. I thought you were a liar. A spy. A devious bitch who would use my family to get what you needed. For a brief moment, I thought you were messing around with Jared Hastings. That was probably the worst part. So it feels pretty good to know I was wrong. Or at least know there were extenuating circumstances."

"Still, I did those things. The lying and being devious. Never Jared Hastings." She shuddered at the thought. "I chose to launder drug money rather than pay for my own mistakes. I'm hardly an angel."

Declan moved toward her, still smiling. "You look like one, though."

She stepped backwards until her back hit the freezer. He placed his arms on either side, trapping her.

"The most tempting one I've ever seen." Declan dipped his head, his mouth finding the tender spot just below her ear. "Who always smells of sugar and vanilla."

She shivered when his tongue darted out.

"Tastes like it, too."

Between the sweeping relief of finally speaking the truth, and whatever he was doing with his tongue, Annabel struggled to stand. One of Declan's arms wrapped around her waist, pulling her against him.

"If you think I'm an angel, you're going to be disappointed," she told him.

He pulled back to look at her, and his eyes seemed to register every freckle. Every eyelash. Every expression she struggled to hide.

"Oh, you're definitely an angel," he said at last. "Maybe a fallen one. Now you want to be forgiven."

Her answer must have shown in her eyes.

Declan grazed his lips across her forehead, his touch almost painfully gentle. "But first, do you need to be punished for what you've done?"

The words were low and seductive, a promise rather than a threat. Annabel's hips arched toward him.

"After three years, you only came to me because someone else told you to do it. That bothers me." One of his hands slid down to cup her ass. The other ran across the back of her neck and twisted in her hair. "So now you're going to do what I tell you."

He tugged on the threads, forcing her head back. "Am I wrong about what you need?"

She shook her head, not trusting herself to speak.

"I need to hear you say it."

"I want this," she told him.

"I know," he replied.

CHAPTER TWENTY

Annabel couldn't remember ever wanting something more.

Declan spun her around. He pressed her flat against the freezer door and used his right hand to pin both arms above her head. The hard muscles of his thighs and chest trapped her.

She tilted her ass toward him, seeking the hard ridge of his cock.

His other hand wrapped around her hips, holding them in place. "Don't move."

Once she stilled, he released her and stepped back. Annabel could almost feel his eyes on her, watching for a single unauthorized movement. She remained in place. The freezer was cold beneath her cheek and chest, while the heat of the kitchen warmed her back.

Declan brushed her hair away from the nape of her neck, then grazed his lips across the skin. It was the only place he touched her.

Annabel shivered. It was torture, not being able to close the distance between them.

"The problem," he murmured against her skin, "is that you never show restraint. You ran when you should have stayed put. You said yes to Hastings when the answer needed to be no. You kissed someone when you were supposed to be working. No one's ever taught you the value of self-control, have they?"

His words held both threat and promise. Annabel's breathing grew shallow and her pussy began to throb, a slow, steady drum of pure need.

Declan grasped the folds of her skirt and drew them up an inch at a time, until the bare flesh above her thigh-high stockings was exposed.

"If I look, I'll see white lace, won't I?"

Annabel gave a single nod.

His hand reached under the skirt and brushed against her mound. Before she could relax into the touch, his fingers gripped the fabric and twisted.

Her torn underwear dropped to the ground.

"You don't get to wear white today."

Annabel sighed in relief, like a costume that no longer fit had been removed.

Declan's fingers settled between her legs, covering her in slow, lazy strokes. "Don't move," he reminded her. Annabel's fingers curled against the hard freezer door. With tremendous effort, she didn't rock her hips.

Declan slid two fingers inside her, then added a third. He didn't thrust. He held his fingers in place, filling her.

Though she tried to remain still, her muscles clenched around him, the movement involuntary. When he withdrew, she bit back a protest, but he wasn't done. With the pad of his index finger, he drew light circles around her clit, never quite touching the swollen nub. The touch was both delicate and maddening.

Annabel's breath came faster, and Declan increased the pressure. Heat rose in her cheeks. Her nipples tightened, and she couldn't stop herself from writhing against his hand, seeking release.

With no warning, he dropped his fingers, leaving her hanging just on the edge of orgasm. Annabel whimpered.

He hauled her away from the freezer. Her back fell against Declan's chest, and he wrapped one arm around her waist to hold her steady. His right hand undid the buttons on her top, spreading it open. He moved both hands to cup her breasts, massaging them slowly. Annabel sagged against him in pleasure.

Declan set her back on her feet, then pulled off the shirt and unclasped her bra. "I said no white," he reminded her. He unfastened the skirt. It slithered over her hips until it lay crumpled on the ground.

"Take off your heels," he murmured in her ear. "I want to see you completely bare. No disguises."

Annabel stepped out of one shoe, and then the other.

Declan spun her around to face him, and for the first time, she felt in control. He stared at her with wonder. He swallowed more than once as his eyes moved from her collarbone to her breasts, to her stomach and hips and thighs and all the way down to her bare feet.

"You're perfect," he managed at last. He pinched one nipple between his forefinger and thumb, then rolled it lightly. "I can't wait to wrap my mouth around this again. To hear you groan as I bite down."

Then his hand was in her hair, pulling her head back for another demanding kiss. He ripped his mouth from hers and placed her hand on his rigid cock. It jumped under her touch. "You're making me fight for control, too," he confessed. "But the difference between us is I know how to win that battle. Do you?"

He tugged her toward the center of the room and positioned her next to the butcher block table. The hand on the back of her neck was insistent, urging her forward until she was bent over the table.

Annabel tried bracing herself on her elbows, but Declan caught her wrists. He stretched her arms forward until her fingers wrapped around the far edge of the table, her chest pressed flat against the surface and her chin digging into the vinyl cover.

Declan walked to the other side and crouched before her. He ran his fingers through the curls that dropped into her eyes. "Do you have a mirror?" The words were low. Purposeful. The sound of a man who knew exactly what he wanted.

Desire pooled between her legs. Whatever he had planned, she knew she wanted it.

"There's one in the closet." She indicated the one she meant with her eyes.

He rose in a single movement, using just his thigh muscles. A second later, he returned with the medium-sized mirror. He positioned it between her arms, then slid it across the table until the edge was only an inch from her chin. Declan propped it up at a slight angle, until she could see both her own face and the room behind her. He moved away, and she locked greedy eyes on the mirror, waiting for him to reappear behind her.

His eyes met hers in the glass. "Don't watch me. Watch yourself. Watch how long you can go without losing control."

On an exhale, she shifted her gaze back to her own reflection. The color was high in her cheeks, her lips were still swollen from his kisses, and her hair was a mess. She appeared halfway to freshly fucked, while Declan looked like he'd just walked out of a clothing ad.

Except for the look in his eyes. The one that said he was as hot as she was.

He leaned forward and wrapped his hands around her shoulders. With slow, steady movements, he ran them down her back. His thumbs outlined her spine while his fingers pressed into each muscle. Even as the touch relaxed her muscles, her skin grew more sensitive. Hungrier.

She was soaking wet. She closed her eyes as his hands rounded the curves of her ass and she imagined his fingers sliding into her again.

He slapped her ass. Annabel's eyes flew open.

"Don't look away," Declan ordered.

She couldn't. Not from his dark blue eyes locked on her face. The way he gazed at her, it felt like he was incapable of seeing anything else.

"I'm going to fuck you now."

Her lips rounded, and his eyes dropped.

"You have no idea how much I want to fuck your mouth," Declan said. "I can't wait to watch your lips slide up and down my cock. But not this time. This time, you get to watch yourself."

She heard the sound of his zipper and the crinkle of a foil packet. When she tried twisting enough to see him, his hand dropped between her shoulder blades, holding her in place.

"Three times," he said. "I'm going to take you to the edge three times. You don't get to come until the last one. Do you understand?"

He waited for her to nod, then he removed his hand. A second passed while he rolled on the condom, then she felt his hands on her hips, tilting them to the angle he wanted. He eased into her.

Once again, his eyes in the mirror were locked on her, registering every minute change in her expression. He saw her sigh of relief as the head of his cock stretched her open, and he saw her impatience when he only entered an inch, then withdrew.

"I didn't say I'd take you there quickly," Declan replied to her unasked question. Again he slid inside, no more than two inches of his thick flesh spreading her wide.

God, he said he had control, but this was ridiculous. She tried to squirm backwards, but his fingers dug into the flesh of her hips, holding her in place. "You look frustrated."

The bastard sounded amused. She clenched her muscles, wrapping them tight around his cock.

Declan's breath came out in a shudder, but he didn't pick up the pace. A couple tantalizing inches at a time, no more.

With no warning, he plunged into her, planting himself fully within her body. She moaned with pleasure.

Declan set up a slow, unpredictable rhythm. Sometimes he entered her a few inches, and sometimes he'd let her feel his entire length for several fast strokes. She never knew what was coming, and the eyes that watched her so intently gave nothing away.

He reached one hand around to stroke her clit. "Watch yourself." He gave a light pinch. Her legs twitched and her breath came fast.

A moment before she lost control, Declan stopped moving. He waited until the flush in her cheeks faded and her breath calmed before he started moving again. "It's your turn. This time, tell me to stop before you come."

There was no way she could obey that order. She was desperate for the release his body offered, and when he picked up the rhythm, moving faster with each stroke, she knew she didn't have a chance. Annabel closed her eyes, moaning as he sank into her, filling her body over and over again.

She wasn't surprised when the slap came. She'd relied on it, she realized. Counted on him to have the control she lacked.

This time, when she looked in the mirror, she didn't meet his eyes. She stared at herself, her red cheeks and soft lips. She watched as her control hung by a thread, but she held onto it.

When his hand again slid under her, she bucked. "Stop." The word was rushed, desperate, and a large part of her yearned to take it back.

But Declan's pleased smile made her regret vanish. He leaned over to kiss her shoulder and stroke her back, his cock still deep within her. "Is that enough, Annabel? Have I punished you enough?"

She managed a groan, but he understood. He drew back, slow and careful, then he slammed into her.

He kept up the demanding pace, one hard thrust after another. His skin slapped against hers, growing slick with sweat as he fucked her even faster.

In the mirror, they locked eyes, and she didn't need to see her expression to know it matched his. Intense and hungry and a little bit lost, as if they both knew there was no going back once they fell over the edge.

It was irresistible. Her body had been well-primed. When he switched angles to hit a new spot, she felt the world stop for just a moment, then she exploded.

Screaming, she rose off the table, her back arching as the orgasm overtook her. Her muscles tightened around him as her arms and shoulders shook and her legs stopped supporting her.

Declan held her in place, gripping her hips as he found his own release. This time, she could see his face as he came. See the way it crumbled under the force of his pleasure. The polite bookseller was nowhere in sight, but neither was the dominating man who managed her body so well. It was just Declan.

After he was spent, he collapsed on top of her, his chest to her back, and she didn't want him to ever leave.

CHAPTER TWENTY-ONE

Only when their skin began to cool and Declan felt himself soften did he pull out. He tied off the condom and zipped his pants, then wrapped the evidence in several paper towels before discarding it.

Annabel rolled over, her face almost dream-like in its easy contentment. She pushed herself upright and gave a little jump onto the table. She crossed her legs at the ankle, still a lady—even though she was sitting on her own butcher block bare-ass naked.

She glanced at the table and ran her fingers across the plastic cover. "It's a good thing I covered this up. I'd hate to have to replace it." With a small, lazy smile, she stretched her arms above her head. "It would have been worth it, though."

Her breasts lifted, and Declan was amazed to feel his cock stir. After all that he'd put it through in the last hour, he hadn't expected it to move again for a week.

God, she'd been flawless. Everything he asked for, she provided. She might be unpredictable and an admitted felon, but for a moment, he'd been able to control her. So long as he could rein in her wild streak, maybe he could manage his own impulses, too.

"That was different." She hopped off the table and walked toward him, completely naked.

He stood transfixed at the sight of her curves in motion.

"And amazing," she added, rising up to kiss his chin. "But next time I'd like to see you undressed, too."

Happiness bubbled up. Next time. That was all he needed to hear before his mind began playing every filthy fantasy he'd ever had about Annabel. They ran through his head like an X-rated slide slow.

"What are you doing this evening?" he asked. "It *is* February 14. I think I need a valentine."

Laughing, she pulled away and retrieved her clothes from the floor. Her skirt was wrinkled, her hair was mussed, and her lipstick had come off long ago. She was absolutely gorgeous.

"I think I'm free. Fowler isn't supposed to send someone for the recordings until Wednesday." She gave him an apologetic look for bringing up the topic. "Wait. You said you've been carrying the pen around for two days?"

Grinning, Declan withdrew the pen from his pocket and set it on the table. It looked so harmless now.

"Then what was all that about gold in a trunk? Yes, I listened. Don't give me that look."

"It's not a look. I'm just waiting for you to figure it out."

Her eyes widened in horror. "It was Niall, wasn't it? He sounds just like your dad. Oh God. Does he know what I did?"

"Honestly, I think he was kind of impressed. My family is under the impression you'd be good for me."

"I always did like your family." Her mouth pursed in thought. "If the Hastings believe you need to cash in the gold to complete the deal, they'll want to…are you trying to get your own car stolen?"

Declan tried not to look too pleased with himself. "Already happened. I checked at five-thirty, and it was gone. Niall will get the camera footage tomorrow."

"You had your car stolen to get footage of one of Fowler's lackeys? What happens when they open the trunk and find no gold?"

"Lackeys talk, especially local lackeys who might know Niall and Gavin and be convinced to confess. And the car is loaded with a safe filled with rocks. By the time they learn they've been duped, hopefully we'll be halfway to arresting Fowler."

She smiled and shook her head. "You probably shouldn't read so many spy novels."

He never wanted her to stop smiling. "Getting Fowler is a start. What will it take to get you away from Hastings?"

Her delicate eyebrows lifted. "Other than twenty-five thousand dollars?"

"Is that really all it will take?" He had most of that in his savings account.

"I don't know." For a moment, she looked uncertain. "I owed them fifty thousand from my last month of money laundering, but planting the pen was supposed knock off half that. Fowler keeps rewriting the rules of my debt, though."

Declan grimaced. "Let's start with the fifty thousand. What happened to the money?" If she could get it back, maybe she could pay off Fowler that evening. Buy herself some time while they figured out the rest.

"I gave it to Erin for the mental health clinic." She shrugged, the movement self-deprecating. "It was a bit foolish, I suppose, but at least it's being well-used."

"You…gave it away?" Declan struggled to keep an impassive face.

"It seemed dangerous to leave it lying around the bakery." Annabel buttoned her shirt and ran her fingers through her hair, then returned the mirror to its original spot. One item at a time, she put the room back together, and with each item, he felt the connection they'd built begin to fray.

"It couldn't have been more dangerous than owing fifty thousand dollars to a gun runner," Declan pointed out.

"As I said, it was a bit foolish. I don't think paying Fowler would help, though. It's not what he wants." Her gaze skittered away, then returned to him. "He says the debt disappears when the Donnellys stop trying to buy Hastings Shipping."

Of course it would be that. The deal his father had dreamed of for years. A chance to expand the business and become the town's preeminent family.

If Declan killed the deal, it might free Annabel.

For far too long, he considered it. It was just a business deal. A couple rich men swapping fortunes. If the deal didn't go through, nothing would change. It would all go on as it had before, and that hadn't been so bad.

It wasn't the deal he cared about. It was his damn father.

"I can't work against my own dad. I just can't."

Her lids dropped for a moment. The tiniest reaction. "I understand. But I can't work against myself. After all, I *am* too pretty to go to prison."

The attempted joke fell flat. "I won't let that happen. I told you, my family has connections. They made an entire car accident, fire, and counterfeiting operation disappear. You don't think they can deal with one pesky lawyer and an old businessman on house arrest? Let's see what my dad suggests."

"No!" The word burst out, a little too strong. "You already told Niall. You want to add your father to that list? The more people who know, the more likely someone says the wrong thing at the wrong time. I won't risk it."

Anger rose, and he needed several seconds to tamp it down. Whatever else had happened in here, he was still the same man. Ironed shirt. Combed hair. Clean trousers. Polished shoes.

When he came back to himself, his voice was level. "What do you suggest?"

Her brow furrowed in thought. "What if we destroyed the deal temporarily? Just long enough for Fowler to leave me alone? As soon as he's out of town, your father can sign whatever contract he wants with Hastings Shipping."

Declan stared at her. "You can't possibly think that will work."

"Is it really a worse plan than arranging to have your car stolen?"

"This kind of contract takes weeks to prepare. As soon as the deal starts up again, Fowler will be right back in town. And that's assuming he means to leave you alone in the first place. How can you possibly trust him to keep his word? Are you really that naive?"

As soon as the words were out, he regretted it. Annabel closed the top button on her shirt, the one she always left open, then grabbed her coat, pulling it tight around her body.

"Naive is another word for stupid." Her voice didn't shake, but she wouldn't look at him.

"No it's not. It's another word for foolish, and you already said you could be that."

She glanced at him then, a quick, sharp glare. Again, he wanted to bite his tongue.

"Look," he tried again, "what reason do you have to think they'll free you?"

"Because Fowler might be awful, but he still speaks for Hastings. Peter was always straight with me, in his own way. No one's come looking for me, not in three years. No one's bothered my mother or cousins. So yes, when Fowler, his representative, says I only need to stop the deal, I believe him. I have to."

"Hastings never played you straight. Fucking hell." He only realized he was shouting when he saw her flinch. Declan forced his voice back to a normal volume, though it still vibrated with rage. "Do you really think you owe a quarter million dollars? Any lawyer worth his salt could have the case thrown out in twenty minutes. No judge is going to award that kind of money to a spoiled brat who's pissed because her husband couldn't keep it in his pants."

Annabel shook her head. "I messed up when I didn't show up to the hearing. They entered a default judgment."

"Which can be overturned. Judgments are overturned all the time. Hastings didn't make Anna Belmont disappear. He probably spent ten thousand dollars to make the lawsuit vanish, so no one would come looking for you. Maybe less. That's all. You made one stupid mistake and turned it into dozens more mistakes. What the hell is wrong with you?"

He couldn't stop, even as he heard each horrible word spill from his mouth. She knew she screwed up. Reminding her of it was cruel.

But he'd screwed up, too. This wasn't the woman he should be with. Declan couldn't remember the last time he shouted, or spoke words without thought. And how many more mistakes was she going to make? He could just see them, strolling around town. The councilman and the felon.

She exhaled, her expression turning mutinous. It was the same expression she'd worn before throwing a cupcake in his face.

"Nothing is wrong with me. I make mistakes. Lots of them. Because I don't spend my life rigidly avoiding any possible error. I don't control every moment of my life because I'm afraid of what will happen if I let loose."

Declan kept his voice low. "You didn't mind it a few minutes ago."

Her eyes flashed at the reminder. "That was sex, Declan. Just sex. We're talking about life, and I'm not even sure you're living yours. You've created an idea of a life, one built out of nothing but fear."

"And you think you're living? Hiding in this town, unable to even use your own name because of the mistakes you made?"

"I did my best," she insisted.

Declan's hands clenched into fists, and he forced them open. "If that's your best, then naive might be the kindest word for you."

He strode through the cafe, unlocked the front door, and closed it behind him with a soft click. Every movement was contained, polite. Nothing that would draw attention from the passing townies.

Not once did he look back.

Chapter Twenty-Two

How *dare* he.

Annabel walked home, her strides longer than usual, the click of her heels a little louder.

Naive. He'd actually called her naive. Twice.

Twenty minutes before that, Declan had looked at her with more adoration and passion than all the other men she'd known combined.

As soon as he was done, he made it pretty clear he only felt that way when she was naked. The scorn he'd shown when he talked about her choices. Like he couldn't put enough distance between them.

She made mistakes, sure. Who didn't? And yes, perhaps she could think ahead a little bit more, but he might as well ask her to have brown eyes and grow a foot taller. She was who she was, and he needed to take it or leave it. She refused to be with a man who wanted her but didn't like her.

As her home came into view, she checked her watch. Quarter to eight. It hadn't even taken Declan two hours to turn her inside out in both body and mind.

She dragged her feet up her front stairs, too aware of what

she'd find inside. A lovely house, decorated to her exact specifications, and empty. A guest room that had never been used, because she didn't allow herself visitors. Her own bed, where no one else had ever slept.

Annabel didn't mind the quiet time she spent at home, reading or watching a movie or puttering around in the kitchen, but she minded doing *all* of it alone.

It was Valentine's Day. Everyone who had someone was celebrating that night, and she walked into an empty house. The chandelier in the living room cast small diamonds of light against the walls, and she tried to take comfort in the beauty she'd created for herself. She took off her shoes and massaged her feet a little, then changed into a silk kimono and slippers. The house was cold, so she turned up the heat and made a cup of chamomile tea. This was her nightly ritual, small tasks designed to fill hours.

Annabel curled up on the sofa and reached for a paperback on the coffee table. Her fingers drifted across the cover. *Gaudy Night.* She'd loved it so much she started rereading it as soon as she finished.

The book was a present from Declan. He'd been horrified to discover she didn't know who Dorothy Sayers was, so he brought her a copy during one of his afternoon visits. He'd known she would love the story, and he was right. Over the years, the man had developed a good idea of her preferences, and he frequently pressed new authors into her hands.

She squeezed her eyes shut, fighting the tears that threatened. She couldn't lose that. Whatever he'd said today, no matter how much it stung, it wasn't the sum total of their relationship. If she could salvage anything from the last week, she had to at least save their friendship. Without that, she had nothing but the bakery and too many quiet, empty nights ahead of her.

Unless she could find a way to change that. Once the deal was dead and Fowler left town, she could have dates again. Maybe find a man capable of ten minutes of afterglow before he found something to fight about. She knew it couldn't be Declan—he'd never forgive her if she continued to work against his family—but there were other men in town. Handsome, single men who weren't as complicated and infuriating as Declan.

Her entire body recoiled from the thought. She couldn't picture another man on her couch, let alone in her bed.

Those were her choices. Repair a friendship and remain in Hastings' debt. Destroy the deal and lose Declan completely.

Whatever their police records might say, the Donnellys were good people. She still remembered Gavin's roguish charm, Niall's mischievous streak, and Bridget's energy. Molly and Richard had welcomed her with open arms, like she belonged at their dinner table.

In contrast, Jared was a weak man who would only act in his own best interests, and Fowler—well, Fowler scared the living daylights out of her. Those were the people she was helping.

"Damn you," she muttered to the empty room. "Don't you dare ruin this for me, Declan."

It was too late. Her mind was already churning, and to her great annoyance, it was telling her he was right.

If Hastings lied to her about the lawsuit, there was no reason to think Fowler told the truth now. Killing the deal was no guarantee of her freedom. If Hastings lied, then she *had* been naive at best—and downright stupid at worst.

If Annabel had taken twenty minutes to speak to an attorney, all of this might have been avoided. But she hadn't known. She went to culinary school instead of college. None of her friends were lawyers. She didn't even watch courtroom dramas. All she knew of the law came from bad lawyer jokes and a belief that even a consultation with a decent attorney was unaffordable to someone of her means.

So when she read a document that accused her of something she couldn't deny doing and demanded a quarter of a million dollars, it never occurred to Annabel that she wouldn't have to pay it.

It didn't matter now if she'd been stupid or naive. The question was, how did she fix it?

Peter Hastings was under house arrest hundreds of miles away, unable to act except through his attorney. Jared was venal but incompetent. Fowler was the wild card. If she learned who he was and what he wanted, maybe she'd have something to hold over his head, the way he held her past mistakes over hers.

It had been too long since Annabel had any leverage, and she rather liked the sound of it.

The next day, not long after the bakery closed, Annabel walked through the front door of the Capital Hotel with a small pink box in her hand and the top button of her blouse undone.

She was glad to see that Jimmy was at the desk. Not only was Lou a jerk, but he'd also proven immune to her charms when she'd tried to visit Fowler. Thankfully, Jimmy had always been susceptible to them.

She winked at the young concierge. Really, he was a desk clerk, but The Capital liked to pretend it was more than a rundown local hotel.

"Belated Valentine's delivery."

Jimmy blushed, no doubt imagining chocolate being spread across skin, and bobbed his head several times.

"Oh, darn." She pushed her lips into a soft pout. "I forgot the room number for Mr. Fowler. Do you mind watching this while I go back to the bakery?" She widened her eyes, pleading without saying a word.

The clerk sputtered. "I wish I could tell you and save you a trip, but that's against hotel policy."

She tilted her chin down and smiled. "Of course. I wouldn't ask you to break any rules."

Jimmy looked torn while he debated whether it was more important to keep his job or to convince Annabel he was a dangerous rebel. After a second's thought, he leaned forward and whispered. "I can't tell you which room he's in, but I can tell you 301 through 304 are empty tonight."

Annabel touched the side of her nose with a conspiratorial smile. "You're a peach, Jimmy." She leaned over the counter and sent a silent prayer of thanks for pushup bras when his eyes dropped down. "Do you happen to have a plate I can use for these? Presentation is so important, you know. It doesn't seem romantic at all to just drop off a box."

Jimmy swallowed once, then dragged his eyes back to her face. "Uh. Yes. One second."

The moment he headed for the kitchen, she slipped

behind the desk. There were upsides to living in a town with little interest in doing things a different way than they always had. The Capital Hotel had yet to switch to electronic key cards. She slipped the spare keys into her pocket, then hurried around the desk just as Jimmy returned from the kitchen.

"Here you go, Annabel." He handed her the plate, smiling at his own daring. He'd always called her Ms. Johnson before. She gave him a coy smile before leaving.

It wasn't a large hotel. Only six rooms on each floor, plus a supply closet, which meant Fowler was in 305 or 306.

Before knocking on the door of room 305, she practiced her excuse. If Fowler answered, she'd tell him she needed to postpone that night's meeting while she cared for a friend with a bad case of the flu.

If she was lucky, he'd turn out to be a germaphobe who would want to avoid her for several days.

No one answered. With a deep breath, she tried the second door. This time, it swung open.

Big owl eyes stared up at her through thick glasses. "Can I help you?"

Annabel wasn't a tall woman, but the man barely reached her chin.

Her eyebrows drew together. "Room 206?" she asked, uncertain.

He shook his head, the glasses catching the light with every movement. "Wrong floor, I'm afraid."

"Oh dear. So sorry." She flashed a smile and walked down the hall until she heard the door click shut.

Afraid to even breathe, she returned to room 305 and

unlocked it. Her ears strained as she listened for any sign Fowler was inside. When all remained quiet, she cracked the door open and stepped inside.

For a second, she thought Jimmy must have confused his numbers, because it didn't look like anyone was staying in the room. Housekeeping had already been through, so the bed was made and clean towels hung in the bathroom. There were no personal items strewn across any of the room's surfaces.

She almost jumped when she opened the closet, but it wasn't Fowler lurking inside. Just two of his identical suits— black, of course—and a neat stack of black turtlenecks.

He kept his bathroom toiletries in a drawer, and she was glad to find two pairs of pajamas in the dresser. While it was difficult to picture Fowler having a relaxed evening, it beat imagining that he slept naked.

There was nothing personal. No paperwork or files. He didn't leave a laptop behind. Even the hotel notepad hadn't been scribbled on, so she couldn't run a pencil over it to reveal a hidden message like they always did in spy movies. There was absolutely nothing here that hinted at the man.

Only the nightstand remained, but she had little hope of finding anything incriminating. The bottom drawer contained the Gideon Bible found in every hotel room in the country. She knew Fowler wouldn't store anything in that drawer. She rather suspected he'd burst into flames if he touched the book.

It was also, she thought, the perfect place to hide a pen. The one that Declan left behind the day before, when he walked away from her. The pen she intended to return to him as soon as she could bear to face him again.

Annabel hesitated. There was a good chance Declan had another scheme up his sleeve. Perhaps he and Niall planned to convince Fowler to rob a bank next, or set fire to someone's house.

This was a different way they might manipulate Fowler, and she didn't want to miss the opportunity. She tucked the pen behind the Bible and closed the drawer.

Before leaving, she checked the top drawer, just to be thorough. That one was a little more interesting. It held a fat stack of twenty dollar bills.

Annabel counted them. A thousand dollars, but that wasn't much for someone who likely paid others to do his dirty work. On a whim, she checked the image of the White House. The flag pointed in the correct direction.

She wondered how many years would pass before she could look at the back of a twenty-dollar bill without thinking of Declan.

Annabel crept to the door and peered through the keyhole. Once she confirmed the hallway was empty, she exited the room.

Exhilaration built as she walked toward the elevator, the restless pleasure of successfully getting away with something. It had been a long time since she felt that rush.

Her finger hovered over the call button when the ancient elevator shuddered to life. Her eyes flew to the arrow above the doors as it counted up. One. Two.

She blew out the breath she was holding when it stopped on the second floor.

It started moving again.

Fowler was the only other guest on this floor.

The stairwell was too far away. Even if she sprinted, she'd never make it. Annabel backed away from the doors. Her hip bumped into a doorknob.

The elevator dinged as it arrived on the floor. Just as the doors began to creak open, Annabel disappeared into the supply closet.

She pressed her ear against the door, listening for the sound of Fowler moving away. His tread was soft, but the walls were thin. She picked out the sound of the key in the lock and the solid thud of the door closing behind him.

The giddy feeling of relief returned as she opened the closet door.

Rather, as she *tried* to open the closet door. Because whoever installed the doorknob hadn't been very good at their job. They'd put the lock on the inside.

And there was no key.

She flipped on the light switch. The bulb sparked once, then went out. Of course.

Annabel felt her way through the closet. It wasn't very large, as it only needed to hold supplies for six rooms. She ran her hands along the shelves until she hit the far wall, then flipped over a metal bucket she'd spotted during the brief flash of light. Sitting on the upturned bucket, she dug around in her purse until she found her cell phone.

The screen provided a welcome beam of light. Even more welcome was the sight of three bars. The signal would be strong enough for a phone call—except her battery was at three percent.

Perhaps, Annabel decided, she *could* start thinking ahead.

Just a little bit.

She typed as fast as she could, ignoring any autocorrects. When she finished, she tapped the recipient window. There was only one person she could contact. One person who wouldn't demand an explanation. Not much of one, at least.

Sighing in defeat, she hit send.

CHAPTER TWENTY-THREE

Trapped in close third poor capital please hell.

Declan stared at the message on the screen. Even without her name attached, he knew it could only be from one person. No, that wasn't true. It could also be from any of his siblings.

But he knew it was Annabel.

Not Annabel. Anna Belmont.

His mind shied away from that thought. She was many people to him—friend, temptress, tormentor—but all were Annabel. Her name had been part of his thoughts for so long, those three syllables had become their own song. He couldn't imagine that changing.

He should leave her there and let her deal with the consequences of her actions. However she'd found herself stuck in a closet at the hotel, odds were good he didn't want to get involved.

The day before, he'd needed to walk away. To put distance between himself and that impetuous woman. He feared rash behavior was contagious, and if he remained in her orbit long enough, it was only a matter of time before he began to show symptoms. Like rushing to help a woman trapped in a damned closet.

If he stayed away from her, life would continue mostly as it had, or even better. He would be a councilman. It would take work, but he could turn Lost Coast Harbor into a draw for writers in need of a quiet, beautiful setting to work in peace. He could only imagine the gorgeous prose that might spring from a month spent surrounded by redwoods or gazing over the temperamental ocean. The adventure tourists and dedicated hikers shouldn't be the town's only visitors.

If he stayed away. Already, it wasn't looking good for him, since he was putting down the book he'd been trying to read—though if he was honest, he'd skimmed the same paragraph for the last ten minutes and still couldn't say what it was about. He lifted Pablo from his lap. The cat protested, then settled back into the warm chair. Declan retrieved his keys and phone from the table by the door, pulled on his coat, and hurried downstairs. Not even a full minute passed between receiving the text and stepping outside. He locked the front door behind him.

Declan crossed the square and strode through the hotel lobby, barely pausing to nod at Jimmy. He took the stairs two at a time.

The closet was directly across from the elevator. As he opened the door, the light from the hallway illuminated a space about the size of a small walk-in closet. Annabel sat against the far wall, using a bucket as a stool. She blinked as the light spilled into the room.

"Why are you sitting here in the dark?"

"Well, it sounded like a bit of fun."

Someday, he might figure out how such a sweet voice could sound so scornful.

She stood, the movement easy and light.

"Watch out for your bag," he reminded her.

It was too late. At some point while sitting in the dark, she'd managed to twine the purse strap around her left foot. As she stepped toward him, she stumbled and tripped over the leather.

Declan rushed forward to catch her before she crashed to the concrete floor.

"The door!" she cried.

He lunged backwards, dragging Annabel with him. His fingers slipped off the handle, unable to get a firm grip before it clicked shut and trapped them both in the darkness.

He didn't need light to know Annabel was glaring at him. "I thought…" he began, but that wasn't true. He hadn't thought at all. He'd reacted.

Still, she said nothing, and the silence grew heavy.

"I'm sorry. Let me call Niall. If he's not in a class, he'll come right over." And Niall would never, ever let Declan forget it, but he'd worry about that later.

An unexpected sound filled the room. Giggling.

Declan pulled out his phone and tapped the flashlight icon on the screen. He shone it on Annabel.

She had her fingers against her mouth, like she was trying to hold in the sound, but mirth bubbled out of her. Her cheeks rounded and her eyes crinkled as she looked at him, the giggles turning into outright laughter.

"I thought you were supposed to be the smart one," she managed at last.

"You were falling," he protested. His lips twitched.

"Oh, so you made a foolish choice with no thought to the consequences?" Her smiled widened. "Which is it? Impetuous or just not very bright?"

The smile still hovered on his lips. "Obviously the second," he said with mock offense. "I made it clear I don't do impetuous things."

He lost the battle against his grin—because whatever else she was, Annabel was still the friend who made him laugh, even when they were fighting.

Shaking his head, Declan phoned Niall, who picked up on the second ring. "Hey, are you free right now?" He explained the situation.

His brother was still hooting with glee when they hung up.

"He'll be here in less than ten minutes."

Annabel nodded at the phone. "You should turn off the light to save battery."

"It's okay. It's fully charged."

For some reason, she found that hilarious. "Of course it is. Turn it off anyway."

Uncertain, he did so, plunging them back into darkness. "Why does it need to be dark?"

"I don't want to look at you."

"Oh." Declan winced. Apparently, a moment of shared humor wasn't enough to erase her memory of their fight. "Is it that bad?"

"Well, I can't decide if I want to laugh at you, yell at you, or tear off your clothes, so it's best if I don't see your face for a bit."

Some distant part of his brain tried to get his attention, remind him that everything he'd said in the bakery was true. He could never trust this woman to make the sensible choice, let alone the safe one. Her interpretation—or understanding—of the law was as flimsy as his family's. She wasn't the kind of woman he ought to have at his side, not if he wanted to maintain his steady approach to life.

But that part of his brain was drowned out by the much louder part that was so happy to be with her again, it didn't care about anything else.

"Well, you already laughed at me," he pointed out. "How about you yell now, and we revisit the ripped clothes idea when you're done?"

"I think I have more than ten minutes of yelling to do."

"Niall could be delayed," he lied. For all his flaws, Niall was never late. "Here's your chance. Yell at me. Tell me why I was wrong before." He found he really wanted to hear her reasons. Wanted any excuse to change his mind.

"I can't yell." She sounded disappointed. "The walls in this hotel are thin, and we're supposed to be hiding."

Declan finally asked the obvious question. "Annabel, why are you in a supply closet?"

"It was the only way to avoid Fowler."

"And why," he said, the words slower, more deliberate, "were you on Fowler's floor if you planned to avoid him?"

"I might have explored his room a little bit." He could almost see the innocent expression she surely wore.

He tensed, remembering why dating Annabel would be a disaster. "What were you thinking? If he'd caught you…"

"He didn't. And don't use that tone of voice."

"What tone?"

"The 'I know better than everyone because I read James Joyce' tone. I'm not stupid, Declan."

"I never thought you were." Her silence spoke volumes. "I mean it. All I said before was you haven't always considered a problem from all angles." He hoped that sounded tactful enough.

"I *was* trying a new angle," Annabel replied. "You were right, at least about this. I have no reason to believe Peter Hastings will let me off the hook, so I wanted some leverage."

"I also said you should try being less impetuous!" His voice rose with his exasperation. "At least tell me it was worth it? What did you find?"

"Nothing." Even in the dark, he could picture her face. Lips pursed in frustration, chin firm and determined. "Toiletries, a bit of money, and two other versions of the same suit he always wears. But at least I managed to leave the pen behind."

"You did what?" Declan caught himself before his voice rose again. "We might have needed to use the bug again, and you just gave it up?"

"How else am I supposed to get the information I need?"

"But leaving the pen with Fowler won't help—" He cut off abruptly. It might not have been his first choice, but it wasn't a bad idea. Knowing about Peter Hastings' plans could be useful. Instead of feeding Fowler false information, now they had a chance to uncover *real* information.

And if they needed to get the pen back in a day or two, he was pretty sure Niall would break into the room for the promise of a six-pack and a hoagie. "That could work,"

Declan admitted.

"Of course it could. I'm not an idiot. Not all the time, at least." Her voice grew quiet. "Why do you do that? Assume the worst of me?"

His chest felt like it cracked open at the hurt in her voice. Hurt he'd caused.

"I don't." He wished for light, so she could see the truth in his face. But she'd asked for darkness, and he wouldn't take that from her.

Instead, he reached for her. She hadn't moved since he put away the phone, and he found her face easily. Declan rested his hand against her cheek.

"I think you're amazing," he said. "I always have, since the first time I saw you. You were so charming. Everyone who visited the bakery left feeling better than when they walked in, and it's not just the food. It's like you carry this light with you, and you shine it on everyone you meet. The day I met you, I returned to the bookstore with a big old smile, already planning when I could see you again." There was something about the dark that made it easier to say such things, to articulate the quiet thoughts that used to live only in his soul.

She was silent for a long time. "It's easy to be happy when you live in the moment," she said at last. The words weren't pointed. They were sad. "The bakery has been the best part of my life. When I'm there, I don't need to think about anything else. I'm surrounded by people. I make things. I'm not alone."

"How could you be alone?" Declan wondered. "People love you."

"It doesn't matter."

No way was he pretending to believe that obvious lie. Declan hit the flashlight button, but instead of turning it on her, he shone it on his own face, so she would see how much he meant his words. "If you're hurting, it matters. Tell me."

Her hand moved into the circle of light. She wrapped her fingers around his wrist and turned it just enough for the phone to illuminate her face, too. Her other hand found the one still cupping her cheek. Annabel threaded her fingers through his and dropped their clasped hands to her side.

"Why do you think I turned you down at the party? Why I was willing to be only your friend for so long? I was never the sort who waited for something I wanted. I went out and got it, until…" She let him fill in the blank.

"Until you got involved with Hastings." Declan finished. "You couldn't date someone, because if they knew the truth, someone might tell the cops."

In the dim light, her green eyes were almost black. "Not just that. Part of it was self-preservation, of course. But I also didn't want someone to look at me like I was a criminal. I didn't want them to see anything other than the woman I used to be."

"However I looked at you after you told me, it wasn't like that. Not like you were a criminal."

"I know." She squeezed his hand. "But you don't see me as I was, either. Before I made one mistake too many."

"Why would I? You're not that woman anymore."

"But you wish I was." Her expression was sad, and though he wanted to argue, he wasn't sure he could. "It doesn't matter," she repeated. "I refuse to think about a past I can't change, and I won't worry about a future I can't control. The present is hard enough."

"Is it really that bad?"

"Not long after I started working for Hastings, I volunteered to help with the coastal cleanup, because I was going out of my mind with boredom. Peter visited me the next day, wondering why I'd been so chatty with Erin Grady. The man viewed every relationship as a potential threat. After a while, so did I." Annabel took the phone from him and turned off the flashlight, plunging them back into darkness. Her expression was once again hidden. "I haven't had a date in three years. I never met a friend for coffee. I don't go out to dinner, because people will gossip about poor Annabel eating alone. Every day, I close the bakery, then I go to my quiet house. That's my life."

He pictured sweet, vivacious Annabel in her empty home, with only her mystery novels and television for company—and, for three years, no hope of that ever changing.

Declan drew her hand to his lips, kissing the knuckles. "It will get better now. I promise."

She drew in a soft breath. Declan cringed as he realized how his words could be interpreted. Annabel might think he was promising that her life would be less lonely—because he'd be with her.

He hurried to clarify what he meant. "It will get better because we'll get you away from Hastings. You can build your life again."

She didn't respond, so he kept talking, hoping he could make her understand. "Part of me wants us to build that life together. But like you said, you live in the present. I like to think ahead. There's nothing wrong with who you are.

But you remind me a little too much of my family, and I avoid that side of myself. You know why that's important to me. You're impetuous, and for you the future is a surprise. I always want to know what's going to happen next—and I want to be able to control it. Whatever's between us, we both know it can never really work. You'd drive me crazy by never thinking ahead, and I'd try to dim the light that makes you what you are. Maybe we'd have fun now, but in the long run, we won't make each other happy."

The door was flung open and light spilled in, revealing Annabel's stricken face. "I didn't know that, but I suppose I do now," she whispered. She disentangled her hand from his.

When Niall dropped his hands on Declan's shoulders with a loud laugh, Declan needed an extra second to control his features before turning around.

"I am telling everyone about this," his brother announced. "Every day, for the rest of my life, I'm telling people about the time my serious brother got locked in a hotel closet with a beautiful woman." Niall peered over his shoulder at Annabel. "One who looks bored? Declan, you really do your best to ruin the family's reputation, don't you?"

Declan elbowed his brother in the ribs. Hard. "Keep it down. Fowler's just down the hall."

"Peter Hastings' attorney?" It was obvious Niall had a hundred questions, but he was smart enough to hold them in while everyone exited the closet.

They moved toward the stairs, not wanting to get caught waiting for the elevator.

"I'll need a way to get the keys back to Jimmy. I don't think I can convince him to fetch another dish for me." She held up a plate of eclairs Declan hadn't noticed in the closet. If he had, he'd have eaten them both by now.

He was glad the desserts had only been a ruse. Fowler didn't deserve an eclair.

Just the thought of that man's unsettling eyes sent a shot of ice down his spine. And then there were the black clothes that made him look like he was constantly on his way to a funeral—possibly one he caused.

Declan swayed on his feet as the memory that had teased him for a week exploded in his mind in full color. A man in black clothes, though not the same ones. Jeans and a sweater instead of the heavy suit and turtleneck. And not a pure black, but one ringed by orange flames as the man rushed past the crumpled metal of Niall's car in search of water or dirt or anything that might douse the flames.

A man who now wore outfits that covered as much of his skin as possible.

Only one person had been caught that night. The other two men had escaped—and one of them had decided to return.

His brother and Annabel watched him with matching looks of concern. He tried to sound calm and normal, wanting to reassure them. His voice came out in a rasp. "You said there was money in his room?"

Annabel's brows drew together. "About a thousand dollars, yes."

She didn't think there was anything unusual. Of course she wouldn't. She hadn't watched Fowler run from a burning building fifteen years ago.

A building where he'd counterfeited money.

"All twenties?" he asked.

Annabel's expression shifted from confused to intrigued. "All of them. But I checked. The flag pointed in the right direction."

Niall made a slight choking sound. "You told her?"

Both Annabel and Niall stared at him, and he realized he was smiling. A big, broad, evil smile.

"He probably wouldn't be using the same plates as before, but Fowler is one of the counterfeiters who got away. I'm sure of it. We need to get him out of the room so I can see that money."

"How?" Annabel and Niall asked at the same time.

"I have a plan."

CHAPTER TWENTY-FOUR

Annabel peered around the corner of the stairwell as Niall's heavy fist fell on the door of room 305. When no one answered, he knocked harder. The door shook.

"I know you're in there, you fucking coward. You think my family wouldn't find out that Peter Hastings' lapdog has been sniffing around town? This is Lost Coast Harbor, you moron. In a small town, people notice when zombie-looking assholes start hanging around. Now get out here and try acting like a man instead of a mouse. I promise it'll only hurt a little."

The door swung open, and she ducked out of sight.

Niall was six inches taller than Fowler and had at least sixty extra pounds of muscle. Any reasonable man would be terrified. Instead, Fowler's voice was coated in scorn.

"The difference is not man or mouse. It is brains or brawn, and your use of mixed metaphor, cliche, and profanity make it clear you have far more of one than the other. You can leave now."

They heard the solid thud of a door closing on flesh. Niall must have got his foot in the door before Fowler could shut it. Annabel winced in sympathy.

"I'm coming in." There was a solid thwack as Niall hit the door, then a cracking sound as he punched right through it.

Annabel stared at Declan, shocked that it worked.

He seemed to enjoy her surprise. "He's been breaking boards in martial arts classes since he was eight," he whispered.

Niall laughed at Fowler. "Well look at that. Guess I do have more brawn than brains. Enjoy your new window." He whistled, the sound growing louder as he moved toward the stairs.

Annabel gasped when he appeared. Splinters poked out of his left hand. Blood welled around the small cuts.

Niall shrugged, unconcerned. "'Tis but a flesh wound," he whispered. "Get down. If he comes this way, I'll delay him."

A second later, they heard the ancient elevator machinery creak. As soon as the doors closed behind Fowler, she and Declan took off running. Hands shaking with excitement as much as nerves, she slipped the key into the lock and ran into the room just ahead of him.

"The money's in the top drawer." She hesitated. "And the pen's behind the Bible, if you want to reclaim it."

"I do. We'll need to put it in his new room." He smiled at her, both sweet and apologetic, and she forced her knees not to buckle.

He slid a single bill from the stack and slipped it into his wallet in a separate section from his own cash. "That's all I needed."

"Do you think he'll notice?" Annabel stared at him. If she didn't know better, she'd almost call Declan's behavior reckless.

Declan looked uncertain for a second, then opened his wallet again. "I don't have any crisp bills. You?"

Annabel ripped open her purse. Her hands, she noticed, were shaking a little. "This is the best I have." She held up a recently-printed bill that only had one folded corner.

"It'll do." Declan slid it into the middle of the stack. "Let's go."

They took the stairs down, joining Niall on the landing between the first and second floors. Declan nodded at his brother, and the other man returned a smile so devilish Annabel understood exactly how the family got its nickname.

Annabel strained her ears, trying to pick up Fowler's low voice as he arranged for another room amidst complaints about the hotel's security.

Jimmy stammered and apologized, which took longer than actually providing another key. "I can put you in room 301, sir."

Declan disappeared back up the stairs.

Fowler continued to berate the poor clerk. "Lou has no business hiring someone so useless. Tell the man I wish to speak with him."

"He's not at the hotel tonight," Jimmy tried to explain.

"And?"

"He's not working, sir. He'll be here tomorrow."

"I assume he is in town? Conscious?"

She winced on Jimmy's behalf, knowing he was likely cowering beneath Fowler's scorn.

"Phone him now. Tell him I expect him within the hour."

Jimmy was still sputtering when Fowler stepped back into

the elevator.

Niall started up the stairs to warn Declan, but the other man was already turning the corner. Declan looked way too pleased with himself. "Turns out lock-picking is like riding a bike. The pen's in place."

No big brother had ever looked more proud than Niall did at that moment. "About time."

"We're not done," Declan reminded him. "We still need to drop off the keys."

"I can help with that," Annabel said. With a wink, she popped open the second button on her blouse. Before, she'd needed Jimmy malleable. This time, she might need him insensible.

Declan looked pained. Niall gave her a thumbs up.

She entered the lobby with her hips swaying and her shoulders back. Jimmy stopped moving when he saw her, though he did blink a lot as she approached.

Annabel positioned herself at the far end of the desk. Jimmy followed her like he was magnetized. "Thank you so much for the plate," she said. "But it turns out it wasn't necessary. I had the wrong name."

"The wrong name?" He tried to understand, but she didn't think most of Jimmy's blood was in his brain.

Declan crept behind Jimmy. He slipped the key to Fowler's old room onto the hook.

The elevator dinged. Declan dropped to the ground, out of sight.

Annabel's heart plummeted at the sound of the awful voice behind her. "You gave me the wrong key. I understand one and two are very close on a keyboard, and you are easily confused, but I am unable to open the correct door with this one."

Annabel put a finger to her lips, letting Jimmy know they had a secret, then spun around. "Mr. Fowler. This is unexpected."

His eyes raked her, lingering on the open neck of her blouse with—what else—scorn. "What brings you by, Miss Johnson?"

She held up the plate of eclairs. "Just a late Valentine's delivery."

She thought she'd actually managed to confuse him. Probably because he needed a heart to understand why people celebrated Valentine's Day.

"Indeed. The correct key, if it's not too much bother?"

Jimmy jumped to attention. Annabel reached for his sleeve, trying to stop him before he spotted Declan crouched behind him.

Niall's voice carried across the lobby before Jimmy could complete his turn.

"Are you getting a new room? Should I stick around long enough to punch a hole in this door, too?" Niall strode toward Fowler. At some point, he'd taken off his hoodie to wrap around his bleeding hand, but he let it drop as he stalked toward Fowler. At least six-foot-four, with muscles bulging from his t-shirt, a scowl that could scare a horror movie villain, and a hand still dripping blood, it felt like Niall had cranked the "intimidating" knob up to eleven. Behind her, Jimmy audibly swallowed.

Niall poked the lawyer in the chest. "Unless you're checking out, I'll be back here every day. There won't be a door in this hotel safe from me. Sorry about that, Jimmy, but I'll pay for it." He circled Fowler, forcing the man to face the far wall in order to keep an eye on Niall.

From his position on the floor, Declan caught her small nod. He sprang up, hung the second key on the hook, then crept toward the entrance, staying as far from the two men as possible. Niall kept spinning, making sure Fowler never saw his brother.

An older man stood by the hotel doors. If there was any question that he hadn't witnessed their farce, his wide eyes and dropped jaw would dispel that hope right away.

Declan gave Otis Spatz a nod, then exited the hotel.

Annabel bit held back a groan. She suspected Declan now had an uphill battle for the Rotary Club vote.

Niall almost looked disappointed when his brother escaped and he no longer had an excuse to torment Fowler. Still, he stepped away from the lawyer, though he didn't drop his menacing glare. "Your call, asshole. Leave town or I'll make your life a living hell."

Though Niall tossed Annabel a small smile as he walked away, she had the feeling he meant every word. The Donnellys might drive each other crazy, but they were the only ones allowed to get away with it. God help anyone else who tried to hurt the family.

She ought to be grateful they hadn't run her out of town yet. At least she was on their side now—and that's where she planned to stay. Somehow.

"Can you make sure these go to the lovely man in room 306?" She pushed the plate at Jimmy and walked away as fast as she could without running.

As soon as she was outside, her fear transformed into a nervous glee. Somehow, they'd pulled it off. She and the Donnelly brothers played off each other like they'd been planning heists for a decade. The rush was extraordinary.

A strong hand wrapped around her upper arm. In the middle of the town square, where anyone could see, she was yanked off-balance and into Declan's arms.

"I'm so sorry about the Rotary—" she began.

He didn't seem to hear her. "Can we skip the part where you yell at me and go straight to ripping each other's clothes off?" he growled.

His eyes were so hot she thought he could burn her skin just by looking at her, and his calm, modulated voice seemed to have vanished.

She managed a shaky nod. "I can multitask."

He threaded his hand into hers and practically dragged her toward the bookstore.

Chapter Twenty-Five

They made it as far as the mystery section. The stairs to his apartment were only ten feet away, but he couldn't wait. At least they were out of sight of the windows.

He had to taste her. Declan spun her against the shelves and fitted his lips to hers. Their tongues tangled together, the movement chaotic and demanding.

Annabel stretched to twine her arms around his neck.

He tore his mouth away to blaze open-mouthed kisses down the column of her throat. "I need you," he groaned against her skin.

He felt unhinged. Unbalanced.

It started when he sent Niall to punch a hole in room 305. It increased when he broke into Fowler's new room to drop off the pen, and intensified further as he watched Annabel saunter toward the desk, prepared to work her magic.

And when he needed to drop to the ground to hide, something within him broke loose.

He should have been horrified by his behavior. Embarrassed. Annoyed. Anything but how he felt.

Alive. Like he'd been swimming underwater for years, and

his head finally broke the surface.

He hooked her leg over his hip and ran his hand up her thigh to grip her sweet ass. Annabel tilted her hips to meet him.

"Take your clothes off," she ordered.

He didn't want to let go of her, not even for that long.

But to feel her skin against his, her softness and warmth, with nothing between them…he couldn't think of anything in the world he wanted more.

He reluctantly dropped her leg as he reached back for his collar and pulled his shirt over his head.

Her hands were already on his belt buckle, but they stilled when she saw his chest, and her mouth rounded into a perfect O that made his cock jump.

She skimmed her fingers over his pecs and down the line of muscles, picking out each one like she was discovering a treasure. "Aren't you something?" she murmured. She made him feel like a god.

"Let me feel your skin." He looked for the control he always knew at these moments, but it had abandoned him. He felt like he was begging.

A second later, her shirt had joined his on the floor and her bra followed. That was as long as he could be away from her.

Declan backed her into the bookcase. It was built into the wall, and he took a moment to be thankful for the sturdy construction. He didn't think he could be restrained right then, not with her soft breasts pressed to his chest, her warmth and sweet vanilla scent washing over him.

She wasn't so easily distracted. "Pants," she murmured

against his lips.

He bit her bottom lip. "Later."

He felt a tug on his zipper, then one of her hands slipped inside. She sighed in pleasure as her hand wrapped around his rigid cock.

"I want to taste you." She pushed against him, trying to drop to her knees.

That red mouth, finally wrapped around his cock. He'd waited three years for that image to be a reality.

And all he wanted was to sink deep inside her. "Later," he repeated, pushing up her skirt and moving her underwear to the side. Declan moaned when he found her soaking wet.

He positioned himself at her entrance and buried himself with a single thrust. She dug her fingers into his shoulders as he lifted her hips and set up a punishing rhythm.

This wasn't lovemaking or even fucking. It was straight-up need. He needed to be inside her. Needed to feel her skin. He needed to make her scream his name.

He needed to mark her.

Declan bent his mouth to the spot where her neck met her shoulder and bit hard.

Annabel gasped and threw back her head, and he drove into her over and over again.

"Annabel?" he asked, his voice strangled.

"I'm…" She didn't finish her sentence. Her body stilled. Already, he'd come to love that moment, the second before she fell apart around him.

Only a few strokes later, he followed. Her hot pussy clenched around him as he pulsed deep within her. His release went on and on, and he let go of everything.

As she came back to herself, she became aware of a slight pain in her back that was quickly worsening.

"Ow."

Declan lifted his head, his eyes still glazed and his brows knit. "Ow?"

"It turns out, when you're not desperately turned on, bookshelves hurt."

"Oh. Oh damn, I'm sorry." He withdrew from her body, leaving her feeling unpleasantly empty. He settled her away from the books. "I wasn't thinking," he said with a smile.

She already knew that. For a few minutes, he'd been nothing but desire, living entirely in his body and hers. The controlled Declan might be the hottest thing she'd ever known, but this one, this man full of need and passion—she could fall in love with this one.

She was afraid she already had.

"I'm never going to look at Agatha Christie the same way again." Declan's smile was as relaxed as she'd ever seen it. He moved to tuck himself back into his pants, and he froze. "Oh hell. Oh fuck. God, I'm so sorry."

She stared at him, not understanding his emotional whiplash.

"We didn't use a condom." His expression alternated between shame and horror. "I didn't stop to think. It never even occurred to me."

"Hey, I was there with you," she reminded him. Her words did nothing to ease his scowl. "I should have remembered, too."

He scrubbed his hands through his hair, the neatly combed strands turning spiky under his fingers.

"I think it's okay." Annabel counted backwards in her head. "Really. I'm pretty regular, and we're in the safe zone."

A fraction of his tension seemed to drop from his shoulders, and she hoped she was right. Still, no point panicking before there was a reason to panic.

Declan gathered their shirts, his expression growing calmer with every passing second. He held out his hand to her, the touch solid and comforting.

He tugged her upstairs, and she followed. Pablo looked up from his spot on the sofa when they entered. He yawned once, then went back to sleep.

"Are you hungry? Thirsty?"

"A glass of water, please."

He kissed her hand once before releasing it. While he was in the kitchen, she shrugged her blouse back on and closed one button, so she wasn't wandering around his apartment in just a skirt. She headed to his bookshelf. "What's your favorite?" she called to him.

He returned with the water. "My favorite book? Might as well ask me to pick a favorite friend. They've all been there for me at one time or another."

On the surface, there was nothing unusual about the conversation. But there was a caution in his voice that unnerved her, like a silent thought was hidden within each word.

Rather than hear that thought spoken, she faced the bookcase and withdrew a volume at random. "I've never read Baudelaire. The language is a bit dense, isn't it?" She set down the water so she could read. The words washed over her, lush and ardent. It felt like the writer gave voice to emotions that could never be defined. She turned the page and smiled at what she found. "*The balcony where veiled rose-va-pour clings—how soft your breast was then, how sweet your soul.*" She was not above reminding him of her body part he seemed to most enjoy.

"*Ah, and we said imperishable things.*" Declan completed the next line. "It's a poem to a former lover."

Oh. She hadn't meant to make him think of *that*. She slipped the book back into its spot on the shelf.

He continued. "I've always thought 'imperishable things' wasn't about love, not exactly. I believe he meant truth, for those are the words that live on. That can't be tarnished or eroded with time."

She gazed at him, the poem forgotten. Declan sat on the bed and removed his shoes and socks, then stood again. His hand went to his buckle, and she watched, mesmerized, as he pulled his pants down and stepped out of them, until he stood before her in a pair of boxer briefs.

Over the last two weeks, it felt like he revealed himself in pieces. What he liked. What turned him on. The feel of his tongue, and then his cock. The glorious sight of him without his shirt. The weight of his hard length in her hand.

But she'd never seen the whole picture. His thighs were as muscled as his chest. She studied his body, from his shoulders to his feet. There wasn't a spare ounce of fat. He was lean, and perfectly made. She longed to trace that trail of dark blond hair that led from his chest all the way down to his cock.

He was so perfect, it took her a second to understand why he was showing her all of himself.

A thick band of ridged tissue ran diagonally across his left thigh, about eight inches long. It was jagged and irregular, with some patches that were almost smooth right below the raised keloid scars. Some parts had faded to a pale white, but others were still an angry pink. It seemed they would be for the rest of his life.

"This is my truth." He simply stated a fact. "It's the one I see in the mirror every day."

Annabel set down the book and crossed the room. "May I?" He nodded, and she dropped to her knees. With tentative fingers, she traced the smooth scar. "Do you feel that?"

"The raised parts are still sensitive, and the muscle underneath hurts if I don't stretch it every day."

The corners of her mouth lifted. "Which you never forget to do, of course." She pressed her lips against the thick, ugly scar that was still beautiful on this man.

He perched on the edge of the bed, and she sat back on her heels, waiting.

"Nothing's changed, Annabel."

Though it was what she feared, even expected, the words still felt like a vise around her heart. "How do you mean?"

Declan swallowed. "I like you, and I think you like me, but if we stay together, we'll wear each other down. Wanting someone doesn't make them the right person for you. What happened downstairs...I never do that. I never forget. It wasn't a small mistake, either. That's the kind of mistake we'd be dealing with the rest of our lives. I don't know what it is about you, Annabel, but I become someone I don't want to be when I'm with you."

The words cut so deep she almost felt her soul crack, but she kept her voice level. "Is it what you don't want, or what you don't *want* to want?"

His eyes looked sad, but not uncertain. "In the end, it's the same thing."

"What does this mean for you? Maddie didn't excite you. I make you feel out of control. Do you think you're Goldilocks, waiting for the one who's just right?" The words were sharper than intended.

He shook his head. "I think I probably need to be alone."

"Trust me. That's not the answer." She rose and turned her back. Tears pricked her eyes, and she didn't want him to see.

She couldn't even say if she was crying for him or herself, or for what they were losing. She wanted to argue, but the words froze on her tongue because, deep down, she feared he was right. It didn't matter if she enjoyed his wild side if he still despised it. If he wanted something else, she shouldn't interfere with that. That afternoon, she'd likely cost him the council seat and everything that came with it. His dream of a writer's retreat. What else would being with her cost him?

Just because she didn't like his decision didn't mean it was the wrong one. Declan had made his choice. Now she had to make hers.

"But I don't want to be alone. Not tonight," he said to her back.

It would be nice. One more night of his touch, a night to taste and touch him, to learn every inch of his skin. She could commit him to memory, a living poem of her very own. A desperate part of her dared hope that, if she stayed with him, in the morning he might even change his mind and give them a second chance.

But she would rather be alone than feel him move within her while he believed, in his heart, that she was the wrong woman, so she did up the remaining buttons on her shirt.

"I'm glad you were my valentine," she said without turning around.

Then she left.

CHAPTER TWENTY-SIX

The bakery was full of furtive glances.

The townspeople looked at Annabel, then looked at each other with raised brows. She knew they were having a silent conversation about her appearance—about the dark circles under her eyes and the false smiles that fooled no one—but she couldn't be bothered to care. She moved through the day in a fog, her motions automatic. Even cooking brought her little pleasure. She made a large pot of cream of mushroom soup, one of her favorite comfort foods, and barely bothered to taste it.

Twice that day, she broke out of her daze a little. The first time was when Otis Spatz entered with several members of the Rotary Club in tow. He gave her a severe stare, then watched her the entire time he ate his cherry danish, as if expecting her to reenact her performance of the day before.

The second time was when she heard Declan's name, spoken in offended tones by a woman in her twenties. Apparently, Declan gave a mocking snort when she attempted to purchase a book of dating advice.

At four o'clock, Annabel flipped the lock with relief and

hurried into the back room. She braced herself against the table and let herself cry the tears she'd been holding in all day.

Then she wiped her eyes, righted herself, and tried to figure out how she was going to get through the next week. The next month. The next hour.

After years of fantasizing about sex with the handsome bookstore owner, she'd finally gotten what she wanted, and it wasn't nearly enough. Declan was so much more than she'd once believed he was—and he didn't want to be any of it.

Annabel couldn't face her quiet house, so she baked. She whipped meringues, mixed the ingredients for fudge, and sliced apples for pie. When there was no room in the case for more desserts, she dug out her gumbo recipe and got to work preparing the *roux*. She moved a little bit slower than usual, and simmered the sauce a bit longer, and she tried not to check the time every five minutes.

Of course Declan wouldn't visit her. People usually took time off after a breakup.

A sob threatened at the thought. Her mind had shied away from the word all day, but that was what it was. A breakup. An ending.

Even so, that afternoon she'd set aside a cup of chocolate mousse and brewed his favorite coffee roast. When no one came to get them, she threw the dessert in the trash and poured the coffee down the drain.

Ten minutes after six, another layer of her heart broke. Declan was staying away.

Annabel wrenched her apron off, balled it, and threw it into the corner. She turned off the stove and chucked the entire pot into the fridge without bothering to cover it.

Tomorrow, everything in the fridge would smell of gumbo.

She opened the closet to grab her purse. Her eyes caught on the mirror hanging inside.

The eyes that stared back weren't the same as a week before. Then, she'd only looked at the present. It had seemed simpler. But life wasn't simple. No one was only their present. People were the sum total of their past actions, their current behavior, and their hopes for their future. For too long, she'd denied the first one and couldn't bear to face the last.

Now, for the first time in years, she thought she knew what her future looked like. It was day after day of pretending she didn't want the man across the street. Pretending it didn't break her heart that he couldn't change even a little to make room for her in his life.

She made him someone he didn't want to be. Every time she recalled his words, the wound felt fresh. Raw.

But Annabel wasn't sure she could change, either, not the way he needed. Better to be lonely than be a worse version of herself.

That didn't mean she couldn't try to be a *better* version of herself.

Exhaling, she pulled the gumbo out of the fridge and covered it up as she should have done the first time. She dried and put away several dishes.

Then, as she did every afternoon, she dropped the vinyl cover over the butcher block. Annabel gripped the edge of the table, needing to steady herself as memories washed over her again. Her body spread across the table, her gaze locked with Declan's in the reflection.

Another version of her future came into focus. She had a

bit of money saved, the honest profit from the bakery. The building was Hastings-owned, and everything inside it had been bought with Hastings' money. She could walk away. Make a clean break. She wouldn't have to walk past this table every day.

She wouldn't see Declan every weekday for the rest of her life, and she wouldn't have to watch him date another nice girl. Maybe marry her, and bring her home to Sunday dinner, where the boisterous Donnelly clan would eat her alive.

It was his town. She'd never been anything but an interloper, trying to escape a past that couldn't be erased.

It was time to leave Lost Coast Harbor. To become Anna Belmont once more, whatever the cost.

Her heart dropped at the thought. For years, she'd longed to reclaim her original name, but now it felt foreign. It was the name of a woman from her past, like an old friend she lost touch with over the years.

At last, Anna would accept the consequences of her actions, but she wasn't so noble that she was willing to do it on her own. Hastings was coming down with her—and his little dog, too.

Annabel withdrew the receiver from its hiding place and set it on the covered butcher block. She flipped the switch from record to play. The machine announced the time of the recording, not even an hour earlier. Fowler's low voice came through the speakers, and she grimaced at the sound.

"We're in good shape." There was a long pause, then he spoke again. "We have the car, but we haven't been able to open the safe. A specialist is arriving in town tomorrow." Another pause. It was the rhythm of a phone conversation.

"Peter, I think it's dangerous to believe the Donnellys won't find more money. Stealing the gold isn't enough."

Annabel gave the machine an impatient stare while she waited for Fowler to speak again.

"It's too risky to wait for their next move. We need to consider other solutions," Fowler continued. "Both Donnelly and your son are determined to complete this deal. If we removed one of them from the equation…" When he spoke again, Fowler almost sounded impatient. "Of course I didn't mean that." Another long pause. "It will never come back to you. I promise."

The recording went silent. She waited the five minutes it would take for the voice activation to turn off.

At four minutes, Fowler greeted someone. A new call.

"Are you ready? Bring Donnelly to my hotel room. What do you mean, which Donnelly? The father, you imbecile. The one trying to make the deal. Bring your cleaning supplies. I'll meet you there."

Annabel struggled to draw breath. She may not have much experience with the criminal world, but she watched TV. She knew what a cleanup crew actually cleaned.

Her mind rebelled. Fowler couldn't be planning to murder Richard Donnelly in a hotel right in the middle of town. Witnesses would see the man being unwillingly dragged through the lobby, and the risk of removing the body was too great. Even clueless Jimmy would know something was wrong, and while Lou was a jerk, even he'd shy away from a guest committing murder in his hotel.

Lou. The man with few scruples, none of them professional, who still refused to give out Fowler's room number.

The one Fowler insisted would phone him immediately, as if Lou was his employee.

A man who worked in a business that accepted cash, where it would be easy to fake how many rooms had actually been used in a given year.

She wasn't the only money launderer in town…and if Fowler owned Lou the way he owned her, it was possible he'd look the other way for all kinds of crimes.

The phone call was made an hour ago. She might still have time.

Her phone's battery had been dead all day, because she hadn't remembered to charge it the night before.

Annabel didn't stop to grab her coat or lock up. She sprinted across the street and banged on the bookshop's door. A warm glow spilled from the second-story window. She knew he was home.

She waited thirty seconds, but no one came downstairs. "Declan!" she shouted up to the window.

"He must not be there, dear."

Annabel spun around. "Mrs. Wandsworth. Do you have a phone I can use?"

"Oh no. I don't wish to spend my life tethered to an electronic device. Why, thirty years ago no one would have imagined—"

"What about a paper? Pen?"

The older woman's mouth tightened at the interruption. "What could be so important?" She looked between Annabel and the door, and she relaxed into a smile. "Have the two of you gotten together? Oh, I do hope so. I never much cared for that Palmer girl. Terrible taste in men, and do you know

I once caught her buying three boxes of condoms? Why any respectable woman would ever need so many—"

Annabel reminded herself that it was wrong to throttle an eighty-year-old woman. "A pen. Do you have a pen?"

Mrs. Wandsworth harrumphed, and Annabel knew there'd be talk around town about that shockingly rude bakery owner, but at least the woman stopped talking long enough to dig through her purse.

The seconds ticked by, each more agonizing than the one before, but at last Mrs. Wandsworth dug out a cheap ball-point pen and a pad of motel stationary.

"Thank you. You're a lifesaver." Maybe even literally.

"If you return in fifteen minutes, he'll open up for book club."

Annabel scrawled a note, slipped it through the mail slot, and prayed that they had fifteen minutes.

She banged on the bookshop door once more, hoping he would hear this time. Nothing.

Mrs. Wandsworth still watched her with shrewd eyes, like she was already constructing a story about Annabel's erratic behavior. Annabel forced a smile and crossed the road. As soon as the door was closed, she leaned against it and tried to think.

A flimsy idea formed, but even a weak idea was better than none. She hurried across the cafe and dug an old phone book from under the counter. No one's cell phone numbers were listed, but the local businesses were.

She stared through the window as she rang Lost in a Book, but no one came downstairs. After four rings it went to voicemail.

In a panic, she made two other phone calls and, when no one answered, she left two more messages.

It would have to be enough. Time was running out.

Annabel sprinted across the park to The Capital Hotel. People still strolled along the paths, and several called out to her. She ignored them.

Lou was at the desk. For a moment, she almost felt sorry for him. It was possible he'd been coerced into their line of work like she was.

Or maybe he'd been too cowardly to say no—just as she had been.

Annabel walked to the desk. "I need the key to Fowler's room."

The hotel owner's eyes bugged out. "No way."

"I worked with him," she said. "Much like you do. For now, I'm the only one who knows about your second job." Annabel refused to look away from the man's shifty eyes and hoped like crazy she was right.

Lou handed over the key.

She took the stairs to Fowler's room. The carpeted hallways muffled her footsteps as she approached.

As she drew near, she heard pained groans. Fear rushed through her, threatening her resolve.

But if she walked away and left Richard Donnelly to his fate, she'd never be able to live with herself.

She swung the door open, armed with nothing but her determination and a pair of sharp red heels.

Chapter Twenty-Seven

S he scanned the room. Her mind rushed to process what
she saw. The television was on, a little louder than normal. She recognized the action movie on the screen. It was in
the middle of a torture scene.

Fowler sat alone at a small desk by the window. In one
hand, he held the remote control. In the other, he held a pen.

Or, to be more precise, a bug.

He pressed the mute button on the remote, and the room
went silent. "Miss Johnson," he greeted her.

They were alone, and there was no sign anyone else had
recently been in the room. "Where's Richard Donnelly?" she
demanded.

"In Eureka, I believe. He had business with a mill up
north."

Fowler placed the remote and the pen on the desk. Her
heart sank as she realized he'd used the bug exactly like
Declan did—to set a trap. One she'd stepped into without
hesitation.

The man's expression wasn't victorious, however. If anything, he looked annoyed. "I'm disappointed you thought

so little of me that you believed you could turn the tables—especially when you made such a spectacle of the process. It makes me question what Peter ever saw in you." Fowler pushed away from the desk and rose. "Peter said it must have been one of the Donnellys, because you know your place."

Annabel's mouth went dry. She took a small step backwards, toward the open door. His strangely pale eyes tracked her.

"It is time for you to remember your place, and it is no longer with Peter. You belong to me now. Close the door."

Not a chance. She'd commit herself to Hastings for another five years before she'd agree to work with this man for a day. Annabel's stomach revolted at just the thought of belonging to Fowler.

When she didn't obey, Fowler drew a small gun from his pocket. His expression never changed.

It was a tiny weapon. Annabel never had much interest in guns herself, but she'd grown up in Texas with an uncle and cousin who liked to shoot, and she recognized the Walther .22. Small-caliber bullets, but at this range, and with Fowler's steady hand, they were plenty deadly.

The silencer attached to the barrel suggested he was prepared to use the gun.

Annabel raised her chin and attempted to stall, just long enough for Declan to find her note. "You don't think Peter will object when he learns I now work for you?"

One side of Fowler's mouth dropped a fraction, a hint of distaste covering his plain features. "You belong to whomever holds the key, and now that's me. It wasn't Peter who threatened to turn you in for identity fraud. He doesn't want you in prison when he's free, and the fool truly believes he'll beat the charges."

"It was you all along, wasn't it? You never planned to give me my name back, no matter what I did."

He stared at her, unblinking. "Your identity doesn't matter in the least. Anna Belmont always existed. You were just too scared to look for her. Hastings understood that much about you, at least. However, your current name is the one you chose, so it's the one you will maintain. It would only draw attention if you changed it now."

Even a conniving, merciless villain could stumble on the truth every now and then, because he got one thing right. This *was* the life she chose—and she was damn sure going to keep it.

"I won't launder money again."

Something flashed deep in his cold eyes. "It's not a choice."

"Everything is a choice," she insisted. "You see, I'm a bit tired of the work. Also, it turns out it's illegal, which has become a problem for me."

His expression darkened at her words, and his finger moved closer to the trigger. Perhaps she should tread a bit lighter.

Fowler's upper lip curled into a snarl. It was a feral expression, and the hair on the back of her neck rose in response. "I have no doubt we'll come to an agreement."

She shrugged and tried to look unimpressed. "Is there a reason you tricked me to come here? Or did you just want to remind me who's in charge?" The words were a little tart, and she knew they would rile Fowler, but she couldn't seem to help herself.

"I would like us to take a short trip."

Her laugh was incredulous. "I'm not going anywhere with you."

"Do you want me to shoot you?" He asked the question much like others would ask if she wanted milk in her coffee.

"I thought you wanted me around to launder money."

Fowler aimed the gun at the outside of her thigh. "I can shoot without killing you."

Annabel cringed, wondering how much longer she could stall before she found herself with a .22-caliber-sized hole in her leg. She thought she might be able to bear the pain, if it meant buying enough time.

The man sensed her uncertainty. "I will only shoot if I need to. It may not even be today. I could wait a day, or a week. I may choose to hire someone to shoot you in the shoulder a month from now, or in the heart in a year's time. Perhaps it won't even be you. It would be just as easy to put a bullet in Declan's skull."

She stared at him, and though she tried to conceal her horror, Fowler's cruel smile told her she failed.

"How do I know you won't do that even if I come with you?"

His smile widened. "You don't."

Annabel considered fleeing. Running as fast as she could down the stairs and into the square, screaming to all who would listen about the monster on the third floor of The Capital.

And then she imagined Declan lying on the ground with glassy eyes, a bloody hole in his head.

Sometimes, being impetuous was the only choice. "Where

are we going?"

Fowler returned the pistol to his inside pocket.

"I'm taking you to the scene of a crime."

DECLAN STEPPED OUT OF A VERY LONG, VERY COLD SHOWER and toweled off. The icy water hadn't helped at all. He still wanted to find Annabel, throw her over his shoulder, and demand she return to him. From the moment the door closed behind her last night, he hadn't thought of anything else.

He'd only spoken the truth. They both knew it. At heart, they were incompatible.

In the last two weeks, he'd invited her to Sunday dinner, discovered she was spying on his family, and slept with her anyway. He'd gotten drunker than he had since his freshman year of college, broken into her house, and told her all his worst secrets. Those weren't the actions of a rational man. If he stayed with Annabel, he'd be running a gambling ring and giving people offers they couldn't refuse by the end of the month.

Yesterday had been a disaster. He'd been locked in a closet, then broke into a lawyer's hotel room and ran around the lobby like he was auditioning for a Marx Brothers' revival.

He'd acted like a Donnelly. Even Niall was impressed.

The worst part was, he couldn't remember the last time he had so much fun.

That morning, he'd made a reluctant phone call to Otis Spatz. His wife attended book club, so he would talk to her husband when Otis picked her up after the meeting. Try as he might, Declan couldn't muster any enthusiasm for that conversation.

Declan parted his hair on the right, then combed it till it lay flat. Next, he pulled out a pair of khakis and a button-down shirt, then grabbed the brown shoes he shined two days ago.

He stared at the clothes, wondering when they stopped being an outfit and became a uniform. A way to signify that he was his own man, separate from his wild family.

Being his own man shouldn't require so much effort. So much restraint.

So much sacrifice.

As he always did when doubt assailed him, he looked down at his leg. This time, another image superimposed itself over his vision, of Annabel on her knees, kissing his scar. His chaotic past and rejected future in one image.

He ran his fingers through his hair, not caring that it stood on end. All this time, he'd treated himself like an addict, as if he was incapable of stopping at a single impulsive act. He'd believed that, if he opened the door to that way of life, he would cross some imaginary threshold and never look back. For years, Declan acted like the Donnelly wildness was a genetic trait, as much a part of their DNA as their blue eyes. If he couldn't cut it out of himself, he would stomp it into submission, one day at a time.

He'd created a damn twelve-step program for being a Donnelly.

Declan paced his apartment, long steps that took him to his bookshelves, where Annabel had discovered Baudelaire, and to his kitchen, where he'd uncorked the wine that he once tasted on her skin. Last, he strode to his bed, but his memory didn't flash to the time he made her fall apart with his fingers and mouth.

Instead, he remembered himself, standing almost naked before her as he explained why an old scar meant he couldn't be with her.

He was a grown man, for God's sake, and he was still paying for the mistakes of a seventeen-year-old kid. Worse, he'd made Annabel pay for them, too.

Annabel was impulsive. Rash. Unrestrained. Everything he swore he would never be again.

And after three years, hers was still the face he wanted to see every day for the rest of his life. One day apart, and he already knew what life would be like without her. Calm, ordered, and miserable.

Declan looked at his leg, and for the first time in years, all he saw was a scar—the healed tissue, rather than the old wound below it. It was meant to be a reminder of his past mistakes, not an excuse to make new ones.

Being with Annabel didn't mean he needed to become her, any more than he needed to dim her light. If she made him a little more like a Donnelly, that was hardly her fault. It was in his damn genetic code.

And really, what had he done? They were trying to expose Fowler, who was a goddamn criminal. No shame in that.

The condom thing was stupid, yeah. He knew better. But would it be so awful to have a little girl with green eyes and blonde curls?

Declan drew to a stop in the middle of his living room as the simple, undeniable truth hit him. He'd been irresponsible because, on some level, he liked the idea of Annabel pregnant with his child. Given the way his heart seemed to swell at the thought, he more than liked it.

He'd tried to make it all so complicated when the truth was simple. They could be themselves with each other and find a way to make that work—because it's what people did when they were in love.

The thought didn't even surprise him. Of course he was in love with Annabel. He suspected he had been for a very long time.

Declan peered through a window. The bakery was dark, but she should be home for the night. There was still time to make this right.

Declan pulled out a pair of black pants instead of khakis. He buttoned his shirt, leaving it open at the neck.

He combed his hair again, then at the last second ran his fingers across the top, just enough for a few unruly strands to act up.

Pablo yawned, unimpressed.

Declan petted the cat, then ran downstairs. He drew to a halt when he saw Mrs. Wandsworth waiting outside. He'd forgotten about book club. This time, their choice was *Like Water for Chocolate*, which he suspected would be more popular than their attempt at James Joyce. It wasn't a mystery, but he knew Annabel would love the descriptions of food. Even if she didn't forgive him that night, he'd bring her a copy tomorrow.

He looked at his watch. Six-fifteen, and book club usually lasted two hours. There was no way he was waiting that long to talk to her. He would let everyone in and trust them to behave themselves until he returned, hopefully with Annabel in tow.

There was a slip of paper just under the mail slot. It was covered in the same handwriting he'd seen written on hundreds of bakery boxes.

Declan's heart no longer felt restricted to his chest. His whole body pounded in time, each beat aware of one simple fact. Annabel had been here. She hadn't walked away. She was also fighting for what they could have.

Then he read the note, and his heart stopped entirely.

I think Fowler plans to kill your father. I'm going to the hotel now.

A wordless snarl filled the room. He should have been there for her. If he hadn't taken such a long shower, trying to drown his emotions under the cold water, he would have heard her knock. She wouldn't be facing that bastard alone.

If Fowler hurt either of them, they'd never find the body.

Declan ripped his coat off the rack and flung the door open.

Mrs Wandsworth started forward. "Your young lady was rather rude to me—"

He sprinted past her without a word.

Time shifted into slow motion. His feet pounded against the concrete path of the park, but he was only halfway to the hotel when Annabel exited the building with Fowler on her heels.

He shouted her name, but neither of them turned. She climbed into the passenger side of Fowler's dark sedan, then the other man drove her away.

Declan drew to a stop, his whole body shaking. It didn't matter if Annabel chose to get into the car or if she was coerced. No way in hell was he leaving her alone with Fowler.

A block from the hotel, the car took a right turn, heading for the highway out of town. Panic rose in his chest. Where the hell would he take her? Declan spun in a circle, searching the town square for a way to follow them.

"I was looking for you."

Declan swung toward the familiar gruff voice, praying to find his father. Instead, it was Niall driving slowly past in his obnoxious yellow sports car.

"Get out," he told Niall.

His brother was confused, but he didn't argue. "Have you heard—"

Declan didn't let him finish. "Go to Fowler's room. Dad might need help."

His brother was still talking, but Declan didn't hear a single word. He jumped into the driver's seat and took off. The tires squealed as he pulled into the street. A horn beeped behind him. He could still hear Niall yelling as he turned the corner and followed the sedan out of town.

CHAPTER TWENTY-EIGHT

At first, Declan tried following Fowler at a distance. When Annabel walked out of the building, she had been unhurt, and he didn't want to give Fowler any reason to change that. Niall's bright yellow sports car was hard to miss.

As Declan drove out of town, he hit a thick patch of fog, and soon he couldn't see more than a hundred feet ahead. His fingers dug into the steering wheel as he tried to quell his fear. Annabel and Fowler were only a minute ahead. He'd see the car soon.

"Fuck it," he muttered, and punched the accelerator. The engine rumbled, and the car shot forward.

He drove much faster than was safe in the weather, and for two miles he sped through the fog, looking for any sign of taillights. When at last they appeared, they seemed to do so out of nowhere. He slammed on the brakes. The seatbelt dug into his shoulder. With a loud screech, the sports car slowed enough to just avoid the other car's bumper.

He was close enough to identify the vehicle. It was a Toyota Prius.

With a scream, he pounded his fist on the wheel. There

was no way to know if the Prius had turned onto the highway between him and Fowler—or if the sedan had already turned off the road, and he'd missed them.

If it was the latter, they could be deep in the trees by now. Lost Coast had dozens of small, twisty roads that didn't seem to lead anywhere. He'd be driving into a maze, and with the fog, he'd be blindfolded, as well.

Declan spun the car around and pulled over, trying to think through this. If he knew why Fowler took Annabel, he might have some idea what the man planned to do with her. Was he giving her a new assignment—or was he eliminating loose ends?

Until that moment, he'd never known terror. It jolted through every organ and lived in his skin. It wanted him frozen and unresponsive, so that he didn't need to think about the horror that might be inflicted on Annabel.

He pushed through it, trying to find a cold center. A place where he could still function. Still consider options that would save Annabel.

Niall's car was fast, but it wasn't built for narrow dirt roads between the trees. Even the Volvo would do a better job, and he couldn't use it because he'd let Fowler steal it.

And he'd let the man steal it because he believed he could get it back. The Volvo had a GPS tracker.

It wasn't much, but it was a start.

Declan yanked the phone out of his pocket and pulled up the app. It only took a second for the small green dot to appear. It wasn't moving. The car was parked.

The Volvo wasn't far from his current location. A mile south at most. Declan pulled back onto the road, only driving a little slower than before as he looked for the turnoff. As soon as he saw it, he picked up speed. The rear tires fishtailed as he made the turn, but the car straightened easily.

It was a curving road, but there weren't any exits. If Fowler and Annabel came this way, they would be ahead.

He pressed the gas pedal to the floor as he rounded the first bend and didn't let up, though he knew how perilous this road was, especially in the fog. The last time he was here, he'd crashed into the side of an abandoned barn and set it on fire.

The dark trees flying past had watched him make this same trip fifteen years ago. Even the crescent moon appeared to hover in the same spot it occupied so many years before.

The road grew rough and he jolted hard to his left. A memory triggered, just in time. He stomped on the brakes a second before the old barn emerged out of the fog.

Again, he was flung against the seatbelt. The hood of Niall's car crashed into the bumper of the dark Volvo parked in the middle of the road, and the airbag expanded around him, filling his vision with powder.

Dizziness struck first, followed by nausea. Declan worked the seatbelt release with numb fingers. It took several tries before he had the strength to press the button.

He clawed at the handle, but the door was stuck. Declan shoved it harder. It didn't budge. On unsteady hands, he crawled across the gearshift and exited through the passenger door. He staggered to standing. The world seemed to spin around him, and he clutched the car roof until it passed.

A light shone in the half-burnt barn. He limped toward the building as fast as he could, his left thigh muscle protesting the recent trauma.

Please, let her be there. Let her be safe.

He exhaled when he saw Annabel standing by Fowler. She was next to a strong wooden post, on the unburnt side of the barn. It almost looked new.

She was alive. Whole. Whatever else Fowler had planned, Declan could handle it, so long as Annabel was safe.

He took in the scene and fought a fresh wave of panic. Piles of paper were arranged around Annabel's feet. Declan peered closer. Not paper. Money. Sheets of twenty dollar bills.

The ruined barn reeked of gasoline, and Fowler held a lighter in one hand. The other hand was wrapped tightly around a small gun.

Fowler flicked the wheel, and a flame appeared. The lid snapped shut, and he repeated the motion over and over again. Each time the fire bloomed, Declan's heart stopped. The man was threatening to burn her at the stake.

Annabel's eyes were immense and terrified, but she kept her spine straight and her chin jutted forward. That was his girl.

Fowler returned his hard stare, and Declan saw something move in the depths of the man's black eyes. An anger so vast it had long since become untethered from its source, until it was nothing but pure, unconstrained hatred.

Then Fowler smiled, dark and victorious, and Declan realized that the anger did indeed have a focal point. Maybe it always had.

"Here I thought you might not take the bait." Fowler's low voice was pitched at least an octave higher than usual, and there were cracks between the words. "That GPS is a handy thing, isn't it?"

"I'm here now." Declan kept his voice level. "I'm the one you want. Let Annabel go."

Fowler made a quiet tsking sound. "Not yet. Not until you and I are finished."

Declan took a step forward. Fowler dug the barrel of the gun into Annabel's side, and Declan froze.

"Tell her," Fowler demanded. "Tell her what you did to me."

"She already knows."

Annabel glared at the lawyer through narrowed eyes. "Of course I do. Accident, fire, you fleeing like the rat you are."

Declan would have been proud of her, if he wasn't terrified Fowler would shoot her just to shut her up.

"What do you want?" Declan glanced at the gasoline-soaked pile. "You're not going to sacrifice that much money."

"This?" Fowler nudged the pile with the toe of his boot. "This is paper. The money will come from you."

"Really? How are we calculating what I owe? What I stole from you, or what I burned?"

Rage transformed the other man's features, the hatred that lurked in his eyes spreading across his face. "You cost me everything. Do you know what I paid for those plates? The fabric? A month later, some snot-nosed kid starts stealing it, and before I can catch him, the brat burns it all down. You owe me fifteen years of money, Donnelly. Millions. Start by offering me that."

Declan watched for any sign the man was joking. There

was none. "Do you think I'm an idiot, or are you one your-self? I've had a few years to research counterfeit money. It sort of became a hobby of mine. You can't spend it. You can't go into a bank with a fat stack of fake twenties. You'll sell it for pennies on the dollar to some moron who thinks no one will notice it's counterfeit. You want real money? Tell me how much. Stop fucking around."

Fowler's eyes gleamed, his hatred right on the surface.

"You won't be willing to pay my price."

"I'll get the money."

"You're both idiots," Annabel murmured, almost too quiet to be heard.

"Excuse me?" Fowler sounded less offended by what she said than that she spoke at all. Bait wasn't supposed to have opinions.

That was her sole purpose—and not just tonight. He saw it now, too clearly. Too late.

There were dozens of different ways Fowler could have destroyed the deal, all of which were more likely to work than having the baker seduce the bookstore owner. Declan didn't know a damn thing about his family's business, and the whole town knew it. By all accounts, he was the least likely target. It would have made more sense to send her after Niall, or even ask her to befriend Bridget. Either of them might have invited her to Sunday dinner.

But Fowler had dangled Annabel in front of him like a tasty morsel he knew Declan couldn't resist, then stood back and watched as Declan fell into his trap.

Annabel rolled her eyes. "This isn't about money. Why on earth would Fowler be trying to extort money in the middle of a gas-soaked building when the hotel and a loaded gun would have worked just as well? Lou wouldn't have batted an eye."

Declan inhaled, the scent of gasoline filling his nostrils, along with wet wood. No matter how clear the day was, it was a cold, still one. The fire wouldn't spread much beyond the fuel.

There was a *lot* of fuel, however. Even worse, there were Fowler's wild eyes, eyes that suggested something had cracked within him. Perhaps the broken pieces had always been there, reined in only by his rigid control.

If Fowler didn't want money, he wanted revenge.

"Whatever you want, I'll pay it," Declan told him.

Fowler closed his fingers around the lighter, and with the same hand, he gripped the hem of his shirt and lifted it several inches above his waistband.

Annabel gave an involuntary gasp.

The skin along his ribs was ruined. The skin puckered and stretched into small ravines, and canyons of inflexible flesh wound around his side and vanished into the man's back. There was no way Fowler didn't live with chronic pain, and even with his hatred for the man, Declan allowed himself a moment of pity for the person Fowler had been fifteen years before.

Fowler dropped the shirt. "That is what I want. I burned, now you burn. Call it poetic justice. Will you take her place?"

"Yes." Declan didn't hesitate. He hurried forward, eager to spare Annabel whatever suffering he could.

"Stop!" Her voice was panicked.

He couldn't. He was almost to her.

Metal clicked around his right arm.

Declan stared at his wrist, now wrapped in a silver cuff. The chain was threaded through an iron ring bolted to the post. The other end surrounded Annabel's right wrist.

He lunged forward. This building was little more than a ruin. The pole was strong, but it was attached to a rotted roof. It would take little effort to rip it free.

Annabel stifled a cry of pain as her half of the cuffs dug into her wrist. He instantly stopped moving and wrapped his fingers around hers.

The man laughed. "You're stuck. Accept it."

He and Annabel were facing opposite directions, so he spun around and placed his body between her and Fowler. She smacked his shoulder and stepped sideways so she could peer around him.

Fowler pointed to the concrete casing that held the post. "This building is a wreck, but I thought of a few improvements."

Declan followed the man with his eyes, looking for any weakness. "How long have you planned this?"

The man gave him an impatient look. Of course. The answer was obvious.

"Fifteen years is a long time to wait. Why now?"

Fowler smiled with grim satisfaction. "No more obstacles."

At last, Declan thought he understood. Until a month ago, Fowler didn't dare act without Peter Hastings' permission. Hastings was an amoral bastard, but he was also a practical one. He preferred to keep up the appearance that he was a law-abiding man in a law-abiding town. He wouldn't have supported an elaborate revenge scheme or arson in the woods—and he would have destroyed any man who attempted it.

For that matter, Hastings wouldn't have been involved in a cut-rate counterfeit operation based in his own tiny town, in a building that any stupid teenager could find.

The only benefit to the barn's location was its proximity to the main road—and to the trucks bound for the docks.

"He never knew," Declan said. "You were on your own, weren't you? Trying to make a few bucks using your boss's shipping lines. He did all the work to keep them protected, and your counterfeit money hitched a ride. Now you're trying to build it all over again. You're trying to kill the deal so you can buy it yourself. Through a shell company, I'm sure, since the Hastings would never sell to you. You've got the plates again." He nodded at the stack of money. "You only need to build a new, safer location along the shipping route and you can start churning out money for those stupid enough to buy it."

Annabel cut in. "And then launder it through town businesses, just like Hastings did. It's about time you caught up, Declan." She smiled at him, her eyes almost playful, and his heart turned over in his chest.

Fowler didn't look bothered by their discovery. "Business, Miss Johnson. Singular. Lou is far more reasonable than you. He'll be happy to continue working with me, and I only need one. My needs are more modest than Hastings' were."

Annabel laughed, the merry sound jarring, given the circumstances. "Have you already forgotten that I said you were *both* idiots?" She leaned forward as much as her bonds would allow. "Wouldn't you like to know why?"

Chapter Twenty-Nine

Annabel nudged Declan's foot. "He is an idiot because I was doing just fine until he came along to 'save' me, but you, Fowler, made a far worse mistake." She lowered her voice, forcing him to strain to hear her next words. "You underestimated me."

He fixed her with a derisive sneer, but his voice wasn't entirely steady. "That seems unlikely."

"I'm afraid you still need my laundry services if you intend to go through with your plan," she said, almost apologetic. "You see, I made a few phone calls before I went to the hotel."

His eyes were pitch black, but the cold scorn was gone, replaced by hot rage. "What did you do?"

His anger made her fear spike, but she kept her voice pleasant. "Well, I was so afraid you were going to kill Richard Donnelly, and then possibly kill me for interrupting, that I figured I had nothing to lose. I left a message with Valerie Childs. You might be familiar with her. She works downtown. Wears a blue uniform and a badge? Took an oath to put away bad guys?"

He took a step forward, and she held her ground. Fowler

fed off other people's fear, and she refused to provide him with a single bite.

"What did you do?" Fowler repeated, the words spoken through gritted teeth.

"I made a little suggestion that she look into the books of The Capital Hotel. Or perhaps look into Lou's personal expenditures. I believe he just bought a lovely new boat."

The man's eyes began to bulge. "I'm going to kill you."

"That's one solution, certainly. But then you'll have to find a new money launderer. I hear it's so difficult to train a new one. However, if you free us, I'm sure we could work out an agreement."

"I'm supposed to believe that? You already refused to work for me."

"That's true," she acknowledged. "However, that was before there was a risk of being flambéed. I feel a bit more accommodating now, though I doubt that will last if Declan dies tonight."

Fowler's eyes bulged out of his head. "No." He strode across the barn, then stopped to point at Declan. "I won't give him up."

She gave a delicate shrug. "Then you'll need to find another employee. I'm sure it won't be too difficult. Of course, you're a stranger in town, so you won't know who would be willing to work with you. Not everyone responds well to blackmail, or so I've heard. But if you ask the wrong person, just try the next. It's not like people in Lost Coast Harbor tend to gossip."

He continued to pace the room, stopping only to throw violent looks their way.

"You may loathe me," she continued, "but at least I'm a known quantity. You know how to control me." She nodded at Declan, ignoring the horror in his eyes.

Fowler bit out a curse and walked away, stopping just outside the entrance to the barn. They watched as he strode back and forth. His lips moved and his gestures were animated. It appeared he was having an urgent conversation with himself.

Declan tightened his grip on her hand. "I think you just waved a red flag in front of a bull."

Fowler cast sharp glances at them, like they were chess pieces who refused to follow the rules of the game. Chess pieces he still wished to incinerate at the first opportunity.

"We're still alive, aren't we? And we'll remain that way until he figures out how to kill us *and* run a thriving criminal enterprise. What on earth are you doing here?"

He craned his neck to see her. "I wasn't going to abandon you to him. Are you insane?"

"You were supposed to make a phone call. Did you even listen to your message? I don't have your father's number. Unlike me, you could have called him. You'd have learned that he isn't even in town and known this was a trap."

"He's safe?" His shoulders sagged in relief.

She caught his left hand in hers and squeezed. He hadn't known. Declan must have been so worried about his father—but instead of trying to find him, Declan had run to save her.

In the middle of a freezing barn in February, the warmth of her heart seemed to fill her entire chest. He came for her.

Even if she still wanted to smack him for it. "We need to talk about your impetuous nature," she muttered.

"Later." Despite the awful circumstances, there was a

smile in his voice. "There's a lot I want to say later, but for now, can you reach into my right back pocket?" He turned his hips to give her better access.

Annabel gripped the keyring. "If you wanted me to touch your ass, you only needed to ask."

"Behave yourself. Feel how the keychain is U-shaped, instead of a circle? There's a catch at the top. Flick it open."

She wiggled her thumb until she hit the lever. It took longer than it should, because she could only use her left hand, but soon the piece of metal at the top of the U popped open. Several keys fell to the ground.

"It's okay. We don't need them. Just don't drop the ring when you give it to me."

She carefully deposited the item in his left palm. "In case we don't have a later, what were you planning to say?"

Declan turned halfway. The new position let him access the cuffs while still keeping an eye on Fowler, who continued to pace angrily outside.

"There's going to be a later," he said with absolute certainty.

"Of course there is, but this is a rather stressful situation. I could use the distraction. Tell me now."

"Oh, you know. I'd start by telling you that I love the way I feel when I'm with you, so that whole thing about not liking who I am with you was bullshit, and I'm sorry for ever thinking it was true. Then I'd add something about how no one's perfect, but maybe we could be perfect for each other, and I'd mention that we might sometimes drive the other one crazy, but it will always be worth it because, somehow, we make each other's life brighter just by being together.

Then I was going to convince you to feel the same way."

Annabel rested her forehead against his back, letting his warm, solid body support her when it felt like her legs weren't up to the job. She gave a shaky laugh. "I expected something more poetic from you."

"You're very exacting about these near-death declarations, aren't you? Very well. Perhaps some Shelley? *Nothing in the world is single; All things by a law divine / in one another being's mingle—why not I with thine?*" He glanced back at her with an expression both amused and sincere. "Is that better?"

Annabel stroked his back. "That will do," she said past the lump in her throat.

The metal shook against her wrist, and he cursed. "This is a lot harder with my left hand."

She tilted her head until she could see what he was doing better. "Why, exactly, do you know how to pick handcuffs?"

At that moment, he found the release, and the cuffs sprang open. Declan flashed her a smile that stopped her breath. "Because I'm a Donnelly." He slipped his hand free and grabbed her wrist. His eyes grew somber as he traced the red marks left by the too-tight bands.

"What was that about doing just fine before I got here?"

"It's true. I was stalling."

"Uh-huh." He cast his eyes toward Fowler. The man was no longer pacing. He stood perfectly still, and though his face was angled away from them, there was a resoluteness to his jaw that suggested he'd come to a decision.

"What exactly were you waiting for?" Declan asked.

Annabel cocked her head, listening to the sound of an approaching engine. "Someone with excellent timing."

~

Declan watched as Fowler spun to face the road.

Watched him raise his gun.

Then he watched Fowler fly backwards as a red Thunderbird convertible slammed into his legs.

Niall grinned at them as he stepped out of Bridget's car, looking for all the world like he'd just arrived at a party.

The handcuffs dropped to the ground, and Niall raised his eyebrows. "Am I interrupting?" His smile fell as he caught sight of his ruined car. "Seriously? Again?"

A deafening crack split the air, so loud Declan's ears rang. Niall's right shoulder jerked backwards, his perpetual smile dropping into a grimace. He stumbled to the ground.

Declan screamed his brother's name and took a step forward. Annabel wrapped her fingers around his wrist, her grip unexpectedly strong. "Wait," she commanded.

Niall crawled to the rear of the car. He only used one arm, because he was keeping the right one tucked close to his body.

"Let me go," Declan growled. "He's shot."

She didn't release him. "It was a .22 in the shoulder of an enormous man, and it's nowhere near any major organs or arteries."

Niall leaned against the bumper and gave them a thumbs up. His enthusiasm was only slightly dimmed by the blood pouring from his wound.

"See? He's fine," she murmured. She tugged Declan backwards, into the same spot where he'd just been handcuffed. "Move your arm."

Understanding, he placed his right arm behind his back and used his body to shield their now unshackled wrists.

Fowler stormed back into the barn, the gun hanging loose at his side. He was more relaxed with it than he had been before—like he'd only needed to try it out to understand how simple it was to shoot another human.

He raised the weapon directly to Annabel's forehead, and Declan felt the entire world narrow to that moment. The metal barrel pressed against her skin. The steady finger, already on the trigger. One twitch, and she would be dead.

He couldn't move. Niall was halfway to standing, but he stilled when he caught sight of the gun.

Only Annabel dared to speak. Her voice was calm. "You can shoot me, if that's truly what you want, but we both know it isn't. I'm nothing but an insect to you. He's the one you want."

Fowler's eyes darted to Declan, then straight back to her. The man licked dry lips. "I don't have to choose."

They all heard it at the same time. Sirens wailed in the distance, the sound growing louder with every passing second.

Panic overtook Fowler's features. His pale irises appeared to shrink as the whites of his eyes expanded. It was the look of a rabid dog who'd just been caged.

She moved so slowly, at first Declan didn't understand what she was doing, not until her hands were on either side of her face in the gesture for surrender. Fowler looked wildly between them.

"You do have a choice," she said, in that same soothing voice. She took a small step, away from the post and away from Declan.

Fowler followed the movement, the gun never leaving her forehead.

"If you shoot me," she whispered, "you may not have time to shoot him, too. He'll fight you for the gun. Even if you hit him, people survive gunshot wounds all the time." She took another step away. Each step felt like she was opening a chasm between them. What the hell was she thinking?

"Don't you dare sacrifice yourself," Declan warned.

Her smile was cold. Unrecognizable in her sweet face. "Of course not. I'm sacrificing you."

His heart plummeted. It wasn't possible. Everything they'd said and felt, it was real.

The sirens drew closer.

"You only have a little time left," she whispered to Fowler. "Maybe time for a single revenge. He's right there. Light the fire. He will escape, and he will live, but he will be ruined. Burn him as he burned you."

Fowler's face grew slack with uncertainty. The man obviously feared it was a trick, but the image Annabel painted was so tempting. She offered him the one thing Fowler wanted above all else. Vengeance.

"Look at him," she whispered. "He can barely walk on that weak leg, let alone run."

She flicked a cruel look Declan's way, and if he hadn't been so terrified, he would have smiled. He'd forgotten how her brow smoothed when she lied. How persuasive she could be when it came to offering men their dearest desire, even when it went against their common sense. Whatever Annabel's actions, her heart was unchanged.

"My leg feels just fine," he assured her. She gave the tiniest nod.

The sirens filled their ears.

"Now," she urged Fowler.

With a scream, he dropped the gun to his side and spun toward Declan, the lighter already glowing in his hand. He flung it toward the piles of counterfeit money.

It never landed. Declan's foot shot out and connected with the small item. It sailed across the room, landing harmlessly on a patch of damp wood.

Fowler roared his rage to the room. The gun swept up, but Declan was already there. One arm caught Fowler's forearm and forced the gun across his body until the barrel pointed at the wall. With the heel of the other hand, he jabbed Fowler's neck and felt a burst of satisfaction at the hard contact. The man gasped for air and stumbled backwards.

Right into Niall's waiting arms.

Declan was fast. Niall was a dervish. He twisted Fowler's wrist until the man dropped the gun, then kicked the weapon away and swept Fowler's legs from under him. He landed facedown with a pained grunt. Before Fowler even understood what was happening, both his arms were wrenched behind his back. Niall snapped on the dropped handcuffs. It was over in seconds.

For a brief moment, Niall wasn't the easygoing man everyone in town thought they knew. His eyes were sharp and his mouth tight, and his muscles were tense. Ready.

Annabel stared between the brothers, her mouth a perfect circle.

"I hope that was what you intended," Declan said. "Because as much as I love you, I'd rather not burn myself alive to make you happy."

"Yes. Goodness." She appeared to be struggling to find the words. "You were as good as I hoped you would be."

Niall stood, though he still kept a boot on Fowler's back. "I'm better," he said with a wink. No one could argue with that. "That was fun. And look how nicely we packaged him for the cops."

"How did you even know where to find us?" Declan asked.

"GPS, of course. I put my own tracker on your car. How else will I know where it is when I want to borrow it?"

Sometimes, Declan wondered why he even asked those questions.

Flashing lights came into view. The siren cut off as soon as the driver spotted them.

Fowler twitched. Niall dug in his boot a little harder, but otherwise gave no sign he noticed the man. "Then the cops saw me rush by the station in Bridget's car and started the chase. They must have been feeling nostalgic for old times."

"That's not why they're here." Annabel's voice was too quiet. It caught both their attention. "At least, that's not why they knew there was a problem. Like I said, I left a message for Valerie Childs." She looked at Declan as if surprised by a new thought. "Did you just say you loved me?"

A knot was forming in his stomach, his relief from a moment before already vanishing. "What did you do, Annabel?"

The cop car drew to a stop behind the Thunderbird and next to the wreck that was Niall's car.

She gave an infuriating shrug. "I'm afraid they'll need another set of cuffs."

The knot tightened, until it felt like he'd swallowed lead. "You didn't. Please tell me you didn't confess to save my family or the stupid deal or any of this. None of that is worth more than you are."

"I appreciate you saying that, but I didn't do it for you. This is for me. I want to know how it feels to live a life without lies. Of course, I will offer to testify against Hastings for a reduced sentence. I'm no martyr."

Declan shook his head, unable to accept what she'd already done. "You'll lose the bakery. Lose everything you've built here. You'll even lose your name."

Annabel reached up to cup his cheek, and Declan leaned into her hand.

"Everything?" she asked.

Declan gripped her hand with his own. Maybe, if he held on tight enough, he wouldn't need to let her go. "Never."

But he couldn't stop time, and at last Annabel turned to face her fate.

The driver's side door opened, and Molly Donnelly stepped out.

Annabel's jaw dropped. Declan covered his face with his hands, feeling equal parts relief and horror. "Mom, please tell me you didn't steal a cop car."

"Of course not. That was Gavin."

Declan's older brother waved as he stepped out of the passenger side. He opened the rear door, letting Bridget out.

Molly took in the scene at a glance. "No one's hurt?"

Niall pointed to his still-bleeding shoulder. Gavin scoffed.

"Wounds heal," said Bridget. "Chicks dig scars. Suck it up."

Annabel looked moderately shellshocked. "Where are the cops? I called Valerie Childs."

Bridget nodded, a little too serious to be sincere. "Yes. It was an interesting message, too. Fortunately, I was hanging out in the chief's office because, ah…the point is, she's so new that she still has all her passwords written on a pad of paper. In her drawer. Underneath her files."

Declan walked to Bridget and engulfed her in a bear hug. What was a little destruction of evidence between siblings? "You did good, sis."

Annabel looked between them, not quite understanding. "But shouldn't Valerie be here?"

Molly took both her hands. "And have her arrest the future mother of my grandchildren? Hardly. Bridget made that silly message go away."

"Poof," agreed Bridget.

Gavin leaned against the hood of the car and grinned at Annabel. "Money laundering, huh? That's pretty hardcore. You might make a decent Donnelly after all."

Every word out of his family's mouth was insane, and Declan found no reason to argue with any of it.

Annabel looked between them all, blinking quite a bit as she tried to process what they had just done. "So you're the ones who chased Niall?"

Gavin almost looked disappointed. "That was one of the patrol cars. They missed the turnoff, though, so they're probably a mile or two down the road by now. We better get them out here to deal with this asshole." He nodded at Fowler, then sat on the hood of the car and pulled out his phone. "While we wait, we should probably get our stories straight."

In his entire life, Declan had never been so happy to be a Donnelly.

CHAPTER THIRTY

Annabel hurried up the stairs between the bookstore and Declan's apartment.

"I'm sorry I'm late," she called, pushing open the door. "I just got back in town this afternoon. I would have been here an hour ago, but I needed to change into something pretty..." She tapered off as she caught sight of Declan sitting on his couch. He wore nothing but a pair of blue jeans and a bemused expression. "You're not dressed."

He blinked up at her, his eyes coming into focus. "You look amazing."

She preened a little while he stared. He ought to stare. This wasn't any old dress pulled from the back of her closet. It wasn't even a new dress bought to celebrate Declan's council victory the week before.

No, this was a bright red, hug every curve, stop traffic kind of dress. The kind of dress one could only buy if they had no reason to hide.

She thought of it as her plea deal dress.

It was also the kind of dress a woman bought when she knew she wasn't pregnant—not yet, at least. Molly Donnelly would need to wait a bit longer for grandchildren.

"Is everything settled? For good this time?" He sounded a bit wary—probably because he'd believed everything was settled once before, after they told Gavin's story to the cops. Considering the money found in Fowler's room matched the stacks of counterfeit money in the barn, no one had any problem believing the Donnellys' version of the facts.

Then Annabel had crept out early the next morning for a one-to-one chat with Spencer Bourne, the federal prosecutor on the Hastings case.

The Donnellys were aghast at her decision. Even Declan suggested that perhaps honesty was overrated, at least in situations that could send her to prison for years. She couldn't even say they were wrong. All she knew was she wanted to live a different life than she had the last several years, and that began with fixing the things she'd broken.

Annabel crossed the room and perched on the couch next to him. "It's truly over," she assured Declan. "I signed the last document today. Three years of probation in exchange for my testimony against Hastings. Now I just need to go thirty-six months without breaking any laws."

Declan tucked one of her curls behind her ear. "You should probably avoid my family, then. They're a terrible influence."

"We can't avoid your family," she reminded him. "They're expecting us at your celebration party in ten minutes. Why aren't you dressed?"

She meant it as a chastisement, but her fingers seemed to have a mind of their own. They traced his rounded pecs and slid down to the defined abs.

Declan caught her hand in his, keeping her still. "God, I

missed you."

"Me, too." She had, so much. She only spent one night in the motel near the federal prosecutor's office, but one night had been too long. The bed was too big, the room too quiet.

She hadn't been lonely, though. They'd texted for hours, and called each other when texts weren't enough. The entire time, she knew he was waiting for her. That she had a reason to return.

She dropped a kiss against his bare shoulder. "Maybe I'll show you how much later."

He leaned forward to nuzzle her neck. "Now."

Annabel pressed herself back, keeping him at arm's length. "After the party."

"I'm not going."

The man was maddening. "I know you've made a career of avoiding your family, but they've put a lot of effort into this. There's a custom banner and everything. Go celebrate your victory. Okay, they're also celebrating that they now own ten percent of Hastings Shipping, but it's mainly a party for you."

"I'm not avoiding my family."

"Then why aren't you…oh."

Declan had lifted her hand to his mouth and nipped her knuckles, temporarily stealing her capacity for speech.

"I'm not going to my victory party," he explained, "because I'm not a councilman."

"That's not what the voters said." She forced her voice to remain level as he opened her hand and pressed his lips to her palm. "Even the all-powerful Rotary Club couldn't defeat you."

"Voters are often wrong. I called the council five minutes

ago and resigned."

Annabel's mouth rounded. "You…but why?"

"Because I've been sitting here for two hours, trying to convince myself to get dressed. To go pull out my suit and comb my hair and smile at the townsfolk who voted for me."

"Well, parties can be rather dreadful. You don't need to convince me. Still, that's no reason to resign." She tried to tug her hand away, but he held on fast.

"I don't want to do it." The words were so matter-of-fact that she couldn't doubt he meant them. "I don't want to hear about potholes and fence heights. I don't care about the timing of the red light on Grove Street."

"But what about the writer's retreat?"

"I needed to keep busy while you were off charming prosecutors, so I did a bit of research. The first retreat will start in six months."

"What about the permits? The red tape?"

"You know, I've spent years watching my family magically avoid charges. My mother stole a cop car and the town acted like it was a bit of a lark. I come from a family of silver-tongued devils who talk themselves into and out of trouble. If I can't convince the town council to allow half a dozen introverted mystery writers to hole up in some cabins in the woods, I might as well change my name."

"Mystery writers?"

Declan tried pulling her toward him. "I thought you might enjoy that more than a bunch of poets."

She resisted, but only a little. "I find I've developed an appreciation for poetry."

A slow grin spread across his face. "Good. I've been

reviewing some old favorites this week. I found a few you might like."

Annabel sprang from the couch and walked across the room. She needed to put space between them before he started reciting verse at her. "Does this decision have anything to do with me? Because just a couple weeks ago, you were really looking forward to taking your place on the council."

Declan watched her with hooded eyes, making it clear there were things he'd rather be doing than talking. Still, he answered her question. "Joining the council was meant to be the culmination of everything I worked for. It was absolute proof that I'd left my past and my family behind. I was my own man. But being your own man shouldn't be so damn hard."

"What do you mean?"

Declan eyed for her a long time. When she didn't move, he stood and prowled toward her, barefoot and shirtless and so irresistible it seemed ridiculous that she'd ever found another man attractive. They were all pale wisps next to the solid, inescapable fact of Declan.

The jeans were old and faded, and his hair was messed up—but his eyes were as intent as ever. As controlled.

He came to a stop before her. "I mean that pushing you away wasn't just the hardest thing I've ever done. It was the stupidest. Far stupider than stealing counterfeit money, or crashing my brother's car. Definitely stupider than spending years so determined *not* to be a Donnelly Devil that I forgot who I actually was."

She swallowed. "And who are you?" she asked.

One shoulder lifted. "I'm a man who likes poetry and

bookstores and cats, who has a terrible sweet tooth. Who forgot how much fun it is to get into a bit of trouble." Declan placed a hand on either side of her, trapping her against the bookcase. "And I'm a man who loves telling you what to do when you're naked and wanting me, and one who loves coming to you with a hunger so desperate it feels like it will never be sated."

Her body came to life under his words. "Well. That sounds like a pretty good man."

He pressed against her, his bare chest warm through her clothes. The dress she'd loved so much just fifteen minutes ago suddenly felt like an unnecessary hindrance.

She twisted against him, wanting him to move, to lift her dress, to rip it from her body. He did none of those things. Declan only looked at her with an expression so open, so honest, that her heart stilled, as if in preparation for a moment from which it would never fully recover.

"More than any of that, I'm the man who loves you. Whenever you want to ask who I am, for the rest of your life, that will be the answer. It's the only one you'll ever need. The only one that matters."

Annabel struggled to find words. At last, she managed a shaky smile. "You should maybe try that poetry thing. I think you might be pretty good at it."

Declan bent his head to hers, and for a long time she listened as his lips and hands repeated what he already said with his words.

Though she answered in turn, it felt incomplete, and when he drew back, the words burst from her, words she thought she'd waited three years to say. "I love you, too. Every part of you. I want them all. I'm greedy that way."

He laughed and tugged her away from the wall. She only managed a token protest as he pulled her inexorably toward the bed.

"Shouldn't we at least make an appearance at the party? Let them know what you've decided?"

Declan tugged her zipper all the way down. "Gavin promised to bring the first batch of the wheat ale. By this point, it's unlikely they'll remember what they're celebrating or, indeed, that they have another brother."

"But…"

Her dress sagged, and Declan urged it to the floor. "If it makes you feel better, we can see them tomorrow."

It did. Her mother and cousins were arriving for a visit next week, but they no longer felt like her only family. The Donnelly clan had a way of getting under her skin.

One of them in particular was quite skilled at that.

Her bra joined her dress, and her underwear followed.

She gasped as he toppled them onto his mattress, landing on top of her with his body braced against his forearms.

"Tonight," he said, "we're having our own party." Declan shifted his weight to one arm. With his free hand, he caressed her bare legs, stopping just short of the juncture of her thighs. "I know you're already wet for me. Is your pretty clit hard and wanting my tongue?"

Annabel tilted her hips toward him. "Maybe you should look for yourself."

His eyes narrowed. A second later her arms were spread wide above her head. "I'm sorry," he whispered in her ear, "did you think you were the one giving orders tonight?"

Annabel exhaled, a fear she hadn't known she carried van-ishing. What she said was true. She loved every version of this man. The one who was kind to everyone in town. The one who memorized poetry. She definitely loved the one she'd just discovered this week, whose control sometimes hung by a thread—a thread she knew how to snap.

Declan was rediscovering that aspect of himself, and she suspected she'd be seeing a lot more of it in the years to come.

But she really, *really* liked this side of the man she loved.

So when he told her to grip the headboard and not let go, no matter what he did to her, she didn't argue, and she didn't argue when he told her to spread her legs and keep them spread until he tasted his fill—though it took him so long to be sated that she soon knew nothing but the feel of his tongue and the sounds of her own cries. And when he thrust into her long and slow, and told her she couldn't look away, it was an order she couldn't imagine defying. She was gazing into his dark blue eyes when she went over the edge, and when he soon followed.

After he was done giving orders, they lay entwined togeth-er. Declan stroked her back, and she ran her fingers across the scar on his thigh. He barely seemed to notice.

He pressed his lips to her forehead. "Now that your name is cleared, I can still call you Annabel, right?"

"You better," she said. "It is my name."

He kissed her again on the tip of her nose. "Annabel John-son or Annabel Belmont?"

She tilted her head to meet his lips once. "I've been think-ing Annabel Donnelly has a nice ring to it."

His answer was poetry, and she was still blinking back tears when he slid into her again, this time with considerably less restraint.

Author's Note

The poems in this book were carefully chosen for a) their descriptions of love and b) their place in the public domain.

Annabel inspires Declan to quote a few lines from "Love and Sleep" by Charles Algernon Swinburne and "Love's Philosophy" by Percy Shelley. The Baudelaire poem that causes so much trouble is "Le Balcon," or The Balcony, as translated by Frank Pearce Sturm.

Were he not constrained by copyright law, I imagine Declan would have a great appreciation for the poets of the mid-twentieth century. By now, he has certainly read e.e. cummings' "may I feel said he" to Annabel. (An audio version of this read by Tom Hiddleston is available online, the best proof I've found that there's a higher power who loves us.)

And whenever he can, Declan reads Pablo Neruda. In particular, Annabel's heart melts when he recites "Sonnet XVII." Trust me on this.

Acknowledgments

As always, I must thank Eve Kincaid, my fabulous co-resident of Lost Coast Harbor. It's not always easy playing in the same sandbox, but she gave me free rein to create the Donnelly Devils and didn't even wince when I handed her this insane family for Bridget's story. She also patiently explained money laundering to me when I kept trying to send the cash in the wrong direction. When we finally begin our lives of crime, she'll be much better at it than I will.

Thanks as well to Sandra Barkevich for her editing prowess and Kaari Busick for her mad copy editing skillz.

And of course, cheers to the many Divas who kept me sane during the writing of this book.

About the Author

Lily Danes write the odd-numbered books in the Lost Coast Harbor series. A recovering city girl, she now lives in the Sierra Nevadas. She has few practical skills and would be absolutely useless in the zombie apocalypse.

Learn more and sign up for the newsletter at lilydanes. com.

www.ingramcontent.com/pod-product-compliance
Lightning Source LLC
Chambersburg PA
CBHW060540180626
46817CB00002B/658